ANNE BRONTË
NIGHTWALKER

ANNE BRONTË NIGHTWALKER

A Brontë Blood Chronicle

GEA HAFF

FIREFOX
PRESS

Anne Brontë Nightwalker

A Firefox Book
Published by
Firefox Press (USA) LLC

Copyright © 2016 Gea Haff
All rights reserved.
Cover design by Patrick Knowles
Library of Congress Catalog Card Number: 2016910951
ISBN-13: 9780997795301
ISBN-10: 0997795301

Printed in the United States of America
www.geahaff.com
First Firefox Edition 2016

For Rob,
my prince

But I would rather be the hare,
That crouching in its sheltered lair
  Must start at every sound;
That forced from cornfields waving wide
Is driven to seek the bare hillside,
Or in the tangled copse to hide,
  Than be the hunter's hound.

ANNE BRONTË

Save as many as you ruin.

SIMON VAN BOOY

Chapter 1

I like my blood warm. I find cold blood as appetizing as an old stale cup of coffee. It's hard to choke down, but then again I'm finicky. Regardless, I've never had access to a blood bank. Our lives are nothing like TV. For us there is no daylight, no friends, lovers or family. We do not travel in packs. We're more like the clouded leopard or spotted jaguar, rare creatures, besieged by modernity, strangely fragile despite our steel strength. We are shy, solitary creatures—especially me. Thus, I haven't seen one of my kind for 50 years, having perfected the art of lying low. Camouflage and evasion are my great skills. Ten years is the length of commitment I give any place or any job. After that, it's hard to explain looking like a 29-year-old. I've spent nine years and nine months in this cold mountain town and soon my time here must come to an end.

As a mortal, I was plain, but since the turning all my physical qualities have intensified, becoming deeper and more striking. My hair is the color of night, cut in jagged edges above my shoulders, evidence of my desperation in the wake of obliterating fever. I wear it pulled back, hidden beneath a low navy work cap. My eyes are blue violet: intense and startling. When light hits them, they shine like a wolf's. I hide them behind a sleek pair of safety glasses, prescription, I lie, that cuts down the sheen. My skin is white. Not cream-colored or fair, but a pure porcelain white like Michelangelo's *Carrera*. Beautiful for a Venus or a Persephone, but unnatural for a human woman. Then again, I'm not human.

Or am I?

Nearly 200 years have passed and I'm still unsure what to call myself. Night Walker is what I've settled on. So much kinder sounding than demon or predator or that most heinous word of all: Vampire.

Long ago I was a teacher and then a writer, but now I am a tender of broken bodies and injured souls. The word they use today is paramedic. Some call me ambulance girl.

Tonight, heaven is brilliantly dark with a net of stars thrown above our heads so incandescent they illuminate the forest. My partner Dana peers through the headlights into the darkness. She is driving fast and lacks my night vision, though her eyes are young and strong. She likes to be in control and so always drives, which is fine with me. I prefer to be in back with the patients. It's easier to ward off starvation that way.

We are, as Dana puts it, "trolling for trauma" in a well-stocked ambulance courtesy of Asheville EMS. I've been a medic since the Crimean War. Dana Fitzpatrick, on the other hand, has been one only six months, and as she goes to nursing school during daylight hours, she is my partner on the night shift.

We are as opposite as the sun and moon. Dana's blonde hair cascades down her back in a silken ponytail she refuses to secure. She's all femininity but there's an assertiveness to her that hints at whips and knee-high, lace-up boots. An alpha female in a Delilah's body, she chafes at my slender, youthful authority.

She pulls out her glittering phone and starts texting.

"Who are you seducing tonight?" I ask.

She glances over at me wickedly. "Someone new and tasty."

"Please tell me he's not married."

"Like Tom? I'm over him. All he talked about was fires and hunting. *Boring.*"

"He was a firefighter. A *married* firefighter."

"That's not my fault. Maybe if his wife wasn't fat, he wouldn't go looking for someone else."

"She's nine months pregnant!"

Dana ignores me and taps at her phone with one hand while steering with the other. Occasionally she glances up at the road. Winter is here and the naked trees flash by in the violet moonlight, spectral as ghosts.

In a flash, I grab the phone out of her hand. Even weak, I'm faster and stronger than any human. "You're going to get someone killed," I say. "Watch the road."

"You have no right to take my phone."

"Texting and driving are against policy and I'm your supervisor. I do have the right."

"Great. You're in one of your moods tonight. Is it that time of the month?"

"Werewolves of London" wells out of the radio and I turn it up loud. After thirty years, this song never fails to thrill me. London and darkness and life. *England.* Dana begins singing at the top of her lungs as she whips the truck around hairpin turns like a demented chariot driver.

"*Ahooooooo,* Werewolves of London," Dana howls. Despite the cold, she rolls the window down to feel the wind rip through her hair. As she howls, her breath puffs with steam. The song infects me and I can't help but move with the beat. My defenses are slipping. Yes, it is that time of month, but not in the way Dana is thinking. I'm famished. It's been a strangely quiet two weeks on the ambulance and I've gone too long without a meal. I'm weakening and if I don't feed soon, I'll become unacceptably vulnerable. I shouldn't have let things get this far, but this is the price I pay for refusing to hunt like the rest of my kind.

"Come on, Anne! Let loose, sister!"

The music sweeps me up, slipping through my near-constant composure. "*Ahoooooo*," I howl long and clear. Dana joins in. Outside, a pack of dogs begins singing in the night. With wide blue eyes Dana looks at me then laughs, head back, voice the sound of shattering glass.

"Are you reading *Dracula* again?" she asks when the song winds down. She's noticed the battered paperback tucked beside me on the seat. For a girl so frivolous, her powers of perception are surprisingly keen. "How many times are you going to read that? I thought you hated genre fiction."

"*Dracula* is a classic. Bram Stoker is hardly *genre* fiction."

"Oh, my bad. I thought it was about vampires. You really should read *Twilight*. It's right up your alley. Vampires with a conscience. Compassionate, pacifist, virgin, vegetarian vampires. It makes me want to puke. I want my vampires slutty and violent."

"Until they rip out your throat. Nothing too sexy about that."

"Unless I'm doing the ripping."

Despite her constant chatter, I'm happy to have her as my partner. She's the perfect foil to work with. All gold hair and abundant cleavage like the quintessential California girl she is. When we're together men look right past me, their eyes finding her like a homing pigeon streaking toward the castle. She is the queen and I am content to remain in her shadow.

"I wish you could take my Lit class for me. It's boring as hell and I'm about to flunk out. I'm gonna be a nurse. Why the fuck do I need to take this crap?"

"Because you're getting an education. A well-educated young lady should be familiar with the classics. What class is it?"

"Nineteenth Century English Lit. Professor Hardcastle expects me to read books that are almost two centuries old. How does reading books written by a bunch of dead virgins help me make a living? Do you realize not one of the women we've read all semester ever had sex?" Dana begins counting them off on her fingers. "Emily, Charlotte, Anne, Jane. Well, actually Charlotte Brontë had sex and then died nine months later. Can you believe her morning sickness was so bad she starved to death? How's that for divine punishment?"

I wince.

"What can they possibly know about life?"

"There's more to life than sex."

"Like what?"

I remain silent, my fallback response to so many questions.

"I was wondering, Anne . . ." She turns and smiles sweetly at me. "My paper is due next week, and I was thinking maybe you could help me with it. All you ever do is read and you're so eloquent."

"Of course," I say, amazed. Never before has she made a request of me other than diverting to the mall for a shopping spree. "What would you like to discuss?"

"Well, actually, I was hoping you could just write it for me."

"Write it for you! That's cheating. I'd be doing you a disservice, not to mention undermining the entire educational tradition."

"God, Anne, don't be so dramatic. People do it all the time. I could just buy something online, but Professor Hardcastle can smell a cyber paper like a bomb-sniffing dog. He already kicked one student out of school for it."

"As he should have. Professor Hardcastle sounds like a man of integrity. A quality you might learn to value, especially when it comes to men."

"He's a stuck-up asshole who thinks he's God's gift to Asheville, North Carolina, just because he has a double PhD from Oxford."

"Oxford? How did he end up here?"

"Hell if I know. I have no idea why he deigned to stoop to our little mountain town. Maybe he can't get a job anywhere else because he's such a fucking jerk."

"What happened?" I demand.

"What happened? When?" she asks innocently.

"Between you and him."

"Nothing." She presses her glossed lips together and resolutely stares ahead. The cold, hard road slips beneath us, fortunately free from snow.

"Then why the animosity?"

"Because he's failing me. He gave me an F on my last paper. So I suggested we discuss my performance over drinks and perhaps I could improve his impression of me. You know, make it clear where my talents truly lie."

"You propositioned your professor! For a grade?"

"It's his voice. That English accent! I cream my panties just hearing it. So I figured why not kill two birds with one stone?"

"And exactly what did he say?"

"He acted all indignant. Said that I affronted his *honor* to think him capable of such a thing." Dana laughs. "'Suit yourself,' I told him. 'Go beat off to Anne Brontë if that floats your boat.'"

"*What?!*" I stammer.

"He totally has an Anne Brontë fetish. It's weird. Guess he didn't like my take on her."

"What was your take?" I ask, unsure I want to know.

"That she's a stuck-up, self-righteous, morally indignant, sexually repressed prude. I don't see anything remotely appealing about her. She thinks she's so much better than everyone else. She's totally cold.

If her character Agnes Grey were my governess, I'd stab her with a pair of knitting shears."

I'm speechless.

"Of course, he didn't see it that way. Said she was a rebel. 'A maverick' he called her like she's freakin' Madonna or something. Said she was way ahead of her time. She wrote of things no one wanted to hear, which is *my point exactly!*" Dana slaps the steering wheel for emphasis.

"Did he say anything else?"

"He claims that she was the bravest of all the sisters. And the strongest. What a load of horse crap. The man has a PhD from *Oxford* and he doesn't even know that Emily was the brave one."

"Why do you say that?"

"*Wuthering Heights.* Any woman who thinks haunting a man to the point of psychopathic insanity is romantic—now that's a maverick. Personally, I think all the Brontës were off their rockers. All those fevers and moors. No wonder Branwell became a drug addict. That poor boy had to grow up surrounded by all those PMSing, sexually frustrated sisters. He sounds like the only fun one of the bunch. I would definitely do him. I would have rocked that man's world."

I stare at her in amazement. "Gosh. I never imagined you gave them so much thought." This is longest conversation we've ever had on an even remotely intellectual subject.

"I don't, but I've sat through weeks of Professor Hardcastle raving about them and he's still failing me. Frankly, I'm glad he spared me from his conceited, snooty self. I honestly think I hate him. Which reminds me, I have some PB tonight."

I flash her a disapproving look. "You know how I feel about personal business on shift. You have all day to go shopping. Why can't you do it on your own time? It doesn't look professional for a woman in uniform to be perusing the shoe department while on duty."

"This PB you just might approve of," she says mysteriously.

"I doubt it." I sigh. After six months of working together, Dana remains staunchly impervious to my influence.

"Professor Hardcastle is giving a talk at Malaprop's tonight." She glances at me when I don't respond. "You know, the coolest bookstore in town? Although the Battery Park Book Exchange is pretty cool too. They have a champagne bar. Anyway, he said if I come he'll give me extra credit and allow me to rewrite my paper." She looks at me imploringly.

I stare out the window. The forest flashes by. I should be out hunting or soon I'll become too weak to work, but I haven't killed an animal in years. I abhor the feeling of a warm, pulsing creature being drained of life in my frozen hands. I no longer have the heart for it.

"Please, Anne. You don't have to go inside. You can wait in the truck and read your book in the dark. It's for my education. I know you hate public places, but this is a matter of me making it through college. My future lies in the balance."

Suddenly a call comes out over the radio and my heart leaps in my chest. Here is my chance to feed!

"Rescue 1, respond to 29 Thornton Road for a one-year-old, fever."

"Damn! Hardcastle starts in 40 minutes and we've got to run on a fucking baby."

My mouth waters and I take a deep breath to settle myself. "We'll make it fast," I say.

Dana looks at me in surprise and smiles.

In a rare gesture, I smile back. "Step on it."

Chapter 2

The call is down a narrow mountain road, pocked and riveted from winter rain. A frigid fog is rolling in and the red flashing lights of the truck throb off it like bleeding moonlight. Dana barrels through the brush, impervious to danger.

She questions my directions. "Are you sure you know where we're going?"

"I delivered a baby here not long ago. Turn right where the road forks, by the Great Oak."

"Women having babies at home? Don't they know it's the 21ˢᵗ century?"

"How can anyone forget?"

"I can't believe people still live like this."

Asheville is a strange mixture of retired Exxon execs and independent mountain folk tucked beneath the Blue Ridge Mountains, each group trying to pretend the other doesn't exist. In a single shift, we might respond to a million-dollar mansion or a dilapidated country shack.

Dana turns right then slows as we come to a broken wooden fence with a gate propped open and a sign that reads, "Trespassers WILL be shot. Turn back."

"Great," she says.

"They're more bark than bite," I say, though I keep my eyes and ears wide open.

"I heard there's bootleggers in these mountains."

"It's true. Some of these mountain folk still make their own moonshine, and I've seen the man of the house, Mr. Granger, partake to the point of violence. He has a nasty habit of slapping his wife around when he's had too much to drink." The urge to give him a taste of his own medicine arises and I smother it, shocked at my violent impulse. Hunger definitely has me in its grip.

"You said he was more bark than bite. I wish Santos were here."

"I thought you were '*done* with him,'" I say, baffled by how easily modern women shrug off their lovers.

"I am, but he's still a cop. It's nice to have backup when you're driving alone to a violent bootlegger's shack in the middle of the woods. This has *Night of the Living Dead* written all over it."

I look at her blankly.

"The zombie movie? You've got to pay more attention to culture. For someone so smart, you have absolutely no idea what's going on in the world."

"Zombies are not an issue here, I assure you. And you're not alone. You're with me."

"Really, Anne. I know how strong you think you are, but forgive me if I'd rather have a pissed-off Army Ranger cop by my side."

Through the mist, a modest log cabin appears. The porch is sagging, yet it holds a broad Confederate flag, faded and tattered. Rangy dogs bound down the steps, barking vociferously. Beside the front door, two wooden rifles form an X. A hand-painted sign beneath them reads, *"A Man's home is his castle and I am King."*

I step out first and shoo the dogs away. In a flash, they vanish. I grab the med box and hand Dana the airway bag, then take the lead as we head to the house. Although I'm ostensibly ageless and impervious to disease, I'm no superhero. My body heals preternaturally fast, but not quick enough to repair a gaping hole in my heart before I bleed out from a bullet wound. Massive trauma can still kill me.

The front door swings open. "Took you long enough," a ropy man in his 30s says.

I give him a nod— "Mr. Granger" —and stamp my old boots against the porch to shake off the dirt before stepping inside. It's time for a new pair. I've worn these far too long, but despite their disparity with my uniform, I just can't let them go. Their soft caramel leather reminds me of when I was a girl running across the moors under a low grey sky, Em by my side, wild as an untamed falcon. Yet no matter how often I oil and resole them, they look outrageously out of date. Although in the Granger home, you'd hardly notice.

Children of various ages dot the room and a cat scurries off. The house has been shut tight against the cold and is permeated with the odors of animals and sweat, urine and dirt. Dana, still unaccustomed to poverty after six months on the job, wrinkles her nose.

"Oh, it's you, thank God." A young woman emerges from the back room cradling a bundle of blankets. Mrs. Granger is visibly pregnant. It seems just yesterday I delivered her last child. "She stopped breathing," she says, throwing the bundle in my arms.

I can smell her. It's the little girl I ushered into life, kicking and screaming like a hellcat. Now she's still, but I can feel her breathing in my arms. Heat burns through the blankets.

"She has a fever," I say. "She's burning up. You mustn't swaddle her so tightly. She needs to cool down."

The mother brushes a strand of wheat-colored hair off her face. "But it's so cold in here."

"Seizures like this aren't unusual in little ones," I say. "They're not like adults. When a baby gets too hot, it's common for her to seize. You must cool her down." I loosen the swaddle. "What have you given her for the fever?"

"Nothing. It all happened so fast. I didn't know what to do."

"How many kids do you have?" Dana asks.

"Six," Mrs. Granger says, bewildered.

"You'd think you'd have this figured out by now."

I give Dana a sharp look. Rudeness will not be tolerated on my truck under any circumstances. "Let's go," I say to Dana, who shoulders all the equipment with a groan.

"Mr. Granger, Mom needs to come with us. Can you handle the kids?" I search his face for signs of intoxication, but tonight he is sober. He's blocking the front door with a group of lean children huddled around him, one clinging to his leg. His face is drawn and hard, creased with worry. His family is all he has and I can tell he doesn't know whether to shout or cry.

His oldest, a lovely girl of 12 with long flaming-red hair and tawny-colored eyes, touches my arm as she peers at her baby sister. I'm startled. People rarely touch me. The girl, Savannah as I recall, looks up at me with a distressed expression.

"She's going to be okay," I say, rocking the babe in my arms. I've unwound the blanket and already the coolness of my body is reviving her. For once, the chill of my skin is a boon. "I promise."

"I know," Savannah says. "I knew you'd come."

Mr. Granger nods and gently pulls his daughter aside. "God bless you, miss. Keep 'em safe."

Chapter 3

Inside the ambulance, I reluctantly turn the child over to Mrs. Granger while Dana maneuvers the truck out of the yard with the precision of a soldier negotiating her way through a minefield. Her driving skills impress me and, coupled with a highly predaceous sexual nature, I sometimes wonder if she isn't a man masquerading as a highly attractive female.

Mrs. Granger sits on the stretcher with the tiny child in her arms. The babe is flushed and damp with perspiration. I long to pick her up and cradle her against my breast. To breathe in the sweet smell of her tender flesh. It is one of the greatest joys of my profession when I am able to hold a child in my arms.

"What's her name?" I ask.

"Lily. Lily Anne Granger. We chose her middle name for you, miss." I look at her, surprised. "If you hadn't been there with her breech and all, she wouldn't have made it. You were so calm and steady. If she has half your nerve I can rest easy knowing she'll survive this world."

I crouch at the side of the stretcher and take Lily Anne's tiny foot in my hands. Thirst hits me so hard, I almost swoon. Gently, I rub my trembling thumb against the delicate ankle, looking for a vein. Nothing is apparent. She is so dehydrated her veins are invisible.

"You, Mrs. Granger, are the strong one. Bringing so much life into the world. You truly are a blessed woman."

"Thank you. Most people wouldn't say so. That's real kind of you."

"Most people are blind to life's gifts." If I had a baby like this, I'd be the happiest creature in the world. How I envy Mrs. Granger, to hold a physical manifestation of love in her arms. And I envy Lily Anne too.

They say I was too young to remember my mother and her long, painful death, but I do. I remember her clasping me, holding me close to her hot, moist body. I remember the sound of her racing heart, the panting breath against my face. Mostly, I recall the agony of being torn from her trembling arms. And I don't know how, because this happened before I knew the words, but I remember someone strong holding me, bringing me to her and Mama's anguished cry, "No, take it away. I cannot bear to look upon her!" A ragged sob bursting forth, a door closing, and the sudden coldness that came with being whisked from the warm-sickened room, away from her. Forever.

A child is meant to be cradled by her creator as surely as a man is made to unite with a woman. To be withheld from one another is unnatural punishment.

What pains me is that my presence increased Mama's suffering. She knew what she was leaving behind—six small children and a love-grieved husband. We needed her! And oh, how she knew it! After she died, Charlotte claimed to see an angel by my cradle. I like to believe it was Mama watching over me.

I glance up at Mrs. Granger, struck by how young she looks. Mama was not far from her in age, nor I from Lily Anne's, when God stole my first love. But I am no longer so powerless. I will protect Mrs. Granger's family so that she will never know an inkling of my pain. I will be *their* guardian angel.

Lily Anne would be a hard stick for other medics but I've been starting IVs for over a century, many on men left virtually bloodless on the battlefield. It's as if, like a divining rod, my body can sense where the blood lies. Quickly, I slide in a needle and secure the catheter, then reach for a box of slender tubes beside the seat and begin drawing the babe's blood for the hospital.

I fill vials with the pungent liquid, my throat tense with thirst, and set them safely aside on the seat for the ER. Now it's my turn, and I reach for the three secret tubes I keep deep in my pocket. Blood from a child this young would sustain me for days. The younger the being, the greater the life force. This is how I survive. By sipping on the injured. Grazing like a fawn. It doesn't take much to keep my heart beating, for our lives are tenacious as weeds. Even in life, I ate little. Always, my sisters would tempt me with treats, fearing my weakness was a result of anemia, but even back then I worshipped self-control.

I have not taken a human life in half a century and did then only as a matter of absolute necessity. Only in the early years of my new birth did I feed upon humans with any regularity, following the wars, taking mostly killers, but still never free from shame.

Now my self-control is secure. Discipline and an iron will have always been my greatest virtues and over sixteen decades I have honed them into a finely edged sword that cuts only me. Of course, there is a price.

There is always a price.

I am weak for my kind. We are a rare breed and I've known only a few, but I'm weaker than any I have ever known. This is what happens when one lives as I do, imprisoned by conscience, forced to feed on the frail.

Lily Anne begins to cry and squirm in her mother's arms.

"She's coming around," Mrs. Granger says. She smiles, gazing at me with a look of absolute trust. "Little Lily Anne is comin' around."

Now is the time to sustain myself. The child's strong, tempered only by fever or flu. A few additional vials of blood are nothing to her. Twice that much wouldn't be missed and might sustain me for weeks. But it's impossible to take such a libation without raising alarm.

My fingers close around the smooth glass tubes in my pocket when suddenly Lily Anne's body locks up. Her breath halts. She's having another seizure. Forgetting my hunger, I draw up medication and push it through her IV line. Mrs. Granger watches tensely until the seizure ends and her daughter resumes normal breathing. I give Lily Anne oxygen and fluids and check her sugar, all the while instructing Mrs. Granger on how to treat her children for fever, and then before I know it we're pulling up to the hospital.

Damn it! I'm running out of time!

I reach for my secret blood tubes, but just as they clear my pocket, Dana slams on the brakes and sends me flying across the bench seat. I catch myself and watch in horror as the vials hit the floor and scatter across the truck. They come to a crash against the wall, breaking into pieces. Fury sparks within me. Fury at Dana for driving like a maniac and fury at myself for losing track of time.

When you are a Night Walker, you must never *ever* lose track of time.

Dana roughly throws the truck into reverse, jolting us all, and backs up to the ER entirely too fast. Mrs. Granger pulls Lily Anne close, kissing the top of her head and wrapping a free hand around her baby's little feet as if to catch and hold her daughter's vulnerability, shielding it from the world.

A wave of protectiveness wells within me. Mrs. Granger need not worry. Lily Anne is my name child and I will perish before I allow a single soul to do her harm.

Chapter 4

Quickly, I sweep the broken shards of glass up and toss them into the trash. Dana yanks the truck's back door open and pulls out the stretcher before I can move to help.

Checking her watch, she says, "Let's make this quick."

I look for the blood tubes I filled earlier for the hospital. My hunger is growing so raw I'll keep them for myself, surreptitiously of course. But thanks to Dana's driving they've slid across the bench seat toward the back door. She sees them before I do and picks them up.

"You need to slow down," I snap. "You're driving like an escaped convict."

"I need to make that lecture," she huffs. "How come whenever there's something I *need* to do, we get a call?"

"That's why they call it a job, Dana." I hand her the report and begin straightening the truck as she wheels the stretcher into the ER, carrying Lily Anne's blood tubes away from me. I long to run after her and snatch them back, but that would look crazy so I stick to my routine. I never remain at the hospital for long. Too much fluorescent light, too many eyes. Dana likes to linger, especially now that there is a new ER doc in town. She must really be worried about school, because tonight she pushes through the doors without even a glance around for him.

I'm restocking the IV kit when Rescue 7 backs in, screeching to a stop beside me. Paul, also known as Chewi for his laconic propensity to communicate through grunts, climbs out moving uncharacteristically fast. Normally, he barely picks up speed for a multiple casualty incident and I wonder what has him hustling. He shuffles to the back and throws open the door. Inside, controlled chaos reigns. A paramedic is at the head of the stretcher bagging oxygen into a patient's lungs while a sweaty fireman performs rapid CPR. Nearby, a terrified mother crouches. Discarded ET tubes, wrappers, towels, and a bloody laryngoscope handle litter the floor.

"Stop CPR," Chewi says, and checks the monitor. The fireman stops. It's Tom, Dana's jilted lover, and I pray they don't run into each other inside. The ECG alarm screams in the small space and the monitor commands, "Check patient" over and over with a grating robotic voice intentionally designed, I suspect, to induce stress. Tom wipes his forehead against his arm. Chewi frowns.

CPR recommences and I move to help. When we unload the patient I see he is only a boy, about 8-years-old, wearing a "Star Wars" t-shirt and PJ's covered in Dalmatians. I place a bare hand on his forehead and sense the current of life struggling within him. CPR is keeping him alive. For now.

Tom looks to me as if for hope, but I can't give any. "Electrocution," he says. "Just a freak thing." There is a bewildered, frightened air to him, and I wonder if he's imagining his own child yet to be born, the potential fragility of life for which he will soon be held responsible.

How vulnerable loves makes us.

The little boy is whisked inside and I cannot help but follow. Just through the code room's double doors, the new ER doc is there listening to the medic's report and giving orders. The hospital staff takes over, but nothing they do is working. The child's heart refuses to beat. Without a pause, the doc cracks open the boy's chest with the ease of a linebacker tearing open a small box. The room falls silent. Stunned, I watch as his gloved hand slips around ribs slender as branches and slides beneath the boy's heart to massage and restart it. My guts clench. The scent of young blood hits my face and I fall back, so caught off guard I can't help myself. I press into the wall, trying to hide.

Upon the doctor's palm lies a tender, glistening heart.

Gently, he pulses the heart with his hand, circulating blood to the boy's brain and body while coolly directing his staff, who remain momentarily frozen. Even the ER's most seasoned veteran looks strained, yet not a gleam of sweat or single strand of hair reveals the doctor's tension. He's impeccable under his white coat, which has somehow survived this impromptu surgery without acquiring a speck of blood. A bright suspended light hangs directly above him. For a split second, he shines like an Aryan god.

This is Dr. Webb, our new physician.

How I long to sink my teeth into the heart he holds and suck it dry. I squeeze my eyes closed at the shameful image. *Dear God, forgive me.*

"Let's go, people," Webb orders, breaking his staff's paralysis. They immediately obey.

A sharp, animal-like yelp cuts the room and Webb looks over. It's the boy's mother, staring horrified at her son's gaping chest. He gives the head nurse a quick glance of disapproval and she ushers out the distraught woman.

Suddenly the energy of the room shifts, as if a faint electrical hum I'd barely noticed swells to fill the space. The scent of blood blooms and Webb's breath catches. The boy is alive! Webb knows the moment of rekindled life, and I see his eyes brighten, ecstatic he made the save. No one notices but me. My hunger flares. Webb contains himself and continues on, remaining methodical and concise.

Dana appears at my side, grabbing me by the arm and once again checking her watch. Tom sees her and blushes, but she doesn't notice. As she pulls me away, I take a last look at the doctor.

"We have a pulse," he says. He stops cardiac massage, letting his fingers fall open from around the boy's heart. In awe, the entire staff stares at the red bundle of muscle beating upon Webb's palm.

Our new doctor has brought a boy back from the dead.

"Get a blood pressure," he orders.

A nurse jumps to comply. The new respiratory tech takes shallow breaths, eyes shining with tears. Dr. Webb says something comforting, I think, but I can't hear. Dana is dragging me through swinging doors.

"Damn!" she says, startling the shock-stricken mother nearby. "I'm going to be late. Mother*fucker*."

Chapter 5

We climb back into the truck and she slams it in gear. I'm certain she doesn't drive her new Camaro this roughly, but I'm too preoccupied to scold her.

"Did you *see* that?" I ask.

"What?"

"Dr. Webb."

"Yeah, he's hot. Most ER docs are total geeks. *Nothing* like TV."

"He cut through that boy's chest like apple pudding. I haven't seen that in a long time. You could work your entire career, Dana, and never see that."

"If I flunk out of school, I sure won't see it then. Though I guess I could be a paramedic like you." She gives me an appraising glance, then grimaces. "Oh, hell no. Navy is not my color, nor is your paycheck an appropriate amount to live on. This job is temporary."

"I don't understand why you're so worried about an English class. Can't you retake it if you don't pass?"

"It will kill my GPA and Daddy will cut me off. This time, he's serious. I can feel it. I have too many expenses to live un-supplemented.

I require patronage. Plus, I refuse to take a class with Professor Hardcastle again. If I have to read another line of Romantic poetry ever again, I'll puke."

"I love the Romantics," I muse.

"Of course you do. You love all those pale sensitive people who die tragically young. Shelley, Polidori, Byron—God, they were all so *weak*. Santos survived ten tours of combat and lived. All these guys did was *write* and not one of them made it past their thirties!"

"Their words were strong. They endured."

"What good are words when you're dead?"

She steps on the accelerator and speeds through town, toward the Art Deco district where my favorite bookstore of all time happens to reside. Dana parks before a fire hydrant, I suspect to irritate her ex, firefighter Tom, and walks into the store. I hesitate.

I've never been inside. Instead, I do my browsing of their titles online. I've been afraid to venture in, lest I enjoy it too much and want to linger and then return. When I'm not running calls in the dark, I keep fiercely to myself. This is how I live: in exile from humanity. Attachment means discovery and discovery all too often leads to death.

Despite our strength, there are so many ways to die. Murder. Starvation. Sunshine. It takes prudence and forethought to navigate our world, no doubt the reason so few of my kind have survived. Young Night Walkers, beset by hunger and fraught with boldness, feel immortal. Enraptured with their strength, they risk too much and perish in the process. Usually it's the sun that kills them, boiling their blood so fast their heart fails like a firefighter fallen from blazing heat. Yes, we have beating hearts, but they're not like yours. Ours tick far too long.

I gaze inside the bookstore. There is a cozy little café on the left where coffee, chocolate, tea and freshly baked muffins are served. In a seating area beside it, an audience gazes at a tall gentleman standing before them. This must be Professor Hardcastle, but I can't make him out from here. To his right, the shop winds around wooden bookcases densely packed with literature chosen by Malaprop's erudite employees. The checkout counter is on the far side and beyond it spills another room with rows of luscious books stacked from floor to ceiling, waiting to be devoured.

It's almost as tempting as blood. I scan the street outside, but see only a squad car idling down the block. My will is weak from hunger and, against my better judgment, I open the ambulance door and step out. No one looks as I cross the sidewalk. My face is thoroughly hidden beneath my cap and my slender frame ensconced in a navy jacket that rarely draws the eye. A wave of warmth and delicious aromas hits me as I open the door: coffee and chocolate and ginger.

Immediately I am struck by his voice. Dana was right. Professor Hardcastle's voice is low and smooth as a glass of scotch. Confident, like a man perfectly secure in his opinions. It is Oxford and England and the moors. Warm fire, brisk air, and the pulse of bodies around a kitchen table laughing out loud. It is home.

Sadness washes over me. Home might as well be on the moon.

All the seats are taken and I take a place against the wall in the back. To my surprise, I find that Hardcastle is in his thirties. He has a disheveled elegance and the sinewy strength of one who doesn't appear to indulge greatly in food or drink, a high noble forehead and impassioned cobalt eyes. His chestnut hair is long, tangled from wind and brushed haphazardly from his face with a strong pale hand. There is an Old World look about him, a toughened Byron, enhanced by his clothes and the old black boots he wears beneath woolen trousers. Ancient boots that look almost as old as mine.

I have not seen a man like this in a hundred years.

I had expected someone older, what with two doctorates and a professorship. Apparently, he is discussing his latest book. My sharp eyes read the title from across the room. *Branwell Brontë, A Man Alone*. An apt title. I focus on the professor's words.

"It has been suggested that Branwell was a homosexual and while living at Thorpe Green, violated his pupil—"

I gasp. "A lie!" I yell. My hand flies over my mouth as the entire room turns to look at me.

Professor Hardcastle's head snaps my way. "Aha! We have a Brontë fan."

I turn and break for the door but a group of college students comes barreling through it in a pack, blocking my way. Instinctively, I pivot and head to the furthest corner of the bookstore I can find.

I pick up a book and try to compose myself. I'm actually trembling. I need to feed! I need to hide. In the background, I hear the professor thanking those for joining him and wishing them good night. I force myself to tune him out. How can he spread such untruths and be so respected?

I sense a presence at my back and turn to find him standing a few feet away with a blinking wire-haired fox terrier in his arms. The little terrier gives me a sniff. He is old with a leather collar around his neck stamped with silver bones and paws, and I wonder what this grown man is doing carrying him around like a socialite with a Pomeranian.

"My apologies," the professor says, with the slightest of bows. In his shirt's breast pocket is a slender volume of Shelley's *Epipsychidion*.

Sweet Spirit! In my heart's temple I suspend to thee, These votive wreaths of withered memory.

"Miss . . ." He glances at the name embroidered on my shirt, "Bell. I didn't mean to offend you." Warm sincerity shines through his voice. My God, that *voice*.

Dana comes bounding up. "Will!"

"Most people, Miss Fitzpatrick, who are my students, refer to me by the title of Professor."

"Whatever. You have a first name like everybody else. Who's this?" Dana asks, nodding to the terrier.

"This is my new companion, Woody. He was my mother's dog. She—" he clears his throat and frowns "—recently passed away."

"Is that why you missed class a few weeks ago?"

"Yes, I returned to England to make arrangements…" he trails off.

"My condolences," I say, meaning it. He gives me a tight nod and his gaze falls to the floor as if burning a hole through the very ground, allowing me an opportunity to study him. The planes of his face are high and true and there's sensitivity to his brow that whispers of sacrifice and responsiveness. He smells of fresh paper and ink and it takes all my strength not to lean forward and breathe him deeply in.

"What a cute little Woody you have," Dana coos nonsensically. "You have such a tiny little Woody in your hands."

Woody is adorable, like a soft little lamb dusted in grey. The old dog's eyes have the milky blue hue of cataracts and he flinches when Dana reaches out to stroke him.

With a vexed look, the professor sets him down and Woody takes a few steps toward me then stops and stares blankly at the wall.

"I'm afraid his sight is going; hence I carry him a great deal more than any dignified man should. Forgive me, Miss Bell. My name is William." He holds out a hand to me.

"Anne," I stammer, not wanting to take it but seeing no civilized way I can refuse. I am literally backed into a corner. Reaching out, I briefly grasp it then shove my hands in my pockets. Why didn't I wear my gloves tonight? I am growing complacent! The warmth of his skin lingers against my palm like a touch of sun.

"Anne . . . Bell? Anne Bell. Interesting. That was Anne Brontë's pen name. Acton Bell, actually." He cocks his head and tries to gaze at me beneath my cap, but I crouch down to give Woody a pat, denying him the opportunity.

Suddenly, a Malaprop's employee walking by stops and stares at me. He is young and earnest-looking, in torn jeans and a faded black t-shirt that states *Born to Read* across the front. "Anne Bell? Do you live on Pearson Street?"

"Yes," I say warily, leaning down and scratching Woody behind an ear. How in the world have I attracted so much attention in under five minutes? Clearly, this venture inside has been a dreadful mistake.

"You're the special order person." He points at me.

It doesn't look like Born to Read boy is going away and I rise, keeping my face tilted down toward the professor's boots. They look vaguely 20th century.

"You have more special orders per month than any of our customers. You are *the* most well-read Malaprop's customer that I know of, and that's saying a lot. You read everything. It's crazy. From the mating habits of vampire bats to obscure 19th century poets I've never heard of. I mean, Cowper?" He waits for a response, looking me up and down. I long to hiss at him to go away. "I've got to say, you're nothing like I expected. I figured you'd be some staunchy old bluestocking that never left the house." He waits for a reply that doesn't come. I have perfected the art of silence. Except with Professor Hardcastle. For some reason, I'd failed utterly with him with my earlier blurting out.

"Hey, your order's here now. Do you want it?" He gestures to the counter where neatly stacked books sit waiting to be picked up by their new lovers.

"No, thank you. I don't want to carry it in the truck. Just mail it, please."

"You know, I always wondered, why do you have your orders shipped when you only live a mile away?"

"Because she's a *recluse*," Dana says abruptly, jolting us all. "She only goes out to work."

William Hardcastle gives her a sharp look, evidently not appreciating Dana's manners.

The kid looks at me with understanding. "That's okay. I'll send them out Monday. Hey, great to meet you." I smile faintly and read the back of his t-shirt before he ducks behind a counter. *Damned to Write.*

Poor soul.

Time to go! I try to slip around the professor but he shifts, blocking my escape. He's a foot taller than me and it's impossible to pass by without physically touching him. I step back, mouth watering.

"So you've read the Brontës?" he asks.

Why is he still here? "A long time ago."

"But you have definite opinions of their character. You take offense with suggestions that Branwell's sexuality was anything less than orthodox."

"I've never heard such a thing in my life! It's gossip and slander."

"I know. Mere speculation." He waves his hand dismissively.

"Exactly! Speculation. The purest form of tabloid journalism. You call that scholarship? I thought you were an academic." I'm shocked at my outburst. Usually the presence of a man renders me painfully silent.

He looks embarrassed. "I was merely answering a question from the audience. I certainly don't support those views, but sexuality does inform our lives. It isn't something to be ignored."

Dana looks at me and smirks, then wanders over to the romance section where she picks up a book with a vampire huntress splayed across the cover in the arms of a steroidal-looking Viking. Shifting,

I glance for the door. How in the world did we land on the topic of *sexuality*?

"I must tell you, Miss Bell, how exciting it is to meet someone who feels as passionately as I do about the Brontës."

"I am not *passionate* about the Brontës. I haven't read them in ages."

"Who, may I ask, is your favorite? Let me guess." He holds up a graceful finger. *"Anne."*

"Anne Brontë?" I remember how my brother described me once, so long ago. "The forgettable nothing?"

"*What?*" He pulls back in surprise and a lock of hair falls into his eyes. My fingers itch to reach out and brush it off his startled face.

"I'm amazed she's still in print," I say, with astonishing composure. "That didactic formula, contrived narrative, it's so stilted and outdated."

"She was writing in the early eighteen hundreds."

"Her sisters didn't write like that. She was clearly riding on the wake of their fame. *Wuthering Heights* and *Jane Eyre* are far superior works, more passionate and sophisticated."

"I beg to differ, Miss Bell. Anne Brontë was deeply passionate, but unlike her sisters, she mastered her feelings. She was a proto-modernist, eons ahead of her time. If she'd lived she would have been another George Eliot, in her own spiritually sensitive way."

"Proto-modernist?"

"A realist exploring freedom and control. Dependency and subjugation. Entitlement and oppression. *Alcoholism*, for God's sake, in 1848! She wrote about things as they *were*. The true and real, not as she wished them to be. *Agnes Grey* and *The Tenant of Wildfell Hall* are rooted in reality, in stark contrast to the romantic fantasies of her sisters."

I stare at him in amazement. Who is this man to think he knows so much? "I read books," I say, "for pleasure and enlightenment. I don't study literary criticism, and I distrust people who claim to know and judge what a writer is thinking and feeling. Is that how you earn your living?"

A blush begins to crawl up his cheeks, my hunger rising with it. "Well, I am a professor of English Literature, but judgment is not my intention."

"Have you published these theories?"

"Um, yes." He shifts uncomfortably. "This is my second book."

"On Branwell Brontë? Calling him a homosexual!" A girl with a nose ring standing in the Women's Studies section turns to glare at me.

The handsome professor puts a hand up to calm me. "I never said he was gay—not that there is anything in the least bit wrong with a person's sexual preference." He gives the glaring girl a nod. "However, I did *not* write that in my book. I was simply answering a question from the audience referring to a popular, if not exactly accurate, biography."

"Well, I'm surprised you would spread untruths like that. I would expect more from an Oxford professor."

I had no idea that any biographies on Branwell existed. I veer far and wide from all Brontëana. Once, in the spirit of morbid curiosity, I picked up a biography on Charlotte. I was, in turns, disturbed and humored by the reconstruction of her life, until I came across a letter she wrote to her best friend, Ellen. It so pained me, I vowed to never read about the doomed family again. I don't want to know what Charlotte suffered, but I cannot forget her words—

It is over. Branwell—Emily—Anne are gone like dreams—gone as Maria and Elizabeth went twenty years ago. One by one I have watched them fall asleep on my arm—and closed their glazed eyes—I have seen them buried one by one and—thus far—God has upheld me. From my heart I thank him.

Now, in the bookstore, before this man, I want to forget all that. And yet I want to remember.

Professor Hardcastle draws a deep breath. "I deeply apologize, Miss Bell, if I have offended you. I assure you I shall tread with far more caution in the future. Please" —he gives me a gracious bow— "I beg your forgiveness."

"Of . . . of course," I stammer, breathless from his chivalry.

Rising, his smile spills over me like the sun's rays after a frigid swim. My too pale hand moves to my throat and his eyes follow. Quickly, I shove it in my pocket.

Woody turns and bumps into my leg. Without thinking, I pick up the soft little dog and rock him ever so gently.

"May I ask you a personal question?" the professor asks.

Oh God, no. I shove Woody in his arms. "We're on duty. We need to get back to work."

"Are you English?"

Dana pops up from a bookshelf and looks at me.

"No," I lie, now determined to edge past him.

"I detect a rhythm in your voice. It's subtle, but I've studied linguistics and you have a hint of Haworth about you."

"Massachusetts," I say, having told Dana I was born there, hating the lie. I will myself not to blush from shame. This is the problem with lies: they go on and on like an infectious disease until you can no longer keep track of whom you've contaminated.

His brow creases. "There's a touch of Yorkshire to your tone, dusted with an Irish lilt. Very delicate. It's quite lovely."

"I lived there a few years." *Eons ago. It's impossible my accent remains.*

"For school perhaps?"

"I was mostly home schooled," I say, refusing to be embarrassed.

"Well, from the sound of it, you're certainly better read than most of my students. By any chance, when you were in England, did you stay in the area of Haworth?"

"I've never been to Haworth," I say, emphatically shaking my head. I feel my skin growing warm, a sensation I thought impossible in such a state of weakness.

While gently rocking Woody in his arms, he watches me. "Interesting."

"I've never been to Haworth," I repeat and shrug with forced nonchalance. I'm increasingly inclined to shove him out of my way and flee.

"Oh, you should go. The Brontë Parsonage is there. Diary fragments, watercolors, poetry."

"Diaries!"

He nods. "Fragments."

"Have you read Anne's diary?!"

"Lord, I wish! Only two small entries remain. What I would give for a glimpse of her journal!" He looks embarrassed at my startled expression. "A strange thing, I know, for a man to say. But, I wrote my doctoral thesis on her. It became my first published book. *Anne Brontë, Child of God.*"

I bite my lip and taste blood.

"I have read Emily's, though. Her last entry is heartbreaking. At 27, she resounds with hope, yet three years hence, she, Branwell, and Anne would all be dead. That family bore more pain than any deserved. Not one lived long, except their reverend father, cursed with unnatural strength to the ripe age of 84."

My tears well like blood.

Professor Hardcastle looks mystified. "I don't know how he bore it. Losing his young wife and six children. He dedicated his life to God only to have his entire family ripped away like Job."

"It was an honor meeting you, Professor. I hope that you will allow Dana some leeway with her paper. She works very hard. Between nursing school and her night shifts with me, it's a wonder she makes it through any of your curriculum at all. Please consider this as you hold her future in your hands. Good day, sir."

I roughly push past him, aware I'm exceeding the bounds of propriety. But I can't help it. I'm *starving* and it's making me cranky and careless. How did I ever become ensnared in conversation with this man? This is why I don't go inside. This is exactly why, when I'm not working, I don't leave the house. When you run on dying people, they don't ask questions like where you went to school.

I walk out of the bookshop, determined never to return.

For once in her life, Dana trails in my wake.

Chapter 6

"I'll drive," I say, climbing behind the wheel. I must do something. I can no longer sit passively beside Dana while she prowls the streets like a huntress. "This is the last time I let you talk me into going anywhere. Though, I must admit, you are correct about Professor Hardcastle. He's uncommonly arrogant."

"He was actually being super nice to you. He apologized twice. You were kind of being a bitch. You on the rag?"

I haven't had a cycle since I was turned, but I don't tell her this. "My physiological state has nothing to do with my mood." This is, of course, another lie. I feel as if I'm starving to death and it's making me overly sensitive. I stare out the window, trying to ignore Dana's luscious fertility. Night Walkers can't reproduce, but even if we could it wouldn't matter. After all this time, I'm still a virgin.

I lay my foot on the pedal with no idea whatsoever where I'm going. My hands are slightly trembling, whether from hunger or the confrontation with Professor Hardcastle I'm not sure. I can't recall when I've had such a long conversation with anyone besides Dana. Especially not a man.

Most of my partners have been male, but no one likes to work the night shift long, so they change rather frequently. Even those who linger come to accept my reticence. I've worked with men for years who know less about me than Dana has pieced together in six months.

Beside my partners and patients, I mostly come into contact with firemen and police, but they're men of action, not intellect, and so rarely lure me into conversation. Conversation leads to understanding and that leads to connection. From connection arises attachment. I cannot become attached to anyone or anything. This is how I survive.

I am silent and perfectly careful. This bores most people. A few people it intrigues—usually men. They are unused to silent, unknowable women, but after a while they move on. No one has more patience than a Night Walker. For us, a decade might as well be a day.

We circle the town and cross the slow, cold French Broad River then I'm speeding onto the interstate, west toward the Smokies, north toward Mt. Mitchell and back south along the Blue Ridge Parkway, skirting the edge of our territory, but I don't care. The night is dead and I'm starving. Dana's on her phone, compulsively texting a girlfriend in California or some new mystery man, I don't know. The Abominable Snowman could cross our path and she wouldn't notice.

Mountains surround me like granite kingdoms, leaning in, forcing me back toward town. I'm driving fast in aimless circles, trying to outrun memories clashing inside me like demons I don't have the strength to fight. Professor Hardcastle has cracked open the coffin of my past and its ghosts are pouring out. I feel smothered by mountains and darkness. How I long for the wide-open spaces of my youth! Horizons immense as the sea. *Endless.* But I'm downtown again, boxed in by buildings, crawling down empty streets until I find myself on Ravenscroft and turning onto Church Street.

Easing off the pedal, I glide before a row of glorious Gothic Revival churches fashioned in limestone and brick, whispering of endurance. Eternity. Transcendence. They're all arches and angles, curves and towers straining to heaven. Stained glass that glows in the dark. And suddenly the spirit of Papa is brimming within me, filling me with tears. God, how I miss him! His stern dignity. His iron love.

No one suffers more than he who lives longest.

My sister Emily may have resembled Papa most in temperament, but I was most akin to him in faith. He alone understood how I struggled with God. Even though we disagreed on doctrine, he never challenged my right to free thought or derided my devotion. When Emily scorned my beliefs and Branwell laughed and laughed at my folly, Papa quietly reminded me to trust myself. God speaks to some more than others, he said, and listening is not for the faint of heart.

Why didn't I tell Papa how much I loved him? Why do words fail me at the gravest moments? So many missed opportunities to express my love, I can barely breathe at the thought of it.

I want to revisit the morning my fate was pronounced; the morning the doctor came to the Parsonage for my final diagnosis. We were in the sitting room: Charlotte, her best friend, Ellen, Papa, and me. My family looked so scared. Charlotte was on the verge of collapse and Papa sat still and stoic. Only two weeks earlier, we'd lost Emily and three months before that, Branwell. Now I too stood upon the precipice of extinguishment.

Papa's eyes burned as the doctor listened to my ravaged lungs. After the examination, I was too excited to hold still, and I circled the room with Ellen for support. I could hardly wait for the doctor to speak, so ready was I to shed this mortal skin.

Call me away. There's nothing here that wins my soul to stay.

The doctor spent an interminable time returning his instruments to his bag, no doubt searching for the right words. There were none.

Not for Papa or Charlotte. But when he declared my fate, a sudden joy seized me, sweeping through me like elation, quickening my pace as I walked back and forth across the small room.

Death was coming. *Soon*! I was to be free at last! Just as Emily and I wrote and dreamed. Yet, instead of becoming one with the moors as she wished, I would become one with God, I was certain.

Lord, I'm coming! I cried, silently. Wait for me! I'm coming!

"My dear little Anne," Papa said, catching me as I passed and drawing me to him. Self-absorption had rendered me heedless to his feelings, but now I saw them. He could say no more, but he didn't need to. All his love was poured into those four words.

My dear little Anne.

I paused a moment before resuming my pacing, too full of joy to hold still. But how I wish I could do it over. This time I'd climb upon his knee, wrap my arms around him and kiss his face. "I love you, Papa," I'd say, even as everyone watched. "I love you so much."

He gave us the greatest gift of all: freedom to be ourselves.

I watch the row of churches shrink in the rearview mirror. "I can't believe it's so quiet," I say.

Dana glances at me. "You're the only medic I've ever known who wants to run calls after dark."

"I sleep in the day. When I'm on shift, I expect to work. I've never seen the town this dead before."

"It's the heart of winter. It's *freezing*. No tourists are here and most sane people are safe inside. Stop wishing calls on us. I've been up all day, starting IVs on geriatrics. A nap would be nice."

The dispatcher comes over the radio. "Rescue 1."

Dana groans. "Anne, you jinxed us!"

I wink at her and pick up the radio. "Rescue 1. Go."

"Respond to the Biltmore for an 18-year-old male. Fall. Possible fracture."

My hand flies over switches as the lights and siren flare. I drive exceedingly fast to the "chateau," an enormous mansion built by George Vanderbilt in the late 1800s so he might more comfortably entertain his friends in the Blue Ridge Mountains. Now that the family trust fund has dried up, the current heirs support the estate through tourism, but at this time of night it is surely closed.

"If I was driving this fast," Dana says, "you'd make me pull over."

It's true, but with my eyes and reflexes I'm a far safer driver. Still, I force myself to slow as we pull onto the estate property. A heavy mist hangs upon the land. We wind for miles down a dramatic drive through naked forest, elegant and dripping in fog while the languorous river slides beside it. The modern world vanishes and we roll deeper into a dreamscape reminiscent of fairy tale castles and hidden slumbering princes. Towering oaks and pines shield the inner sanctum as we curve our way toward the estate's heart.

Against my will, I am awed by the invisibly contrived harmony such outrageous wealth willed into being. At last, the road spills open revealing the property's crown jewel. My breath catches. It *is* a fairy tale. Gondal and Glass Town and Cinderella. Looming up out of the mist, the Biltmore House with her heavy stone and peaked dormers dwarfs me. Gargoyles peer down at us, watching, guarding.

I almost feel mortal again.

On a walkway that zigs and zags up a high stone wall, I see a blonde teenager in a beanie sitting beside an overturned skateboard with two friends off to one side. Sergeant Atticus Santos is there along with the Biltmore's night watchman and to my great surprise, Professor Hardcastle!

His hair is ragged from the wind, and he wears a high-collared, double-breasted wool coat, navy with brass buttons. It looks old and military. With each breath he takes, the air turns to steam. The little pooch, Woody, stands close beside him in a Kelly green parka with matching booties on his feet.

What in the world are they doing here?

I pull in front of the police car. Santos gives me a piercing look. He is dark and sleekly muscled, caught between black and white, war and peace. His eyes look haunted, as if he has demons and they are winning. Since his first day on the street, he's treated me with a barely concealed hostility I've never understood. Perhaps he finds me unnaturally evasive.

As much as possible, I avoid police. Their work has made them suspicious and given them a finely honed instinct for detecting lies. Santos has been back from the war for years, yet hasn't transitioned from hunting terrorists to running down troublesome teenagers with much grace.

He turns to gaze at Dana as she steps out of the truck, golden and glowing in the flashing lights. Only months ago, she told me she was completely in love with him. Now she flips her flaxen ponytail over a shoulder and ignores Santos, walking past the patient up to the professor. "What are you doing here?" she asks.

"I was on my way to visit a friend when I noticed this young man in need of assistance."

"What were you going to do? Lecture him to death?"

"I've had a bit of medical training and thought I might be able to help."

Dana gives him a skeptical look.

"First aid in the Royal Navy. Nothing extensive, but I'll venture a guess he'll live." He nods to the boy, who is sitting slumped on the curve, looking somewhat abashed but otherwise unharmed.

I'm surprised the professor has a military background. Other than his patrician posture, it's difficult to detect. I thought he was all literature and poetry. How has one man accomplished so much in so few years?

He acknowledges me with a nod, which I ignore.

I walk up to our patient. There is a youthful, rich, athletic look to him. His jeans are ripped at the right knee and I can see that it's scraped, but otherwise undamaged.

I want to throw him in the back of the truck, climb in and sink my teeth into his throat.

The urge shocks me. Stupid, stupid, stupid, not to sip from Lily Anne. By missing my chance to feed, I've put more lives in danger. I cannot continue to assume that calls will keep coming.

Santos walks up. "Old Man Vander here," he says, indicating the night watchman, "caught this kid riding the wall and chased him down. The kid fell as he was evading capture. Need you to check him out for my report."

The night watchman is a sprightly man in his early 50s wearing the dark green uniform of a park ranger. *Biltmore Estates* above a heraldic emblem is embroidered on a patch over his heart in expensive thread. His snow-white hair is pulled back in a low ponytail and despite the park ranger uniform, his lyrical mustache lends him a marked refinement. I can't help wondering how he chased down a teenage boy on a skateboard.

Vander smiles at me. "Good evening. This young man was trespassing on private property, and as I hope I have made myself perfectly clear to everyone present," he says, pointedly looking at the boys who stare down at their feet, "trespassing on Biltmore grounds will be tolerated under absolutely *no* circumstances. The next time I catch any one of you riding slipshod over Biltmore stone as if it were common concrete, I shall give you the flouncing of your life and have you incarcerated for as long as legally possible."

Santos nods and glares at the boy.

"I'll take him off your hands," I say, moving to grab the stretcher.

Dana's head jerks up and Santos looks surprised. "You're taking him to the hospital for a scraped knee?"

"It could be cracked. It wouldn't hurt for him to get an x-ray."

Santos squints at me, but I dip my head as I bend to palpate the boy's knee. I rip his jeans open wider so I can get a better look. The muscles of his leg are firm beneath my hand. Everyone watches, including Professor Hardcastle.

"What's your name?" I ask gently.

"Garrick."

"Any pain or tenderness?" I squeeze harder than necessary.

"*Ouch!*" he cries.

"See," I say to Santos. "Unusual tenderness." I fear he senses the lie. As a mortal girl, I *revered* honesty and still after all these years deception does not come naturally. This is why I usually remain silent, but it's not always possible to do so.

To my relief, Garrick doesn't argue. I suspect he's grateful he's not being arrested. Quickly, I pull out the stretcher and help him onto it. Then, by myself, I pull it over to the truck and slam it in. I'm being reckless, revealing too much of my strength, but I want to get out of here right away. I'm famished.

Dana is saying something to the professor, clearly flirting. I must admit, I understand her attraction. He *is* handsome. There is an air of Shelley about him, but with an edge of discipline the Romantic poet never had. Even my sister Emily, immune to male beauty, might not be so blind to William's charms. She craved Shelley so powerfully, called to his spirit so passionately, I worried for her sanity. And she thought *my* grasp on reality was tenuous because I loved Jesus. Shelley drowned when she was but four-years-old.

I feel the professor's eyes on me and try not to fidget. I have the sensation he sees right through me. His gaze is unsettling. Santos is watching Dana while the professor, deaf to her words, stares my way. It's almost rude.

Rarely have I been looked at so openly and it makes me slightly dizzy. My body tightens, ready to flee. There's something about this man. Woody takes a step toward the truck, and in a flash Hardcastle catches him and holds him lightly in one arm. Woody blinks.

Old Man Vander watches everyone, taking in the entire scene. A cold sweat breaks over my skin. There is too much keen observation here. People are usually heedless to their environment. How is it I've come to be surrounded by the most observant men in town?

Panic starts to grow, beginning in my belly and snaking up my chest. This is how it always begins. This is how I know it's time to leave. Decade after decade I have moved on before people grow too cognizant of my eternal youth. Before they fully grasp my never-failing health. In the past, I never bought property. Never owned pets. I didn't make friends. But now I own an old Victorian house with a cat named Ivanhoe and feel a strange connection to a man I met barely an hour ago.

"Dana," I bark. "Dr. Webb will be waiting." This gets her attention. Ever since the new ER doc arrived, Dana hasn't complained about a single patient transport.

I climb into the back of the truck, but before I can pull the door closed, Santos grabs it, stopping me. His grip is strong, even for a mortal man. He looks at William and motions him over, then puts a hand on his shoulder like he knows him. Old World Professor and New World Cop seem a strange combination, but William is perfectly relaxed under Santos' touch.

Dana is heading to the driver's seat. "Dana," Santos says, stopping her. She gives him an impatient look. "You'll want to hear this."

"I doubt it," she says.

Santos frowns. "You'll want to hear this too, Will, with all the kids you see on campus."

Will? Do they know each other? How? What can they possibly have in common? Santos has spent the last 12 years in the Army. Ten tours of war have left him hypervigilant and angry, a sure sign of PTSD.

Santos takes a deep sigh. "A young girl was killed today. On her way home from the bus stop. Up off Barker road, toward Trust. Someone slit her throat from ear to ear."

My breath stops. Even Dana falls silent and a shadow crosses Will's face. This type of thing doesn't happen here. In Atlanta or Charlotte maybe, but not in our sleepy mountain town. I speak first, "Was she . . . Did he . . .?"

"No evidence of sexual assault. Some bastard just slit her throat and left her there to die. Her parents called her in missing when she never made it home from the bus stop. I went to check it out and found her lying in the dirt, scratch marks in the ground where she clawed at the earth while she bled out."

"How old was she?" the professor asks.

"Just turned 12."

"Dear God, man."

"If any of you come across anything suspicious, let me know."

Santos has that veiled look I've seen on so many men's faces. The look that comes from trying to shove all the horror down and lock it away. The look that shows they're failing.

"I'm sorry you had to see that," I say. "How horrible."

"I've seen worse."

Dana shakes her head. "Worse than a 12-year-old with her neck slit from ear to ear? God, Atticus. No wonder you're so fucked up."

Before anyone can speak, Dana slams the door closed, shutting me in with the patient. I feel her climb into the front seat and we speed off to the hospital. Pulling away, I catch Professor Hardcastle's eye through the rear window. He's looking straight at me with an expression of disturbing intensity. Instinctively, my hand flutters to my face, checking that my glasses are there.

I glance away, turning my attention to the teenage boy sitting compliant before me and swallow as my mouth begins to water.

Chapter 7

"Take off your parka," I order Garrick. He gives me a perplexed look but obeys. He is wearing a grey, long-sleeved waffle t-shirt with a radiological symbol splashed across his chest. For someone so young, his shoulders are broad. I take his arm in my hands and slide his shirt up his bicep, grab a tourniquet and secure it.

"You gonna stick me?" he asks, sounding alarmed.

"I'll be fast."

He looks nervous. "Is this really necessary? I'm not crazy about needles."

"The hospital might need to give you medication for the pain."

"It really doesn't hurt that much," he offers. Ever so slightly, he tries to pull away but I hold him firmly in my grip.

His veins are full and plump. The blood courses through them beneath my fingers, teasing me. I plunge in the needle, then pull it out, leaving a soft catheter. Grabbing blood tubes, I pierce the vials and watch them fill with blood, deep red and luminescent. The color of sunrise and death.

"How much you gonna take?"

This is the problem with the wealthy. They're always asking questions, demanding to be informed of one's every move. The poor don't question me like this. I want to reach for the three clean tubes that rest in my pocket, free of the preserving chemicals the other tubes have, but Garrick will not stop watching me. I slip back behind his head as if I'm reaching for something and grab the tubes.

Now is my turn. I fill my vials as Garrick watches. He is unusual. Most people afraid of needles do not look so closely.

"If you're afraid of needles, why do you watch?"

"Because I'm afraid." He looks at me and grins.

I finish and connect the IV tubing to the catheter in his vein. Next I take vitals and get a patient history. This is completely backwards, but I will not let this opportunity to feed pass me by. Three vials will hardly make a dent in my hunger, so far have I let it slide, but they'll sustain me until I can feed again, hopefully soon.

When we arrive at the hospital, Dana helps me roll Garrick inside while she scans for Dr. Webb. The intake nurse, whom Dana has taken to surreptitiously calling Nurse Ratched, looks at me like I'm crazy for starting an IV and transporting a boy with a scraped knee. Normally, I do not make such poor transport decisions, but my hunger has rendered me desperate. I contemplate keeping all the blood tubes and choking down the five full of chemicals even though they taste like rat poison. If I can get it down, my body cuts through the nasty peripherals straight to the hemoglobin.

The ER is quiet and the nurse has no reason to complain about this transport, yet she gives me a critical look anyway as we roll Garrick into a room and I give the report, emphasizing the exceptional tenderness to his knee and that I suspect a possible fractured patella. Her brow creases as she listens, an indication of doubt she does not voice.

I've survived this profession for so long because of my unnatural talents. I don't call in sick or take vacation. I can smell illness that others cannot see. From working in countless wars, I can cut and sew and clamp. Since 1853, I've been ministering to the sick and injured. I may not have not seen everything, but I've seen enough to diagnose the mysterious and save the unsalvageable. Despite my frosty personality and unusual solar affliction, my supervisor adores me, gladly working around my unorthodox schedule, having me relieved without fail an hour before sunrise.

Tonight however, I've compromised my reputation. My freedom to work unsupervised and unquestioned is firmly rooted in the trust of those with whom I work, and by the look in the nurse's eye, I've now injected doubt into the equation. This never would have happened if I hadn't stopped hunting in the wild. A deer would sustain me for weeks. Charlotte always warned, if I'm not careful, I'll die of idealism.

My fingers wrap around the blood tubes about to hand them over, yet I hesitate.

I cannot bring another unmerited patient here tonight without raising undue suspicion and I cannot count on the calls continuing to come.

I release the tubes and let them rest against my thigh, warm in my pocket. Making an effort to slow my movement to human standards, I head to the truck, where I will knock the blood back fast as a shot of scotch.

"Medic!" A voice cuts through the ER's hush. I turn to see Dr. Webb with an irritated look in his eye marching toward me. This is a first.

"Aren't you forgetting something?"

"No," I say carefully.

"The blood. Give it to me. I want it all."

Chapter 8

Dr. Webb stops before me and gives me an accusatory look. He is shorter than he no doubt desires, but fit and muscular with a confident face. His skill is exceptional—a force of calm amidst the chaos. I've witnessed him cut with surgical precision through his staff's swirling stress as a life circles the drain before them. He doesn't falter through doubt or indecision. He doesn't second-guess himself.

The hallway's fluorescents are bright; one reason I never linger long here. I cock my head as if confused, tilting my cap down just so. I have elevated the technique of concealing my gaze to the level of art.

"The blood you drew from the boy." He holds out his hand palm up. It is smooth and white.

Anger flashes through me. Garrick must have told them. I should have forced him to look away. I should have taken control. I shove my hand into my pocket and grab the blood, my fingers feeling for five tubes. "Sorry," I say, "I must have forgotten." Dana has appeared behind the doctor and is giving me a strange look. I place them in his cool hand.

"All of them," Webb says. "The boy said you took eight."

I know doctors all too well. They are accustomed to being sought after and worshipped, but they are mere mortals, perfectly capable of fallibility. I have saved their asses more times than I can count, and their power to intimidate me died long ago. Yet under the ice blue edge of Webb's gaze, my confidence falters. I feel like a poor cleric's daughter standing before the Magistrate of Blake Hall, accused of stealing his daughter's supper. Lamely, I feel about in my pockets, then, as if in surprise, hand over my stash. I pray I am too anemic to flush with shame though it burns my very blood.

"I've heard of you, Bell. How you exceed the protocols and violate your scope of practice. I don't care how many crikes you've done or bleeds you've staunched. That means nothing. I don't want to see sutures or cut downs. You are a paramedic and will adhere to your department's protocols or I will have your license revoked."

Dana's mouth drops open in surprise. I stare at the doctor. I can see his pulse beating in his throat. His pressure is up, filling him with life, flushing him with heat, and the desire to suck him dry flashes through me so strongly my stomach clenches.

"If you want to be a doctor, then go to med school like the rest of us," Dr. Webb says. "But if you think two years of school qualifies you to diagnose and perform surgical techniques, you are seriously deluded. Nothing is more irritating than a paramedic who thinks he's a doctor. I *will* be watching you, Bell." His eyes drill into me cold as missiles.

Abruptly he turns and collides into Dana, gripping her waist to stop from knocking her over. She lights with lust and briefly he hesitates before releasing her and striding back up the hall. An image of WWII strikes me. Berlin. All those self-righteous men stomping about like overdressed bullies.

Oh, the immaculate discipline it took not to feed on them all.

Chapter 9

I walk to the truck and climb in the passenger side, my energy spent. "What was that about?" Dana says, starting the truck.

I don't answer, just stare out the side window into the never-ending darkness that is my life. Always hiding. Always running. Always lying.

"You seem all out of whack today and you don't look so good either. I thought you were the Terminator. Never tires, never eats, strong as a man. I've got to say, Anne, you're not living up to your reputation. You okay?"

I shake my head, not knowing what to say. Tears are threatening. I'm so hungry I could cry. This is how an addict feels, damaged and desperate, unable to extinguish the insatiable craving raging inside, burning away dignity and sense of self. My poor brother. Is this how he felt?

This is why I will never drink directly from a human without killing them. To feed upon a human and let them live is to inject them with a thirst that can never be quenched. It will turn them into a degenerate manifestation of their former selves. A wretched, quivering shadow. This is why Branwell fought his addictions for years before finally succumbing. Now I know he was fed on, played with, *savored*, before he was ultimately taken by a soul thief.

I will not do this to another living being. But, oh I am sorely tempted to erase this need and restore my self-control.

I look over at Dana. Even through her uniform, her breasts swell, soft and ample. She is a picture of healthy fertility. How would she recover if I drank from her? I could knock her out so fast she wouldn't know what happened. Sedate her with an amnesiac from the med box and drink. When she awoke, I could say she had fallen asleep.

Shame washes over me. How low I have fallen! I am not this girl. I am gentle and good. Humane. No one has more reverence for the sanctity of life. I am dying for it.

If I don't feed again tonight, tomorrow I will have to call in sick and hunt. Search through this smoky wilderness for life. Can I even do it? Have I let my strength fade so far that I can no longer chase down a deer? Can I drain a life, even an animal's, in order to live? Will God forsake me longer if I do? Is this all a great test?

If Thou should bring me back to life, more humbled I should be;

More wise—more strengthened for the strife—More apt to lean on thee.

My own words haunt me, reminding me how I fail my vow. I'm weaker and more ignorant than ever.

Dana drives back to the station and goes inside, falls into bed, hoping we're done for the night. Sunrise is hours away, and I sit in the truck, staring blankly into nothingness. I consider pulling out my sketchpad and drawing, but all I see are varying shades of black and grey. How I miss the rosy pink and sunlit gold and glowing orange of dawn. Green grass and blue skies. The neon yellow of a butterfly. My world now is a thousand shades of shadow. For hours I sit in cold solitude, succumbing to weakness while sunrise crawls closer with a pull as sure as gravity.

Are these the symptoms of a heart, of heavenly grace bereft—
For ever banished from its God, to Satan's fury left?

Everyone I have ever loved is dead and I will never love again. This isn't despair; it is fact.

I've heard modern souls astonishingly suggest that those who lived long ago, encircled by death as we were, grew numb to it, that perhaps we suffered our losses less. This is not true. Our attachments were stronger, deeper, and more enduring. We knew from hard experience that no one can be replaced.

After Mama died, Papa never loved another woman again. That must have been hard for a man in his prime. Branwell had one engulfing love, whom he claimed to die for: the married Mrs. Robinson. Charlotte had her professor. Emily, her dead poet. And for me, there was the heartbreaking rogue, Reverend William Weightman. I can't help smiling at the vibrant memory of him. His passion for Greek and Latin. His youthful enthusiasm for life. Every time he entered the Parsonage, it was like clouds dispersed and the sun burst forth. His light drew even Emily from her self-constructed cage—some feat!

Charlotte warned me his charm shone for many girls, not only me. Always the protectress, she was. How was I to know he wrote sweet letters to other more beautiful, worthy subjects? And so I waited at Thorpe Green, feverishly hoping and praying for his promised visit, that he was traveling near my place of employment and would stop in. So long had I been removed from family and friends, so starved for a single ray of warmth, the thought of his presence was like oxygen to a drowning sailor. I prayed so relentlessly for him to come, my knees grew bruised and black and bled.

He never came. Apparently, I didn't fit into his social schedule.

Two years later, cholera took him at 28, transmuting my anger into forgiveness and purifying the memory of him.

Yes, thou art gone! And never more, Thy sunny smile shall gladden me;

But I may pass the old church door, and pace the floor that covers thee
May stand upon the cold, damp stone, And think that, frozen, lies below
The lightest heart that I have known, The kindest I shall ever know.

All our loves were unrequited but they endured. Death did not break them. Time did not sunder them. It's modern love that is shallower than a grave.

The curse of being a Night Walker is not living forever—it is living forever in perpetual darkness. Alone. If I could sense divine love, I would bear this purgatory with grace, for I once was a holy girl and though God has exiled me, I've not lost hope one day He'll gather me back again. I want restoration of my soul. I've patiently endured my penance and I won't stop striving for salvation, even though it is killing me.

Only one thing is certain. I have accumulated too many attachments. I must sell my house and possessions. Tomorrow I will call the Realtor and list the house as is, with my library, antiques, and art. Such foolish extravagances! I have currency stashed in strategically placed safety deposit boxes throughout the country. It will hold me until I acquire new I.D. and find another job.

I will revert back to the life of a nomad as I once lived, with few possessions and no indulgences. With a trembling heart, I know my time here is over. Too many eyes watching: Santos, Dr. Webb, Professor Hardcastle.

I think of William Hardcastle looking at me as if he has known me all his life. And, I remember William Weightman, sitting across from me at church, catching my eye and sighing in transient longing. He is gone, but the professor is here.

He has read my words.
He thinks I'm the strong one.

Chapter 10

"Rescue 7, respond to Whisper Mountain Road off Highway 63 for a 24-year-old male, attacked by a wolf."

I jerk out of my oblivion. Attacked by a wolf? It's not our territory, but I lean over, start the ignition and crank up the heat for Dana.

"Rescue 1 to Central. Cancel 7. We'll take that call. Do you have a more specific location?"

"Negative, Rescue 1. Call came from a cell phone. The caller was confused and unable to state his specific location. We triangulated the call with GPS."

I pull up the map on the computer mounted on the dash. The location is up a high mountain road and sunrise is an hour off. Dana climbs in the truck bleary-eyed, pulling her hair back. "Did they say attacked by a wolf?"

"Yes. It's probably a wild dog."

She takes a quick look at the map then looks at me. "You sure you want to take this? Seven can take it. Lucien relieves you soon."

"I'll be fine. It's a trauma call. We'll make it quick."

She gives me an uncertain look. Despite the rare diagnosis of XP, xeroderma pigmentosum, I claim to have, she thinks my aversion to sunlight is purely psychological. No doubt this risk I'm taking is solidifying her theory. But if I don't feed tonight, I won't make it long, sunlight or not.

⌘

Dana follows the mountain road, slick with icy frost, at a relatively reasonable pace. We don't have a specific location and she doesn't want to miss it. All I see are miles of wilderness, trees so thick they form an impenetrable barrier to my vision. Sunrise is still a ways off and the night is the violet black of dying darkness.

I roll my window down to sniff the air. Dana doesn't complain. She has the cold tolerance of a Viking. Suddenly, the scent of blood hits me.

"Stop."

She glances over at me and slows. "Did you see something?"

"I think I heard yelling. Pull over here." Blood fills the air, hitting my brain with the intensity of light. We're close.

Dana finds a spot to pull over on the narrow shoulder. To our right, the ground falls off sharply into a tilt of trees and brush. "Stay with the truck. I'll check it out and let you know if I need anything." She opens her mouth to speak, but I'm slipping down the incline, through the trees into darkness.

The air is chill with the scent of pine and blood. It floods my head. I follow the scent over cold-hardened ground, my boots breaking through the frost. All my senses are alive. I can hear the beat of a heart, getting louder and louder as I near. I pray it is strong enough to sustain the trauma. I smell no wolf, nor hear one. The night is silent save for my breath and boot falls, and the beating of a heart louder than sirens swelling in the night.

I fall through the trees.

In the splintered moonlight I find them: a father and son in camouflage, rifles within reach. Hunters. The father is dead, his neck torn open leaving him drained. Blood is everywhere.

A few feet away, a young man lies semiconscious on the forest floor, panting with quick shallow breaths, his back propped awkwardly against a tree, one hand clutching a rifle. His gun is hot. I can feel the heat reaching out to strike me. He looks like a thick country boy, now drawn and diminishing. His femur is broken with a jagged edge of bone jutting out of the flesh like wet white coral. The break has lacerated his femoral artery and it oozes hot blood in the crease where his thigh meets his hip. A t-shirt is wrapped tightly around his leg, but it hasn't fully staunched the bleed.

I crouch down and untie the bandage, exposing the wound. He is slashed but not entirely drained. His skin, the bone-white color of shock, gleams with cold sweat as his eyes begin to dim. He is fading. There isn't much time. Sirens howl through the night. Soon Santos will arrive. I sense him coming like a storm.

Crouching, I rip the boy's jeans open wider, fall to my hands and knees, press my lips against his wound and drink.

Chapter 11

I'm flooded with life. It sweeps through me like liquid flame, searing through weakness, kindling my veins. The blood is storm-heated lightning jolting my body straight into my brain, electrifying me.

I press my mouth deeper into his thigh, careful not to pierce him with my teeth and pump him with my venom. My tongue reaches out, tasting, licking, loving. Pure pleasure floods me.

The tug of life comes. The final tether holding a soul to the world lies on the tip of my tongue. One long pull and I would hold it in my mouth and swallow to be reborn again.

It is the source.

The life force.

Immortality.

In a rush, my spirit knows itself and I remember everything.

Chapter 12

I am Death Walker, Grief Bringer, Daughter of Carnage.
I have walked through fields of blood, nimbly stepping over corpses the way a dancer steps onto a stage. I am the Queen of War, knee deep in fallen life, up to elbows in warm failing flesh. The slip of intestine against my fingers, the feel of once strong hands gripping at me, begging me to save them.

War draws Night Walkers the way the sun draws life. In the beginning, desperate and new, I stumbled upon Crimea and preyed upon killers, as if somehow that would right the wrong. It seemed to me that if a man were so willing to take another's life for a god, country, or gold, if he could cut down his brother for some narrow vision of manhood, then why should I not kill to survive, to sustain a species that was our Lord's creation? For if God had sired everything upon the earth, even the vilest creature: the cockroach, the worm, the vampire bat, and if He had assigned them all a part to play in His plan, why should I not live?

Yet it seemed that we Night Walkers existed for no reason other than consuming life. Our contribution to the world was impossible to understand. We did not sustain another species through symbiosis. Nor did we contribute to civilization, so confined were we to the darkness, fearful to show ourselves, fragile despite our unnatural strength. Always poised on the verge of extinction, hiding even from each other, especially the males—our hell-brothers and the greatest Alphas of all. My purpose remained a mystery, but my faith burned brighter in death than it ever had in life; if I walked this earth, then I was a creature of God's and surely my purpose was somewhere to be found. I would trust in my Father and in time He would show me the way.

I was young.

So I thought if to kill a killer were to save my species, if it were to give me more time to learn my purpose, the purpose of our existence, then surely that was a worthy sacrifice to make. A means to an end. Isn't that what those in war always say? It is a means to a better end?

So I fed and fed and fed. And the girl I once was grew smaller and smaller until she was obliterated beneath the weight of corpses, until that fine noble girl was completely obscured, becoming only a concept, a memory existing solely in my mind. And finally it dawned on me; maybe I wasn't a child of God's at all. Maybe, instead, I was Satan's child.

One night I came upon a field hospital where I saw a young doctor, worn and thin, flung across a bed in fitful sleep. Creeping close to study such broken beauty in this rank domain of mud and disease, I gazed upon his face and to my surprise smelled the sharp scent of blood. Curious, I studied him to see from where it came. His pulse beat strong in his throat and he had no wounds.

I brought my face close to his and slowly breathed in his scent. I wouldn't harm him. I chose only killers, not saviors. Searching him, I found the source in his pocket: three test tubes of blood. Dark red. Iridescent in the moonlight seeping through the window. I held one up to the light. It shimmered like scarlet sunshine. Then I opened each one and drank.

A new life was born. And since that moment, I've been struggling, striving to get back that girl who I once was, before she drowned herself in the blood of soldiers.

I became a nurse and followed the wars. They came like waves, one after the other, all over the world. The sun was not yet such a ferocious enemy and I traveled across many seas, gathering languages along the way. There was always a need for strong, enduring hands. Others faltered in the night, yet I thrived in it. I was strong as a man, they said. Never flinched or turned away. I didn't get sick or hungry or attached. I was perfect.

And so I moved from Death Bringer to Death Walker. And I saw that those hardened killers on the edge of death, lying shattered in their cots, were really just boys beneath all their muscles and scars. Hundreds, *thousands*, cried out for their mothers before death came to carry them away.

I held their hands. I knew when death was coming. I clasped their hands in mine and told them it would be okay. And for those in too much pain, I sunk my teeth into their wrists and drained their pain away.

Chapter 13

The country boy's life lies against my tongue, but I cannot take the final pull. I will not be the extinguisher of his life, no matter how faintly it glows. I release him, resecure the tourniquet and, with his tattered jacket, wipe my face clean. He is now thoroughly unconscious but his heart beats faint and fast, sustained by the tenacity of youth.

"Rescue 1 to Central," I say. "I have one adult male trauma alert to Mission Hospital. Broken femur and lacerated femoral artery. Requesting air transport. LZ is Whisper Mountain helipad. Be advised, one fatality on scene." I switch over to simplex. "Dana, pull out the stretcher and backboard, then help me get him up this mountain." I don't need help, but I won't be able to explain carrying this strong young man all the way to the top on my own. I'll bring him up part of the way, though.

I pull him onto my shoulder, stand, and begin my climb toward the truck. Smoothly, I make my way up the mountain, weaving through naked trees, my breath steaming the chill air like a dragon with a heart full of fire. As I near the edge, I carefully set him down and call out to Dana.

"I'm coming," she says, crashing through the brush and slipping a few feet before regaining her footing. She slides to a stop beside me, panting, hair a tangle from the brush. Unlike me, she is wearing latex gloves and trauma sleeves.

"We need to backboard him," she says, indicating his broken leg.

"No time. Life over limb." I pick up his arm and pull it over my shoulder. "Grab the other."

She does so. Despite her femininity, she is strong. I've never seen her flinch when faced with blood or death. Together we pull the boy up through the brush toward the road.

Sirens grow louder and louder, a scream in the night.

As we reach the top, a squad car screeches to a stop. Santos. We lower the boy on the backboard. Dana is breathing hard and it doesn't take much effort to imitate her. Quickly, we package the patient and heave the board onto the stretcher.

Santos strides up. "What happened?"

"Looks like they were attacked by an animal," I say. "Not sure how he broke his leg. Maybe a hard fall."

"You called in a fatality?"

"An older male. His throat was torn open." Santos moves toward the lip of the mountain, his hand resting on his holster. I've carved a path of broken brush through the trees and Santos starts down it.

"Do you need help?" Dana asks me after the stretcher is loaded and I've climbed in the back.

I shake my head. "No time. Head to the LZ. I'll work him en route."

Under the bright lights of the truck's interior and stripped of his bulky clothing, the patient appears even younger than before. He's only a teenager, poised on the cusp of manhood. His blonde hair is plastered to his forehead like damp straw and his skin has the unnatural pallor of shock. It is Night Walker white. He's on the edge of death, circling the drain, broken in my hands.

What was he doing hunting out of season?

I work fast. I do everything Dr. Webb has forbidden me to. From my own surgical kit, I remove a clamp and scalpel. I clamp his bleeding artery and perform a venous cut down on his other leg in order to start a large bore IV. He'll need blood immediately. I can't give it to him, but the flight crew can en route to Asheville's Trauma Center. There's no time to lose.

Dawn approaches. I feel it warming the frigid air, heating the entire truck. I'm running out of time. There's no way I can transfer the patient to the helicopter and make it back to the safety of my home before sunrise. Panic grips me. Dana was right; I should have let Rescue 7 take the call. I've cut it too close. I close the UV shades I've installed on the truck's windows. Even if I stay in the back, protected from the sun, its ultraviolet will penetrate the truck's skin, through my own and into my blood.

I look down at the young man and place my hand against his forehead. Bending to his ear, I whisper. "It's okay. Everything will be okay."

But even as I say it, I know it's a lie.

Chapter 14

I stay deep in the truck as Dana makes the patient transfer. "Please hurry," I plead as she pulls out the stretcher with the help of the flight medic. Behind her the sky shifts from dark grey to soft smoky violet, a color I haven't seen in so very long, yet one that now terrifies me. I push deeper into the truck.

Dana gives me a concerned look and shuts the door. I know she has always thought my so-called disease purely psychological. Most people do. XP is so rare and my skin so flawless, they think it a figment of my imagination. Few of those acutely afflicted, as I claim to be, live past twenty. Yet we are kin, perpetually exiled from humanity.

In our world, the sun does not bring life; it takes it.

By the moment, the heat grows more intense. I reach for my backpack and the silver UV blanket I've placed inside for this sort of emergency. I have not been in a scrape this tight since I was young. The door flies open and I throw myself against the furthest wall, huddling like a trapped beast beneath the blanket.

Santos stares at me with eyes of black fire.

"Close the door," I hiss.

He doesn't move, only hovers there watching, waiting, I suppose, for my skin to erupt in lesions as I have claimed it will when touched by the sun's rays. My blood burns. The truck is filling with heat, leeching me of strength as if I am in a small stone oven being cooked alive. I'm faint with sweat and growing more exhausted by the second.

Behind Santos, my own black Mini Paceman races up, windows covered in dark tint far beyond legal limits. The car slides to a stop beside the ambulance, causing Santos to whip around. The passenger door flies open. Fellow EMT Lucien leans over from the driver's seat and says, "Need a ride?"

I flash through the truck, take a running leap past Santos and throw myself into the passenger seat, the blanket billowing out behind me like great silver wings. I slam the door closed, shutting out Santos and throwing down the lock.

Lucien stares at me, wide-eyed. "Hope you don't mind I took your car, but I thought you might be ready to go home."

He's not yet 20, sleek and with a glow beneath his deeply black skin as if lit from within. His eyes are a luminous jet black and when he smiles, he is dazzling.

He's never been late for me once.

"Lucien, you're my guardian angel," I whisper, breathless. "Now get out."

He smiles and slips out the door with a graceful spin. I slide to the driver's seat, throw the car into first and shoot toward home like a comet. My turbo Mini is a shield, custom designed with UV protection on all sides. It hugs the mountain as I flee past the death scene. Police cars and a fire engine line the road. Men stand on the lip of the mountain, gazing down. As I fly past, they crane their heads to watch me.

Flashing lights appear behind me and a squad car comes up fast. Santos. He can't see me through my tinted windows, but I see him. His jaw is set and he pulls up dangerously close. Briefly, I wonder if he is pursuing a subject and wants to pass, but then it occurs to me, I'm the one he wants. Who knows why?

I stomp on the pedal and leave him in a cloud of frost.

My Mini grips the road like a race car and is just as fast. In town, I dart across the river and hightail it to historic Montford while deftly avoiding the occasional cat or early morning runner. Past old Riverside Cemetery, I tap my garage door opener. Arts and Crafts, Queen Anne, and Colonial Revival homes flash by in whips of blues and greys and greens as I dash past down Pearson Street. Once more, I push the garage remote, this time to close it. I gun for my house. The door jerks and begins to lower. I may have miscalculated. It's closing faster than I'm covering ground. If I'm too late, I'll have no choice but to crash through my garage door.

I haven't been this scared in decades.

I downshift and press my foot against the gas; the Mini jumps, kicking into higher gear as my house looms up, a dark Victorian violet. I love this house entirely too much. Past the Great Oak perched on the edge of my drive, I pull the emergency brake, spin my car a quarter turn and punch it for the garage at the back of the house. I slam my foot on the brake, afraid I may shatter the pedal as I slide beneath the door. Mere inches from the inside wall, I screech to a stop while the acrid smell of burnt rubber reminds me of young women burned alive at the stake.

The door descends, bathing me in blessed darkness.

My breath comes fast and jagged. My heart is lurching in my chest, trying to break free. I'm so hot, I feel fried. Despite the cool darkness, the sun's heat clings to me like a leech. It singes my veins. My skin is on fire. I'm burning alive!

Throwing myself out, I stumble to the passage leading off the garage. My keys feel like dripping metal in my hands, and when I drop them, I curse God.

When the door is finally open, I run for the bathroom and turn the shower on to full cold. Ice-cold water pours out of the freezing pipes. I scramble beneath the water, falling to my knees, and rest my head against the cool tile. For minutes I stay like this, trying to catch my breath and cool myself. Slowly, with shaking hands, I strip off my clothes and push them out into a wet heap on the floor.

Ivanhoe appears in the doorway, vivid as a flame. The cat gives my drenched boots a disdainful sniff and looks up at me, unaccustomed to such dramatic behavior.

Standing, I let the icy water stream over my face and skin. It hisses with steam when it touches my flesh. I run my hands over my body, hard as polished granite. There are no lesions or burns, only cold white skin gleaming beneath the water. Somehow I've survived this wretched shift. The winter, with its dim pale sun, has spared me.

A powerful banging at my front door shakes the wooden frame. I know it's Santos. From the sound of it, he's on the verge of punching through with his bare fist.

Suddenly all falls silent. I turn off the water to listen. A hinge moans like a hungry ghost and a heavy footstep falls on my hundred-year-old oak floors.

He is inside.

Chapter 15

Wet and dripping, I slide on my long velvet robe and meet Santos in the living room before he's made it too far. I keep back. Light streams through the open front door, turning my walls a rich, deep amber, a color I've never seen them. The golden edges of my books glint. Ivory keys of my piano glow. The deep violet of my robe gleams. How beautiful it all looks in the light.

"Get out!" I demand. My eyes flash. I step toward Santos, wanting to tear him to pieces.

He reaches for his Taser and I freeze. I'm torn between fight or flight, but either way is hopeless. There's nowhere to go and I cannot kill a deputy and leave his car, lights flashing outside, undiscovered until nightfall. An image of men surrounding my house, breaking down doors, assaults me. It will never happen because no matter what Santos does, I will not kill him.

I'm doomed.

The door opens wider and I shrink back. It's Professor Hardcastle, haloed in light. His eyes are a dark blue, wide with surprise. He steps inside and stops when he sees Santos, hand on his Taser. "Atticus, what in God's name are you doing?"

Santos catches himself and lowers his hand, yet remains tense as a viper ready to strike.

"Shut the door," I demand.

Hardcastle complies, then fumbles for a light switch in the darkness. A chandelier lights high above us, bathing the room in antique light. Crystals twirl and tinkle from currents swirling through my once peaceful home.

The men look around and Santos narrows his eyes suspiciously. A grand piano graces the living room, which is lined in tall bookcases from floor to ceiling with a slender ladder placed before one. Heavy embroidered drapes cover the windows. Persian carpets adorn the glossed oak floors. Before an enormous fireplace sits an umber velvet couch along with two vermillion wingback chairs. William Hardcastle looks momentarily dazed.

Other than contractors, no one has been inside my home. Beneath me, my legs tremble, and with all my strength I try to steady myself.

"What in God's name is going on, Atticus? Why are you accosting Miss Bell in her own home? You're terrifying her."

"She ran. She refused to pull over," he says, a restrained fury in his voice. He looks wild inside my living room, as if a feral dog has sneaked inside.

"I can't," I say. "I have XP."

"I know all about your fantasy ailment. It doesn't cause one to burst into flames. It's against the law to evade an officer."

"That's hardly reason to Tase someone," Hardcastle says in a tone of aristocratic authority. He steps between Santos and me, his tall body forming a human shield and reminding me of Papa. My head comes to the lower blades of his shoulders and I long to rest my forehead against his back, place my hands upon the soft wool of his coat and collapse into his strength.

"What are your reasons for detaining her?"

"I have questions. There was another attack in the woods. She carried a man twice her size up a steep mountain. Not dragged him, but carried him." Hardcastle glances over his shoulder at me, perplexed.

"I helped the boy walk up with me. He lost consciousness near the top and Dana and I carried him the rest of the way."

Santos' eyes blaze. "You're lying. There was only one pair of tracks, not two."

I shake my head in denial.

"What reason would she possibly have for lying?" Hardcastle asks.

"Because there's something about her that's not right. She's not normal."

My heart sinks. Santos has discovered my secret, even if he doesn't know it yet.

"Exactly why I find her so appealing and hardly grounds to chase someone down in your squad car. You must take a breath, man."

"Remember Afghanistan," Santos says.

Hardcastle quickly shakes his head. "I'm trying to forget."

"You need to remember." It's an order, not a request, but beneath the words I hear an undercurrent of fear.

"What in the world can that possibly have to do with Miss Bell?"

"Jadallah."

Hardcastle drags in a breath as if struggling for patience. "Jadallah was an insurgent. Anne Bell is a paramedic. I hardly see the connection."

"He wasn't normal either. Remember how he died?"

"How can you compare him to her! Have you gone completely mad?" Hardcastle's voice shakes the chandelier. The crystals clatter above us like breaking glass.

"Don't be fooled by the look of her, William. Don't let your attraction blind you."

Hardcastle falls momentarily speechless. Even in the dim light, I see a blush crawl up the back of his neck. Santos' words surprise me. Attraction is not a state I normally inspire in men, at least I certainly didn't before, and since my turning I have allowed no man close enough for the impulse to kindle. Especially not Night Walkers. Our males are the most dangerous creatures on earth.

Is it possible Professor Hardcastle could feel such a thing?

The darkness has changed me.

"You've said quite enough," Hardcastle says. "Ten years of combat is more than any man should endure. It's clearly taken its toll."

A hurt look sweeps Santos' face. "If you suggest this is PTSfuckingD our friendship is done."

Hardcastle starts. "I said nothing of the kind, but it wounds me you'd so easily relinquish our friendship after everything we've endured."

"This isn't *easy* for me. But, she's lying, Will. I *know* it. I survived ten years of war because I listen to my gut and when I don't, people die. My friends die. She claims to be born in Boston but there are no records there of her birth or education."

Hardcastle looks at me, uncertainly. Turning to Santos, he says, "We've all done things we'd rather forget. If Miss Bell wishes to conceal something from her past, I am sure there's a valid reason. That doesn't make her a criminal."

I want to reach out and touch him. Place my hand on his back and steady myself.

"Why do you trust her?" Santos asks. "Because she looks young and innocent? Because of the uniform? After all we've seen, how can you believe in that?"

"You have your instincts, and I have mine. I understand you have questions, but this is neither the time nor the manner in which to ask them. As your friend, I'm asking you to leave. You can discuss these things with Miss Bell at a later date when you've both had an opportunity to compose yourselves. Surely you have an investigation to conduct before all the evidence erodes. Miss Bell is not going anywhere."

How I wish it were true. My home cradles me in beauty and comfort and I don't want to leave it. I've always felt safe here in my fairy tale Victorian and this curiously eccentric town sheltered by forest and mountain, insulated by a community of free and radical thinkers. *Keep Asheville Weird* posters proclaim, no doubt a reason I've been so easily tolerated. Dreadlocked artists and grateful patients have lured me into a false sense of security.

Yet in one single night, I have been tragically exposed. A soldier, an officer of the *law*, threatens me in my home, while no doubt Dr. Webb, at this very moment, stands over my patient, scrutinizing the evidence of my disobedience.

Maybe the anarchists are right; authority is the greatest danger of all.

Santos glares at me. So much anger swirls through him, I can hardly see his soul.

"Stop scaring her, Atticus," Hardcastle says softly. "It has never been your way to intentionally frighten a woman."

Without a word, Santos turns and walks out, leaving the door gaping open behind him. Seconds later, I hear him drive away. Professor Hardcastle walks to the door, removing the hide-a-key I clearly didn't hide well enough from the lock. He gently shuts the door and sets the key on a delicately carved end table.

"I apologize, Miss Bell—"

"Call me Anne. I think we're over formalities now." I collapse into a chair by the cold fireplace and pull my knees tight to my chest. My hair is wet and my robe is damp. It occurs to me I'm no longer wearing my glasses. Did my eyes shine in the dark? Is that why Santos reached for his weapon?

Suddenly I feel naked and acutely aware that I am entirely alone with William. With one hand, I pull my robe closed at my neck, and wrap the other around my knees, curling up like a little girl. I can't seem to stop shaking and hug myself for support.

"What are you doing here?" I ask.

"I live nearby. I was taking Woody for his outrageously early morning walk when I witnessed your vehicle fly by like a bat out of hell with Santos not far behind. Needless to say, I sensed something amiss." He looks at Woody, who has been standing beneath the piano this entire time. "What I would give for that dog to sleep past sunrise."

"Why does Santos hate me? What happened in Afghanistan?"

William takes a deep breath. "For that, we will need a fire. It's freezing in here. May I kindle a flame and make us a cup of tea? Woody appears a bit frozen. If I let him catch cold, my mother will haunt me from the grave with a ferocity to rival Catherine Earnshaw's."

He looks down at me, waiting for my response at his mention of the *Wuthering Heights* heroine. There is color in his face and his eyes are bright. A ring of midnight blue, so dark it's almost black, encircles their irises, imparting an intensity that makes me feel exposed beneath his gaze … and yet strangely safe.

He has protected me.

Against all my better judgment, I say yes.

Chapter 16

I escape to my bedroom to dress after William begins a fire and places Woody before it. Although my house is three stories high including the steeply peaked turret, my bedroom is in a broad basement built deep into the ground. Ivanhoe follows softly as I descend the narrow staircase. I'm dazed. I'm alone with William Hardcastle in my robe. What would my sisters say? A smile breaks over my face and I can't help giggling like a schoolgirl.

Always, I was the proper one, impeccable with propriety, the strictest lady and the loneliest. Our natures didn't appeal to men, nor our features. Desire burned within us all, yet the potency of our imagination, our greatest power, eclipsed us. Who can compete with Heathcliff or Rochester? It was far more thrilling to consummate our desire in dreams than to settle for an all too common man.

But, there is nothing common about William Hardcastle.

I enter my bedroom. In spite of the 19th century antiques, it's more simply furnished than above. An armoire stands against one wall, carved and dark in the Gothic style. The other wall holds a demure English dresser with a simple wooden box upon it. Near the fireplace a pale grey chenille chair sits beside a small table, upon which lies *The Gospel of Mary*. In the corner stands a dressmaker's mannequin. She is made to my exact measurements and pinned and draped in swathes of dark fabric.

The bare walls are painted a soft cream. And in the room's center looms the crowning jewel: my sanctum. A source of security more psychological than physical.

It is a tall, oak-paneled bed with great hand-carved doors and a paneled ceiling enclosing a deep mattress within. When the doors are shut and secured with heavy locks on the inside, I'm encased in a cocoon of perfect blackness. I have covered the mattress in the softest sheets and cashmere throws and draped an old silk comforter of faded burnt orange across it to remind me of the dying sun.

Emily would be intensely jealous. She dreamed of a bed like this and depicted one, albeit much simpler, in *Wuthering Heights*.

For now, the doors are open and Ivanhoe jumps onto the bed and stares out at me with glittering emerald eyes. It's almost as if he's mocking me.

"I know," I say, smiling, "there's a man in the house. And a dog." It occurs to me that Woody is perhaps a greater affront to Ivanhoe's sense of normalcy than William. I bite my lip. This isn't good. I should not be entering into conversation with a college professor. In no way should I be fostering understanding.

"This isn't about connection," I tell Ivanhoe. "This is about intelligence gathering. Knowledge is power. I must find out why Santos suspects me so that I can avoid this sort of situation in the future. And I must know what happened in Afghanistan."

I slip on a simple black dress, T-backed and trimmed in lace, and high, grey knit slippers that hug my calves like soft woolen boots. In my former life, I was fiercely modest, and have sewn my own restrained clothes since my mortal days. Lately, I am succumbing to vanity with more and more ease, cutting dresses out of the softest velvet or silk, trimming them with lace or satin ribbons embroidered with the finest metallic thread.

My self-righteous morality falters with each passing decade. After all I have seen, a velvet ribbon hardly seems like a crime. With each fallen life I catch and swallow, my compassion for human frailty grows. We are fallen angels, all of us. And the longer I live in darkness, the harder beauty grips me. It no longer seems like an evil, but a blessing, a balm against the carnage and ugliness of the world.

I glance in the mirror I've placed in a corner in order to check my handmade work. It's the only mirror in the house. Despite the legends, Night Walkers have reflections, but I rarely look at myself. Tonight I'm pale with hunger. My shoulders are bare and my skin looks pearl white against the narrow strip of lace that runs down my back. Again a sensation of nakedness arises, and I smile at myself with a tenderness I never found in my first 29 years. It's only a sleeveless dress I'm wearing, falling below the knee, trimmed in a slender band of lace. To a 21st century college professor, I'm sure it is nothing risqué.

Still, I gather a shawl about my shoulders and slip on a pair of tortoise shell glasses to conceal my eyes, glowing like blue amethysts. I feel like a young librarian on her way to rendezvous with a dashing hero from a Gothic romance.

Have I gone completely mad? A low voice whispers in the back of my mind. *Dangerous. It is too dangerous.* But I push my brother's voice away.

Silently, I ascend the stairs to find that William has built a large fire and set tea out before it. Ginger. It is one of the few items of consumption I have in the house. Does he find it odd my pantry is bare? Besides a tin of hot chocolate and a few canisters of loose fragrant teas, my cupboards hold only small cans of cat food stacked in tidy rows. And in the fridge there is nothing but a bottle of farm fresh organic cream—an occasional treat for Ivanhoe.

The scent of spicy ginger saturates the air. The sound of flaming pine crackling and popping fills the room. Ivanhoe jumps upon the piano to survey Woody from a safer vantage point. Woody has stretched out before the fire and William stands at the mantle with a serious expression, staring at one of my paintings. It is ocean bleeding into sky in shades of iron blue and smoked violet tinged in tender rose, the sun about to rise or set upon a vast expanse of loneliness. A girl stands before it, gazing out to sea, looking small as a snowflake amidst the empty grandeur.

Such a place of refuge for me, that sea. Now stolen by the sun.

William turns as I walk in and looks almost dazzled when he sees me before quickly composing himself. He's removed his coat to reveal faded jeans and a worn Oxford sweater with two daggers crossed over the heart lending him the air of a lean mountain poet. In his presence, I fall immediately shy.

"I hope you don't mind, but I took the liberty of making tea that I found in your cupboard. I thought it might help settle you. I feared Atticus had shaken you a bit. He honestly doesn't know how savage he can sometimes appear."

"Thank you for coming to my rescue," I say, my voice barely above a whisper. I have never drunk tea with a man beside my fireplace. This is new, but I will be gone soon so I'll allow myself to enjoy the moment. I'm certain it will never come again.

I pour steaming tea into a china cup and slide it to the edge of the table nearest him. Then I make myself a cup and savor the aroma and warmth wafting off it before I curl into the velvet chair before the fire.

When did I become such a sensualist?

A myriad of emotions sweeps across William's face. Worry. Curiosity. Desire? Finally, he clears his throat. "I must apologize for

Atticus' behavior. I assure you he is a good man. He would lay down his life for you without a thought if you were ever in harm's way."

This I do not believe.

"He's been too long at war. A decade in combat. And I mean real combat. He actively sought out the most violent territories, and as a result has lost more friends than anyone should ever have to."

I stare into the fire. Against my will, my heart softens. Few people in the world today have lost more loves than me. Helplessly, I watched my mother, brother, and three sisters perish, and from immortality's wake, I witnessed my only remaining sister, on the cusp of love and motherhood, fall far too young. I saw my father crack with grief, his entire family dead before him. My heart has broken so hard and deep, it's a wonder it even beats at all.

Modernity shields people from such pain until war rips those layers of protection away.

"That doesn't explain why he hates me so."

"The war has left him suspicious. We saw such strange, inexplicable things."

"You were there too?"

"For a short time. My family has a long tradition of naval service and I, not without reservation, took a break from my studies to follow in their footsteps. I worked in military intelligence and found myself encamped with Sergeant Santos in a remote mountain range, searching for insurgents. It was my job to gather intel, upon which Atticus and his Rangers would hunt down our targets and bring them back to me for interrogation."

I must look shocked because he says, "I know. One would not think me skilled in such things. It does not come naturally, I assure you. I am simply adept at knowing what questions to ask and recognizing when someone fails to answer truthfully. In this particular way, Atticus and I are similar, though he takes it to another level."

"I detect a hint of Haworth."

"I have never been there."

I turn toward the fire. William, like Santos, must have known all along that I was lying.

"One night, Atticus brought in a wild and ferocious enemy. Jadallah. Atticus claimed he had come upon him drinking a fallen comrade's blood, from his throat no less, and that it took three high-caliber bullets and four men to bring him down. When Jadallah came to me, despite his wounds he was still surprisingly strong." William looks at me to see how I'm taking this. "If this upsets you, I'll stop."

"Go on."

"For three nights, we kept him locked in a windowless room. No food, little water, constant interrogation; yet no matter what we did—" He stops and stares into the fire. "No matter what Atticus did, Jadallah wouldn't break. On the fourth morning we dragged him outside to stage a mock execution, hoping to wear down his will. Jadallah fought like a demon and then to our surprise collapsed on the ground and died while lesions erupted over his body."

"What do you think happened?" I ask warily.

"I think his heart finally gave out. He wasn't as strong as we thought."

"And the lesions?"

"Clearly he had some latent illness or allergy of some sort. It was Afghanistan, for God's sake. Every sort of disease thrives there."

"Why doesn't Atticus see it that way?"

"He has never once strayed from the claim that he saw Jadallah drinking from a Ranger's throat like a rabid wolf."

"But you don't believe him."

William rubs his hand over his face and through his hair. "There is no telling what Atticus saw. There had been a battle long into the night. Rangers had been up for days hunting Jadallah through vicious mountains at high altitudes. They were dangerously low on food. In the heat of combat, one's mind can play strange tricks. And it's a well-known fact that prolonged sleep deprivation and fasting cause hallucinations. We all assumed Santos was traumatized from the battle. He had lost four men that night at Jadallah's hand. Good men he'd led for years. Brothers. He never seemed to fully recover, and after 12 years in the military, he didn't reenlist."

"What a sad story," I say. "In this job, I've seen strange happenings too." William looks at me close, and I glance away. "Nothing I'm sure as dramatic as that."

"It's a place to which I wish never to return. But others must. There is a darkness in the world that must be contained lest it devour the light of humanity forever."

Afraid, I look at him. Is he speaking of me?

"Atticus Santos sacrificed a part of his soul to protect that light. I ask you, Anne, to forgive him, if he sometimes sees darkness where there is none."

With a sigh, I give a small nod. I've seen it before—the imprint of carnage. War leaves the sound of madness ringing in ears long after its battles have ended. It is the itch in fingers for triggers that never entirely vanishes. A shame that never fully fades. The darkness burns within Atticus, reflecting out to the world. This is the price of killing, the knowing, whether you want it or not, that violence slumbers in your soul. If Santos is not vigilant, the *knowing* will devour him and extinguish his light. That is the battle he must fight and win now.

I don't say this. Why has William survived the war emotionally intact, while Santos chafes beneath its weight? Is it a matter of time spent at hell's door? Or is it because Santos has taken life and William has not? At least I hope he has not. I hope he doesn't have that burden choking his heart as I do.

"How does Atticus explain Jadallah's behavior?"

"He believes he was a demon."

"A demon?"

"Yes, a literal demon escaped from hell." William smiles. "Atticus doesn't have our education. Though raised in Miami, he hails from Cuba and superstition runs in his blood like lightning. Once, over far too much whiskey, he let slip his abuela and madre are Santeras, which I believe, is a sort of secret priestess, so the idea of dark spirits isn't foreign to him. It's some Santeria mix of Catholicism and African religion. I don't understand it. He doesn't talk about it much."

Anxiety slithers beneath my skin. I understand it all too well. Cuba and Haiti have fed me generously through revolution, hurricanes and earthquakes, and I have seen the power of Santeria and Voodoo up close. Their priests are especially adept at recognizing Night Walkers and can be shocking in their fearlessness. Possession. Zombies. Sacrifice. They dread none of it. We are a great prize to them, and they have been known to offer far more than goats and chickens to their enigmatic gods.

"And you?" I ask. "Do you conceive it could be a possibility?"

"I'm a historian and an atheist. I find truth in facts and guard against flights of fancy. As a wise person once said, 'Speculation is the surest form of tabloid journalism.'"

"But you're a scholar of literature and poetry. How do you reconcile that with facts?"

"I find immense enjoyment in expressions of the human imagination, but I don't take them literally. I don't believe Count Dracula walks the streets of London or Quasimodo swings from the bells of Notre Dame. Or that the man, Jesus of Nazareth, after a vicious death, rose fully restored in a cave before Mary Magdalene. I do, however, believe she was his lover and greatest disciple."

"Heretic!"

He gives a slight bow. "At your service."

"But what if all the stories are true?"

"Then we are living in a world of madness."

"I thought that was evident." I smile.

His voice goes soft. "You are the truest thing I have seen in quite a while." I feel my face flush and look back to the fire.

"I must say Miss B—" he corrects himself "—Anne, you have an exceptionally beautiful home."

"For a paramedic, you mean."

"For anyone."

A lie is on my tongue, how I am blessed to have received an inheritance from my aunt. It's what I have told others, but I cannot lie to William when I know he may see through it. And I don't *want* to lie to him. His nobility pulls at me, gathering me in. I want to be worthy of his protection.

What am I thinking? I will never be worthy.

"Your collection of books is astonishing. I understand now what the young man in Malaprop's was saying about your taste in reading. For one so young, you certainly have an eclectic and extensive library. *And before my dreaming eyes, still the learned volumes lay. And I could not close their leaves, and I could not turn away.*"

My breath catches. He knows my words by heart!

He steps to my bookcase and gently caresses a book. "May I?"

"Of course."

"*The Book of Universes.* Are you a student of astronomy?"

I give a noncommittal shrug. "According to Barrow, the theory of relativity suggests our universe is one amongst millions. We live not in a universe, but a multiverse." My voice grows excited. "Imagine, millions of universes containing gazillions of galaxies swirling about out there. The possibility for life is limitless." I wonder again if I am a cross-species alien experiment, and shudder at the thought of a race so cruel.

William stares at me a long moment before slowly sliding the book back in place. "Have you ever considered applying to UNC Asheville? I'd be happy to write a glowing recommendation."

"You've only known me for one night."

"And yet it feels like I've known you for centuries, as if we've met before and the memory is poised on the edge of my consciousness, but I can't quite place where or when. It's maddening."

"I thought you were a man of reason," I say, teasing.

"Somehow in your presence, reason dissipates."

I cannot hold his gaze. My dress has risen above my knee and I run my hand over the lace again and again, smoothing it against my cool flesh while my heart thrashes in my chest like a wild bird. I draw my shawl close. I no longer feel safe.

This is a danger I am completely unaccustomed to. This is a mistake. Branwell's words come back to me over the cold, dark years: *"Trust no man but me. I am the only one who will protect you."* Dear brother, where are you now? I want you back with all your broken desires and fierce misguided loyalty.

Suddenly Ivanhoe leaps from the piano and stalks over to Woody, who is snoozing, oblivious, by the fire. Ivanhoe shifts his stance to that of a lion hunting prey.

"Ivanhoe," I demand, "behave yourself." As usual, he ignores me and crouches before Woody, ready to pounce. To my relief, he gives him a sniff, then curls up on a cushion placed for him by the fire.

"He's not accustomed to guests," I say. "His manners have grown a bit rusty."

"I will take that as a hint to leave."

"That's not what I meant at all."

"You've had a long night and I'm sure could use some much needed rest. I shall go home to write."

"What dead virgin are you chronicling now?" I ask with a sad smile. So many memories he swirls up. When he is near, the past feels close.

He looks away, embarrassed. Curious, I wait.

"I'm writing a novel." He blushes, appearing to brace himself for my laughter. I give him a look of infinite compassion and he continues. "It's my first foray into fiction, and I find it far more terrifying than the mountains of Afghanistan. It will be a catastrophic failure I'm sure, but I plan to put the finishing touches on it today. By the way," he says, abruptly changing the subject, "you may like to know that I've decided to take your advice and give Dana an extension on her paper. She has until Monday morning to turn in her rewrite."

"That's generous of you. I keep hoping a college education will refine her character."

He raises one eyebrow doubtfully then swoops Woody up in his arms, who growls at the indignity of being awakened. William gives me a slight bow. "Thank you, Anne, for listening to my story. I have no doubt you will guard it well."

"I will guard all your stories well, I promise."

His eyes darken and then he is gone.

The door shuts behind him and the crystals of my chandelier clatter and clash in his wake.

Chapter 17

Long after he has gone, I stay curled before the slow-burning fire. Ivanhoe is a ball of sunlight in my lap. William has brought warmth and life into my quiet home. I had forgotten what it is to feel gentle heat upon my skin and I vow to build more fires.

Only not here.

My heart clenches with fear. I should be planning my escape, readying myself to leave, but I am paralyzed with indecision and doubt. Running will only draw more attention I tell myself, and I am weak with hunger. I must play it cool and careful. The last thing I need is an angry Ranger and an Oxford historian tracking me. Better for them to think I have chosen to move than to mysteriously vanish. But how can I stay any longer?

I stroke Ivanhoe's soft, velvety fur and try to imagine where I would like to go, but nothing comforting comes to mind. Vancouver perhaps? Milwaukee? Only the New World is accessible to me now. It is not so easy as one thinks to travel in darkness. The sunlight is always waiting to trap me with its relentless punitive reliability. Transatlantic flight has made matters easier, but airports today abound with glass and windows. Delays are deadly. I cannot lock myself in a bathroom forever. I get tired too.

The older we Night Walkers become, the more sensitive to light we grow. Fortunately, my wisdom and wealth increases, giving me an edge, but it's getting harder and harder for me to do my job. I could not bear endless nights of idleness and I would rather die in service to humanity than walk eternally without purpose. But it hurts. It drains me. As my UV intolerance has grown, my shifts have shrunk from twelve hours to ten and soon eight may be too long. If I can no longer preserve life, what purpose shall I have? How can I redeem myself if not through service? Saving lives is the only way I know to justify my existence, for I still believe,

That even the wicked shall at last be fitted for the skies;
And when their dreadful doom is past, to life and light arise.

Before the turning I knew only drawing, music, literature, and a few tentative languages. My gifts were not practical earthly skills geared toward survival. The humanities aided me little in the early years of my rebirth, though I now see they shielded the lit flame of humanity within me. My love of civilization was so great, the well of collective wisdom to draw upon so deep, it guarded me from the beast within.

But it was nursing that inserted me back into the living. In a century ravaged by war, the preservation of the injured was a skill desperately sought. Never before had I been so needed. It was a blessing to contribute, to *serve*, and I thought if I could hold on to it, I might regain God's grace once again.

There is a rest beyond the grave, a lasting rest from pain and sin,
Where dwell the faithful and the brave; but they must strive who seek to win.

I would strive harder in death than I ever had in life. With courage and faith, I would endure!

Years passed, then decades. The 19th century came and went followed by the 20th. Wars erupted and bodies piled beneath my hands like discarded treasure. With every revolution of the moon, the anvil of darkness grew harder. As my nights grow shorter and the sun more brutal, what will become of me? Shall I end up groveling in a crypt, feeding upon rats? Can hell be worse than that?

Night, the holy time of peace, is killing me.

William has conjured up the past as surely as a sorcerer summons a spell. There is no room in my crypt for him. He curses me with memories. My words rise like fragments from the deep, crawling out of the grave, shaking off the dust before slouching toward consciousness.

How can my spirit soar away confined by such a chain as this?

Why has God forsaken me?

After years of endless darkness, I'm still uncertain of my mortal sins. Why was I denied entrance to God's kingdom? I died an innocent virgin. I never stole a single thing in my life and I did not lie. I didn't worship other gods. At times, I questioned the Lord's existence, it's true, yet dutifully I said my prayers every night like an obedient girl. My sins, I think, must have been the self-righteous arrogance of the just. Pride. I took too much pride in my discipline and honor. Yet eternal darkness seems a harsh price to pay for one so young.

One thing is certain: this tentative friendship with the professor must end. It was stupid for me to allow him to stay and talk. He, more than anyone, is capable of divining my identity and discovering how *not right* I truly am. This makes him more dangerous than Sergeant Santos or Dr. Webb. They may distrust me but they can't possibly know I'm almost two centuries old.

The longer I stay, the harder it becomes to leave. I'd forgotten the intoxication of conversation; the simple joy of drinking tea before the fire with a friend. The spark of energy that flares when two people come into intellectual contact. Companionship is a pleasure to which I've grown unaccustomed, but with William's strong, tall form fresh in my mind, the way he looks at me, the sound of his voice turned to me, the need flies back sharp as hunger.

When the fire collapses to ash, I silently descend to bed and lock myself into sleep.

Chapter 18

Hours before sunset I wake, slip into my robe and ascend the stairs. I am regimented with my time. When you live for centuries you must be, or else the years will slip like water down a drain, sucking your intellect and discipline dry with it.

When I'm not reading, my predawn hours consist of painting in my turret studio. My art once helped support me, but as the 20th century marched on, romantic landscapes and somber portraits became increasingly less popular. Although I've painted for two centuries and studied with masters, for some impenetrable reason I'm unable to break free from the styles of my youth and evolve as an artist.

Manet said I must let go, step into the void of uncertainty and feel free to fall. But what if letting go means death?

After the first Boer War, I made my way to Paris and was stunned to view the sensually vigorous renderings of battle by Meissonier. He alone captured the chaos and degenerate eroticism of war. How I longed to find expression for the carnage I'd seen! To turn the horror into something meaningful, beautiful even. Yet despite my time with him, the images failed me and when they did come, as soon as my brush touched the canvas, they vanished like a wisp of smoke. It seemed there was an iron curtain draped across my memory between each war and every time I pulled back the veil, my mind thrust it down again.

I make my way to the living room, lighting lanterns as I go. Although I no longer write fiction, my Dickensian desk is covered in notebooks and scribbled pieces of paper. Instead of writing narrative, I take extensive notes on what I read. Quotes and ideas. Words. Just because I no longer write doesn't mean I no longer think.

How can I part with my notebooks? They are enough to fill two great trunks. And what will I do with my desk and my bed? I should be making arrangements for my move, listing the house as is, looking for another job, but I am overcome with lethargy. I must feed. The boy warded off starvation for a night, but it's back with a vengeance, growing inside me like a wild beast. I'm desperate to see what tonight brings. I pray it will be busy and that I'll have no common calls with Santos. Perhaps passions have died down and William has convinced him I'm not a demon.

Santos appears in my mind with that look of his—hostile and direct—and I stumble upon the edge of a rug, which unnerves me even further. If one quality defines me now, it is fluid grace. Santos threatens to take even that from me.

My thoughts are broken by the sight of a broad, thick envelope slid through the front door's mail slot. I bring it to my nose and my stomach tightens. William's scent is on the paper. In amazement, I turn it over in my hands knowing the heft and shape before I even open it.

A manuscript.

Inside there is a handwritten note on heavy ivory paper. With trembling hands, I read.

Dear Anne,

This is my manuscript. Today, in a fit of despair, I almost threw it in the fire, but at the last instant decided to place it in your hands instead. Before I lose courage, I shall run it over and slip it through your door. If I hesitate, it is the fire for sure.

I have lost all reference to my story's worth. I am like a child lost in the forest, unsure which way to turn or whom to trust. In a blind act of faith, I turn to you.

Please do me the great honor of throwing this manuscript in the fire if you think it unworthy of life. Your courage will protect me from a greater injury. As a member of academia, I am well versed in having my work incinerated by superior minds, and I entreat you, Anne, to grant me your honesty no matter how fierce it may be. I promise that in the end, it will spare me a far greater humiliation.

Yours,
William

Butterflies flutter in my belly. William has offered me a glimpse of his soul, an honor I have not been granted since I was a human being. No one knows more than I the fear that comes in sharing one's creation with another burning mind to see if they divine any meaning within its pages.

The memory of my work's reception turns my face hot. My hand presses my cheek and I squeeze my eyes closed, trying to blot out the embarrassment, but ancient accusations slip through my fingers, whispering across time. My writing was *immoral, coarse,* and *brutal.* Morbid manifestations of a degenerate mind. Even Charlotte, my own sister, claimed it was a "mistake" and endeavored to erase *Wildfell Hall* from public consciousness and forbid its reprint. But the truth *is* coarse and brutal. Hurt and fury rise like a wolf in my chest, contracting, looking for a place to lunge. I reach out with an arm to brace myself against the door, take a long ragged breath and force my feelings down. Despite Charlotte's betrayal, I won't stop loving her. She, with all her success, suffered more than any of us, for she had to go on utterly alone.

Suddenly, I'm afraid for William. What if I hate his novel? What if it *is* terrible? How can I possibly deliver this news? All my family were writers. We shared our work with one another and we all had talent. I, less than my sisters, but not so bad as to warrant the fire. Time and again, Emily saved my words from destruction. She alone understood them and saw their worth. When she died, I could not write another word.

A hand flies over my mouth, stifling a sob. Her absence pains me more than the night.

Oh, to be separated from my dearest loves for so long is the harshest punishment I've ever known. What I would give to hold a single hand once more, to feel a warm breath on my cheek, to hear a soft, familiar voice in my ear. I would burn for all eternity if I could see but one of my family for a single moment and say, "I love you always and I will never forget."

Through a veil of tears, I look down at the manuscript and tremble from all the memories it has wrenched loose. All the love it has let fly into the heavens like a wave of shining darkness.

My shift does not begin for hours. In the spirit of my brother and sisters, I place a kettle upon the stove for tea and build a bright, roaring fire before which I will sit and read William Hardcastle's manuscript.

Chapter 19

I drive to the station assaulted by violent images of William's novel. His written words whisper through the night, sticking to me like snow. I try to brush them off, but the mood of his blood-drenched dream clings to me. Maybe it's only hunger gnawing at me like an angry fox. Trying to shove it all out of my mind, I pull my Mini into the truck bay and park. I must forget his words. I must not think of him. I cannot see him again.

Jadallah scared him more than he admits.

I go to the truck and place my things in it: *The Book of Imaginary Beings* by Borges; my surgical kit; and a new UV blanket, although if I need it a second time I'll probably not live much longer, a Night Walker only has so much luck.

I begin checking out the truck, wiping everything down and making sure the narcotics are in order. Lucien always leaves the truck immaculate, but the routine comforts me. A shadow falls and Lucien appears at the back door in sleek jeans and a closefitting t-shirt accentuating his lithe, muscular frame. Most people resign themselves to my strangeness and eventually surrender the attempt at conversation, but Lucien has always gone along as if I am completely normal.

"I see you haven't erupted into flames," he says, looking at my arms for evidence of irritation. He has always believed my story of XP.

I glance at him from beneath my cap and push my safety glasses higher up my nose. "Yes. Thank you, Lucien, for coming to my rescue."

"Anytime." He slaps the side of the truck. "Gotta go. Got a hot date." I wait for him to spin off, but he doesn't move.

"Let me guess. An ER nurse captivated by your supreme heroics."

"No." He smiles. "She's not a nurse, but she is from anatomy class. A white girl. If you don't see me in the morning, it's 'cause I didn't make it past her dad and his shotgun."

I can't help but smile. "I hope you have a fine night."

He nods stiffly in the doorway, glued to the truck, gripping the handrail hard enough so the knuckles beneath his skin appear as pale knobs of bones. Usually he is smoothly confident, and I wonder who has him ruffled.

"Nervous?"

"Nah." He shrugs and looks away, then back again. He sighs. "She's so pretty, Anne. All golden like a princess. Long blonde hair down to her waist. I don't know what she wants with me."

"You're beautiful too, Lucien."

"She actually asked *me* out. What if she's trying to piss off her dad or something?"

"This is Asheville, one of the most liberal towns in the country."

"This is North Carolina and she's not from Asheville. She's a mountain girl. I just hope she's not havin' her little Christian rebellion before she marries a country boy with a gun safe bigger than my Fiat." He rubs his forehead.

"What are you really afraid of?"

"That I'm going to have a taste of her and want more." His voice is so soft only I could hear it. "But hey" —he throws up his hands dramatically— "what's the worst that can happen? Only heartbreak and death. What do I have to lose?"

"No one amongst us will escape that fate. Have courage, Lucien. You're one of the most special people I know. Intelligent, disciplined, compassionate. You are a prince. Any woman would be lucky to have you."

He looks suddenly guilty. "I told her I'm applying for med school. At first I said it to impress her, but then I thought, why the hell not? I'm getting my associate's in EMS. Why not go for a biology degree? And if I get the grades, I could apply for the MCAT." He gives me an uncertain look.

"That sounds like an excellent idea. You'd make a fine doctor."

"You think so?"

"Yes. In this day and age, anything is possible. We're only limited by the greatness or smallness of our dreams."

"No one in my family has even gone to college. They think I'm a rock star just for being an EMT."

"Then you will be the first, and you will pave the way for your descendants so they too may climb the ladder of success and serve humanity. Heartbreak and death will come to us all, Lucien. The best we can do is face it with courage so that those who follow can learn how to bear it."

He takes a deep breath and slowly lets it out. "Thanks, Anne. You don't say much, but when you do, it counts." He laughs. "I'll see you before sunrise. If I'm still alive."

⁂

Dana appears twenty minutes late for shift, throws her purse behind the driver's seat, and climbs in. "I know, I know. No lectures, please."

Peering into the rearview mirror, she applies cherry red lip gloss. She looks pale with dark circles beneath her eyes. Jittery. Her hair is a tousled flaxen mess, whether from lovemaking or a restless sleep I can't tell. She attempts to smooth it back into a ponytail then pulls crumpled sheets of paper from her cargo pocket and thrusts them at me. "I've been working on my rewrite for Hardcastle all night. Mind looking it over?"

I smooth the paper against my thigh and read the title: "Dominance and Submission in *Wuthering Heights*." "Sounds interesting."

"Heathcliff's a total psychopath. He makes Christian Grey look like a pussy."

"Who's Christian Grey?"

She gazes at me in disbelief. "*Fifty Shades of Grey*?"

I stare blankly back.

"Unbelievable," she says in disgust, starting the truck and peeling out of the station. "I need coffee now or I'll never make it through this shift. And I don't want any of that cheap mass-produced crap. I want my beans handpicked by indigenous people high in the mountains and hand roasted under the sun."

"Where can you get that?"

"Malaprop's. They have a ginger mocha latte I've been lusting for all day. I am fucking beat. When I wasn't at clinicals, I was racking my brain, trying to think of a new spin to put on my Lit paper. I just don't know what to say. I don't care about those people. Give me a vampire hunter with tits and a bow and lots of hot lovers. That's what I want to read, not books about controlling abusive men and the poor delicate women who love them. *I* want to be in control, goddamnit." She nervously runs her hand through her hair, sweeping escaped strands off her forehead. "Do you have any chocolate?"

I arch an eyebrow.

"Oh, I forgot, you don't eat after sundown. Part of your strict vegan diet, no doubt." She sighs. "God, I could go for a steak right now. I'm starving."

She's not the only one.

The ambulance curves through frayed shadows, down empty, brooding streets. The town hunches frigid and bare, waiting for snow to fall like a whip. Green lushness has fled, revealing naked limbs and dirty yards. Winter strips secrets away, revealing cracked foundations and crunched dreams. Iron-grey earth juts out from train tracks, reminding me of Northern England. Where is everyone?

Dana drifts through downtown, gnawing at her soft lip. I smell blood and briefly imagine running my tongue along the tender inside of her mouth. She parks down the street from Malaprop's and gets out. I stay, but roll down the window for the cold, fresh air. I'm not going in there again. In 24 hours, I've drawn entirely too much attention to myself. Time to go silent and still until I leave.

The moon is waxing, yet even the redbrick and Art Deco buildings look dim tonight. Faded. I worry about Lucien. This does not seem like a propitious night for love.

"Anne."

William Hardcastle appears at my window with Woody tucked under an arm. The professor's hair is windblown, trailing over an eye, and his breath mists frosty clouds in the cold. He hands me a steaming cup of hot chocolate.

"I thought you might be in need of some fortification. It's absolutely freezing out here."

Reluctantly, I take it. "Thank you," I whisper. I am famished. It may give me a little sustenance. I sip, enjoying the scent of chocolate and the heat of it on my tongue. Woody is staring at me, wrapped snuggly in his parka, and I can't resist reaching out a gloved hand and giving his head a little stroke before withdrawing into aloof silence.

I am determined to harden my heart against Professor Hardcastle. I have allowed him too near, but I *will* recover from the lapse.

Tonight, however, he appears shy. Embarrassed. I suspect he's terrified that I disliked his novel. I understand his fear perfectly. It's the vulnerability that comes from exposing your inner self, demons and scars, so thoroughly to another human being.

"Enjoy your evening," he says in a cold, clipped tone. "May it be quiet and safe." Turning, he vanishes into the bookstore before I can even speak.

"Let him go," I whisper, eyes closed. *Let him go.* I will deliver the manuscript tomorrow evening on my night off. I've written detailed notes to give him. I'll place it in his mailbox. He can wait one night. No one reads as fast as me anyway.

The thought of his anguished uncertainty breaks my heart.

I pull off my cap and smooth back my hair. Snow begins to fall, delicate as lace and when I step out of the truck it lands against my skin like soft, icy kisses. Inside the store, I find William in the back by the classics. Woody sits propped against a bookcase. My glasses are wet from snow and I remove them to wipe them dry.

William looks up, surprised to see me, and a delicious warmth travels over his cheeks and down his throat. I swallow. If I don't feed tonight, tomorrow I must hunt.

"Anne," he says then stares blankly at the book in his hands. "You mustn't say anything. Really, it isn't necessary. I should never have burdened you with such a weight. It was an impulse I failed to check. Normally, I'm not a spontaneous man." He's staring at the book, turning it over in hands: *Paradise Lost.*

"William, it was extraordinary."

He looks up.

"Powerful. Beautiful. It's brutal but tender too."

His voice comes out a hoarse whisper. "You read it?"

I gaze at him, amazed. He's *brilliant*. He captured it: the horror and *love* of war, the ineffable quality I could never express in my paintings. "It's a masterpiece," I say, shaking my head in astonishment. He must know before I leave that his work is important. "For your first work of literature to be so powerful . . . It seems you and Emily Brontë have more in common than I would have imagined."

"Literature?" he asks, looking about ten years old.

"Yes," I smile. "It is most definitely literature."

Suddenly he's kissing me, drawing me into his arms. The little boy is gone and the man is here. Heat wrenches me, piercing me like a bolt of lightning, burning through my belly into my heart. An electrocution. I wait for him to recoil from my coolness, but he leans into me, pressing me against the stack with an arm behind me, steadying. Even beneath his thick coat I feel the hardness of his body, the energy of it, and I'm helplessly melting. All my strength vanishes. He could do anything to me and I wouldn't stop him.

I'm dizzy. Falling. I'm falling into a dark place, all hunger and need and want. I want more of his warmth, his hardness, his pulsing beating heart.

"Anne!" Dana says, regarding us from the aisle. "We have a call."

Her voice snaps me back to myself and I am slipping out of his arms. He catches me by the hand, reluctant to let me go. When I look up at him, his eyes go wide and he releases me, taking a step back. He is looking into my eyes, looking into me, and confusion washes over his face.

My glasses. I remember my glasses. In a flash, I put them on, but it's too late. He's seen me.

Chapter 20

Dana climbs behind the wheel with a smirk on her face, but, miracle of all miracles, she doesn't say anything.

My fingers long to touch my lips, but I'm determined to pretend nothing out of the ordinary happened. "I didn't hear a call come in," I say, searching our dash-mounted computer for the reference.

"Like you were paying attention." She gives me an arch look, then sucks at her coffee. "Santos hurt himself. He called my cell. He doesn't want it going out over the radio." She drives uncharacteristically slow, which appears to be an effort. She's fidgety, tapping the steering wheel and continually scraping a loose strand of hair off her face. I really must talk to her about her hair. "That man has more pride than a tribal warlord. It must have *killed* him to call me." She giggles.

Great. Santos.

"What happened?" I ask, worried. "He must really be hurt to call us." I remember last night and my breath kicks up a notch. The accusations. Maybe this is all a ploy to get me cornered. I'll let Dana deal with him.

"I didn't ask and I don't care," she says. "This one's all yours."

I stare at her.

"*What?*" Dana barks at me. "Just because I fuck someone doesn't mean I love them, Anne. Every time I have a boyfriend you think I'm going to marry him and have his babies."

"It just baffles me how you can be so in love one moment and then utterly indifferent the next."

"When it's over, it's over. I don't go back."

Santos is obviously a sore subject, but I can't help wondering why their relationship ended. Before I have a chance to ask we're pulling down a narrow back alley, brakes groaning as we roll to a stop behind a row of restaurants and bars. Dana squints to see through the gloom. Two squad cars sit shrouded in fog, motors idling but lights off, dusted in a fine layer of snow. Trash is piled in cans and steam puffs from rooftops. A keen wind whistles through the alley and Dana zips up her navy jacket as she steps out of the truck. My cold tolerance is preternatural, but for appearances sake, I follow suit.

Bundled against the cold, Santos braces himself on the edge of his driver's seat, but with his legs outside the cruiser. His right pant leg is pulled up, revealing a deformed knee and the thick muscle of his quad bunched above it in spasm. A small holster rests against his ankle and a slender blade is slipped in his left boot. I stay back. But I can see his brown skin is whiter than it should be and there's a sheen on his brow. I want to lay the back of my hand against his forehead to gauge his skin, but I don't. He gives me a hard look, and I'm tempted to turn and wait in the truck, but I refuse to back down. Beside him stands a magnificently tall officer, blacker than Lucien, leaning against the car. He grins at Dana as we walk up.

"Glad you're amused, Samson," Santos says between clenched teeth.

"A chick kicked his ass," the deputy says with an enormous smile.

"Jesus Christ." Santos shakes his head. "Let the stories begin."

"What happened?" I ask

"I rolled up on a scamp skulking about in the shadows and when I stopped to check it out, she bolted. So I chased her. I jumped a wall and landed wrong. Popped my fucking knee."

"That's his story and he's sticking to it," Samson says.

"That's the truth."

"She outran him," Samson chortles. "Hey, those crack monsters are fast."

"Why'd you chase her?" Dana eyes him like he's a psychopath, or worse—an asshole. "Since when is 'skulking' in the shadows a crime?"

"She ran."

"You chased her because she ran? What are you, a *dog*?"

"I'm a cop," Santos spits out.

I take a slight step forward, distracting him, and notice a jagged scar on his inner knee. "Has this ever happened to you before?"

Samson erupts in laughter.

"Your knee, I mean," I say. "Have you dislocated it before?"

"Once, but I forced it back in. This time, I tried, but I . . ." He shifts and flinches. We all wait.

"You . . . what?" Dana asks with the same smirk she offered me earlier. How this woman loves to see us squirm.

He looks at her grimly. "I can't do it."

Dana cups a hand to her ear. "What did you say? I didn't hear you?"

"Just do it, Dana. Slam it back in place. Get off on the pain. I figured you'd be all for this."

"*I* can't do it," she says, shocked at the idea. "That's not part of my training. Have Samson drive you to the hospital. He's good at driving." She gives him a wink.

"I offered," Samson says, "but he refused. Said he wanted you."

"Not my exact words," Santos says. "I don't have time for a ride to the hospital and all the bullshit paperwork. Can't you just slip it back in?"

"It's not that simple," I say. "Relocations are beyond our protocols. If she does it wrong, she can make it worse."

"Oh, what the hell," Dana says. "It's worth a try." Licking her lips, she steps forward and lays her hands upon Santos' knee. He freezes. She's not wearing gloves, and her red fingernails feel for the edge of his kneecap. Santos grips the seat of his squad car, fingers digging into the vinyl. He holds his breath. Dana drops to her knees and dramatically pauses with his knee cupped between her hands.

This is so wrong. I should say something, stop this, but they're both consenting adults. I remind myself that Santos wouldn't be so kind to me. As he chased me down a mountain road beneath an ever-hotter sun, my well-being was the last thing on his mind.

Dana's fingers tighten and Santos goes pale. He digs his fingers deeper into the seat. Suddenly struck with a conscience, she turns to me. "You're the one who should be doing this, Anne."

"Neither of us should be doing this. You heard Dr. Webb. This is completely outside our protocols."

"Like that's ever stopped you before," she says.

"Dr. Webb wasn't here before." And I've only broken protocol when a life hung in the balance. Santos is safe. He suffers from pain and an impermanent injury that I know he can take.

Santos jerks as Dana shoves at his kneecap, her eyes glinting with determination. His body goes rigid, but he doesn't scream. For a second, I think he's going to pass out. Dana seems to enjoy his pain as she tries to work the kneecap back in. Samson and I wince. She's doing it wrong.

"*Fuck*," Santos groans.

"Enough!" I say, pulling her off him. "You're going to do permanent damage. Santos, you're coming with us. You'll be out of the ER in a few hours." I grab the stretcher and drop it beside him.

He kicks it away with his good leg. "I don't have a few hours."

"Then drive yourself," I say, vexed. How *dare* he treat us like this.

Samson shifts uneasily. "Just go," he says. "It's dead out here. You ain't missing anything."

Santos stares at him helplessly. "The paperwork's gonna take hours."

Try writing a novel.

"Look," says Dana. "We don't have all night either. Don't be such a baby. Get your ass on the stretcher."

Simultaneously, she and I step forward. I slide my hands beneath his shoulders and Dana takes his legs. With surprising grace, we lift him and place him on the stretcher.

"That's how you do it," Samson says as we load his sergeant into the truck. "Break him down like a double-barreled shotgun." For once, Santos seems at a loss for words. "Enjoy the ride, Sarge. I'll have someone drop your car at the hospital."

Dana pushes the stretcher forward to lock it in, but it snags on a loose seatbelt we failed to secure around Santos. She pushes and jerks at the stretcher trying to free it, jostling him. His knee slams against a rail.

"Are you fucking kidding me?" he yells.

With a frustrated sigh, I climb inside, free the stretcher and belt in Santos. "I'm driving," I tell Dana, snapping my hands back from Santos' waist as fast as I can.

But she closes the doors and smiles gloriously at Samson, leaving me alone in the back with a man who is carrying at least two guns, two knives, a pair of handcuffs, baton, and a Taser.

"I told you, Anne," she says, before shutting me in, "this one's *all yours.*"

Chapter 21

I sit on the bench seat beside Santos so I can take a blood pressure and get vitals, but I hesitate. He's encased in a Kevlar vest, thick jacket, and laden duty belt. I, on the other hand, feel defenseless. The sharpest thing I have on me is a pair of trauma shears and I'm so famished, I feel faint.

Santos looks as tense as a lion ready to spring. We're not going to fight, I tell myself. For all he knows, I'm a paramedic and we're just taking a short ride to the hospital.

There's something about her that's not right. She's not normal.

I brace for his accusations, afraid any move will open the floodgates.

Finally, I pick up a blood pressure cuff and reach for his arm.

"Don't touch me," he whispers.

I drop the cuff beside me on the seat and draw a hurt breath. I would never harm a patient. *Ever.* Patients trust me. The one thing I have going for me as a female paramedic is the trust that comes from looking young and harmless. The most hardened criminals, suspicious of any touch, relax beneath my hands. Somehow, despite the lives I have swallowed, there is still an innocence about me.

It is an illusion.

A sensation of being studied crawls across my skin. He's watching, observing my body language, trying to examine my face beneath the cap and glasses. This is the closest we've ever been to each other and in the brightest light. How did I end up in this situation? I should be driving! I should be *leaving*. Why isn't Santos saying anything? Demanding explanations for my unnatural behavior?

Curious, I look at him, but he looks away. Cops may be good at reading people, but so are paramedics and there is an uneasiness to him that is more than pain. Then with a start, I understand.

Santos is afraid of *me*. It's not anger that has rendered him silent, it's an undercurrent of fear that only a Night Walker could smell.

I should say something to reassure him. I've done this for thousands of patients, but with him I'm at a loss for words. Then I remember how he confronted me last night in my home. How frightened I was. And angry. Instead, I pick up my report.

"Any meds?" I ask.

"No."

"No psych meds?"

He looks at me like I'm insane.

"Allergies to medications?"

"No."

"Medical history?"

"No."

"Injuries? Surgeries?"

"Nope."

"No knee or shoulder surgeries?" I ask skeptically. Twelve years in the military and no injuries? I find that unlikely. I wonder how many head injuries he's had. That might explain his infernal temperament.

"Nothing."

"Have you ever been in the hospital?" I'm kind of prying, but this time it's *my* turn to ask the questions. Let him see how it feels to be cornered like an animal.

He sighs. "Twice with a TBI. Traumatic Brain Injury. From an IED. Improvised Explosive De—"

"I know the acronyms."

"I was only in a few days. I have a hard head."

I start to make a note of it when he reaches out and grabs my wrist. "Wait, Bell. Scratch that. I don't need that in my records."

"It's in your military records."

"I don't need the department to know."

"This report is private." Indignant, I try to extricate my arm, but he grips it so hard, I can't free myself without revealing my strength. "This is an entirely inappropriate way to treat a paramedic and you know it. If a civilian ever touched you this way, you'd throw them in jail."

"Delete it, Bell. *Erase* it." His voice is growing louder, his grip on my wrist tighter. "This has nothing to do with my knee."

"Alright. Take it easy." I rip my hand out of his grip.

He gives me a suspicious look.

"I'm very thorough with my reports. I assure you, you're not special. I can't take a blank report to the hospital." I set it down and cross my legs. I can just see it: all his medical history pouring out to the intake nurse while she shakes her head at my empty report.

"What's that scar on the inside of your knee?" I ask. He stares at me as if deciding whether or not to answer. I wait.

"A bullet ricocheted, hit my knee and dislocated it." Empathy rises, but he shoots it down. "It was just a flesh wound. Somehow I forced my knee back in, but it hasn't been the same since." His face is impassive as if none of this bothers him at all.

"When was that?"

"Oh-two."

"Operation Anaconda?"

He looks at me, surprised. "How'd you know?"

"I read about it."

Two gods at war in the remote mountains of Afghanistan. The god of Abraham and the god of Ishmael. And a great serpent was their image.

I wasn't there but I can picture it. Overturned trucks and broken bodies. Bombs of friendly fire incinerating their own. No time for grieving, get back in the fight. A mountain peak. Helicopters crashing. Men pinned down for days, dragging their wounded through graves of snow to be refused medevac. Mortars raining with chaotic consistency. Reinforcements that didn't come. Fighting hypothermia and an enemy five times greater than what they'd expected.

One of the chinks in a vivid imagination is the ability to envision all the horrors others have suffered.

"That must have been early in your career."

"It was my first time in combat. I was straight out of Ranger school. So fucking green and gung ho. Way to pop your cherry, huh?" He laughs without humor. "We lost awesome guys that day and all I got was a dislocated knee."

"You sound disappointed. You were lucky." I correct myself. "Not lucky. That's not what I meant—"

"That's all it was. Dumb luck. I don't want it. I lost a lot of guys and all I ever suffered was minor bullshit. It's not right."

"And parted friends, how dear so ever, will soon forgotten be.
It may be so with other hearts, it is not thus with me."

He gazes at me and frowns.

"It's not your fault."

"You have no fucking idea whose fault it is," he snaps.

I lean back to give him space. If he only knew how many men have shared their shame with me. Survivors suffer the greatest guilt of all. The injured are too busy healing and the dead don't feel blame.

I look him straight in the eye. "I know you're a brave man who has dedicated his entire adult life to protecting others."

He scoffs. "A lot of good it's done. People keep dying. Everyone except me."

I think of Papa. "That, Sergeant, is the price life reaps on the strong."

He stares out the rear window into darkness.

"Perhaps you have a powerful guardian angel," I tease to lighten the mood.

"She can go fuck herself."

"That's no way to talk to an angel."

"I know," he says, staring down at his hands.

"I suppose it doesn't matter. They don't listen very well anyway."

"What do you know about angels?" There is a wary expression in his eye that comes from having others scoff at your beliefs. A feeling I know all too well.

"After my mother died, when I was little, my sister swore she saw one by my bed."

"Did you believe her?"

"I don't know. My sisters were always seeing things—ghosts, angels. Emily said she could hear the dead whispering." *Shelley, in particular.* "And my brother heard voices." *The opium didn't help.* I look at him to see if he thinks I'm crazy.

"Yeah, my mom too," he says.

"Did she give you that?" I indicate the small Catholic medallion he wears around his neck. On each side are colored beads, emblems of Santeria I suspect, but I'm afraid to ask.

"Yeah." He looks a little embarrassed. He takes it in his fingers, the brown of his hand dark against the silver. "St. George. He was an officer in the Roman Army. Now he's the patron saint of soldiers. Mom gave it to me after boot camp. For protection. The damn thing works too good."

"St. George, the dragon slayer, rescuer of fair maidens," I say. "He chose torture and sacrifice over conversion to paganism." Santos' faith intrigues and frightens me. To a true believer, I must be an abomination. More daughter of Satan than child of God.

He tucks the medallion beneath his bulletproof vest. "You know a lot for a paramedic." The tone of suspicion is back.

"I *read*. It's amazing what you can pick up from books."

He stares at his boots.

"Despite your disdain for life, I see you're wearing your vest. That's wise."

"My mom made me promise to wear it. She can be hardcore when she gets something into her head."

"And you keep your promise?"

"Of course." He looks at me like I'm clueless. The hospital lights shine through the window as Dana pulls in and deftly backs up to the ER. Santos groans in frustration, laying his head back against the stretcher, revealing his pulsing throat. "I don't have time for this shit. Goddamnit!"

His heart throbs in his neck and my mouth waters. He snaps his head up and looks at me. I glance away, down to the thick vein in the crook of his elbow and long to start an IV and draw his blood, but I'm afraid. With another patient I would, but with him I just can't. Anyway, we're here. I'm out of time.

Little passive Anne.

How perfectly I embody my childhood avatar, a tiny soldier Papa brought home from one of his trips—*Waiting Boy*. Waiting to eat. Waiting to die. Waiting for salvation.

When will I take control?

Santos' breath kicks up and he shifts, inadvertently moving his knee and flinching. I have to get vitals. I can't drop him off with an empty report. Before he can protest, I reach for his wrist and take his pulse. He lets me. His flesh is surprisingly cool beneath my hand, and his pulse bounds beneath my touch, elevated, whether from pain or fear I'm not sure. He's the armed one, but he's nervous with me. Vulnerable. And though they are physical opposites, he reminds me of Branwell, with that same sense of wounded idealism wearing at his fractured pride.

Who is more idealistic? The poet or the soldier? I have known both to die for their beliefs, and still, after all this time, I cannot decide.

Chapter 22

Inside the ER, Santos and I are immediately shown a room, one of the perks of his being in uniform. Dana has refused to move from the truck. Even the lure of Dr. Webb can't entice her inside with her ex. Santos edges onto a hospital bed and when I look around for the nurse to give my report, Dr. Webb is standing right beside me. Santos is certainly getting uncommon attention.

Webb extends a hand and I place the report in it. His brow creases. All that is upon it is a name and a pulse rate.

"Sergeant Santos, what seems to be the problem?" I start to leave, but Dr. Webb stops me with a hand on my arm. I look at him, astounded by the presumption, but he ignores me and turns to examine Santos' knee. Two men have touched me in one day. I have become too familiar to them. It's definitely time to leave.

While I wait, I gather my composure. Webb will *not* intimidate me. The room is freezing and I could choke on the sharp scent of antiseptic, which comes from the war Dana says that Webb has waged on MRSA. I can't smell a single bacterium anywhere.

"I threw out my knee jumping a fence. Listen, Doc," Santos says, his voice turning warm with a charm I didn't know he had. "Can we forgo the x-rays? We're riding short out there." He nods his head, indicating the street. "And I'd really like to get back into service."

I try to inch away, but Webb stops me.

"Bell, wait. There's something I need to say to you." My heart drops. I think of the hunter and all the things I did to him after Webb's proscription. Damn! Why didn't Dana make this patient transfer? I've really had it with her. She's the rookie. *I'm* the supervisor. I have about as much control over her as a panic attack.

Webb touches Santos' knee, and before the officer knows what's coming, slides his knee into place with such ease it's almost like he's showing off. My eyes widen in disbelief. So much for *his* protocols.

Santos lets out a deep sigh of relief.

"You're free to go," Webb says, slapping him on the shoulder. Santos tenses, then gingerly slides off the bed, testing his knee when his feet hit the floor. He bends his leg a few times. Puts weight on it, then looks at Webb.

"Thanks, Doc. I appreciate it."

"Professional courtesy," Webb says. "Now, if you'll excuse us, Bell and I have some matters to discuss."

Santos' cell rings. He answers it and walks out without the slightest hitch in his stride. For once in my life I want him to stay.

With a hand lightly against my upper back, Dr. Webb steers me into the hall. Struggling to hide my fury, I pull away from him. My composure is cracking. *Stay cool, Anne. Calm and cool.* I push my glasses higher up my nose.

We are almost eye to eye and his edge is back, yet he speaks in a low, intimate voice. "I just thought you should know, I'm filing a complaint with your supervisor regarding the trauma patient last night. You blatantly disobeyed me and acted way outside your scope of practice. You violated your agency's protocols against my specific instruction."

"Did he live?"

"Are you listening to me?"

"The boy. Did he live?"

"That's beside the point."

"That is hardly beside the point."

"Whether he lived or died is irrelevant. You acted irresponsibly. Just because you got away with it today doesn't mean that tomorrow you won't find yourself out of your depth. If paramedics start performing *surgery* in the back of their ambulances, there are legal ramifications for all of us. It only takes one time to screw up. Believe me, I know."

I study him through my glasses. Why does he dislike me so? Most physicians are happy to have my help. And if not at first, they eventually come to respect my ability. But for Webb, my proficiency is a great affront.

"Listen," he says, "we've gotten off on the wrong foot. I'm not your enemy. I appreciate your talents. I simply want you to follow your protocols. I'm the doctor. You're the paramedic. We all have our assigned roles to play. I'd rather work with you than against you."

My eyes narrow. "Hard now that you've filed a complaint against me, endangering my job and certification."

"I haven't filed it yet. I'll withhold it if you'll admit your mistake and agree to stay within your bounds."

"How is saving him a mistake?" I throw up my arms in frustration.

Anger flits beneath his gaze. His voice is low, soft. Anyone witnessing our conversation would think it personal, even intimate. "You have absolutely no regard for my authority. You think you can do whatever you like. This conversation is over." He turns to leave.

"Wait!" I reach out and grab him. Surprised, he stops. I release him as if I've been burned. How hot I feel. I've just grabbed a physician. "I hear you, Dr. Webb. You needn't file that report. I'll follow the protocols. No problem."

He pauses for what feels like an eternity. I stare down at his shoes, ashamed I can't hold his gaze. He's wearing expensive leather loafers with tassels on them. My boots look a wreck in comparison. Finally, I look up.

"Okay then," he says, trying to read my face hidden beneath my cap. "I see you restrained yourself with your last patient. I appreciate that."

"I could have saved him the trip. Saved you the time." Not that Santos would have let me, but Webb doesn't know that.

"Not without risk. If anything had gone wrong or the sergeant complained, your position would not protect you. Let me protect you. Let me incur the risk. I restrain your actions, Anne, not because I think you're not capable, but because I want to protect you. While I'm here, I will not allow you to continually put your career at risk. You know how litigious this society is. If I came on strong, it was only because I was trying to scare you straight."

"I don't need to be scared straight."

"There's no other way to get through to you. Your history makes that all too evident."

"How do you know my history?" *How does he know my first name?* "You don't know me at all. You've only been here a few weeks."

"Your reputation precedes you. I'm a good judge of character and I know an intractable idealist with tendencies of martyrdom when I see one. I have no doubt you would sacrifice yourself for one of your unworthy patients. There are plenty more where they came from and only one of you. You are too skilled for me to allow you to fall on your sword."

Now he's flattering me. Who *is* this man and why does he care what I do? "I've survived this career for a long time, Dr. Webb, without your protection."

"The world is changing, Anne. Our patients will hang us out to dry before we even get our gloves off."

"Then why fight so hard for them? You cracked a child's chest open to save him."

"Because when you have the power to ward off death as I do, it pisses me off when God intervenes."

"So you believe in God?" I ask, off balance.

"Yes, but I prefer Him to stay in heaven where He belongs and leave those on earth to me."

I'm silent. What is there to say to that?

Webb gives me a gentle smile. "I'm only here for three months. As you know, I'm filling in for Dr. Fisher. All I ask is that you obey me for three months."

At the word "obey," I bristle.

He sighs at my reaction. "Wrong choice of words. All I ask, Anne, is that you accept my offer of protection and stay within the bounds of your license."

I've never witnessed such arrogance in my life and yet his confidence tugs at me. His skill. I remember my early years as a nurse— how raw I was—and the pleasure that came from submitting to a brilliant doctor who burned with blood and experience.

Webb reminds me of my first mentor.

I gaze at him, then turn my back and walk out.

Chapter 23

Santos is gone, but Dana is waiting, watching me in the truck's side mirror as I leave the ER. When I climb into the truck, she asks, "What did Webb want? I saw him talking to you."

"To chew me out about the hunter."

"Is that all?" she asks.

"What else would it be? You know I don't like to hang out and talk to doctors."

"Well, apparently they like to talk to you."

"Let's get something clear, Dana. *You* do the patient transfer."

"That's not the way it's done, Anne. The medic in the back with the patient gives the report and makes the transfer. You know way more about the patients than I do."

"I'm your supervisor. It's done the way I say it's done. I don't like hospitals and I'm not going inside unless I have to."

She looks at me as if I've lost my mind. "Strange choice of professions, don't you think? I can't believe Jimmy puts up with your, your . . . *eccentricities*. Sometimes I honestly wonder if you're blowing him."

My mouth falls open in shock. "I don't blow my supervisors."

"I know. I doubt you've given a blow job in your life." She slings this at me as if it's a crime.

What would she say if she knew I was a virgin? I rub my hands over my face. I've got to eat. Tonight. For real.

"It's just that every time I'm interested in a man, all they ask about is you."

"What?"

"It was the same with Santos. I swear he was more into you than me. *What does she eat? Does she nap on shift? Does she drink? Is there a man in her life? A woman?*"

"A woman?" My face grows hot.

"Yeah, the rumor is you're a closet lesbian."

Again, I'm speechless. After all I've experienced tonight you'd think I'd be impervious to surprise, but Dana never fails.

"Believe me, Anne, you could *never* handle him. Sex with him is like a battlefield."

"Handle who?"

"Santos. I'm all for rough sex. I love it, but I prefer to wield the whip, not take it on my hands and knees."

"He *whipped* you?!"

"No." She laughs the thought away. "I'm kidding. He's actually quite conservative. No porn, no toys, nothing. An Army Ranger who doesn't watch porn? That" —she jabs at the steering wheel for empha-sis— "Is. Not. Normal. I think he has a Madonna/whore complex. Typical Latin, which explains why he talks to his mother every day. What kind of man does that?" she asks, perplexed.

"A man who loves his mother?"

What a dream it would be to talk to Mama every day.

"Cut the cord, for fuck's sake. There was something cold about sex with him. Detached. He's like a machine in bed. God, the stam-ina! And you should see his cock—"

"Alright!" I put a hand up to stop her. "Enough."

"I'm all for friends with benefits, but he was scaring everyone else away. I want to be worshipped. Obsessed over. Not casually fucked."

"Battlefield sex does not sound casual," I say, confused. "Maybe he wants more."

"I'm telling you, he's schizo. Guns all over the house, a *life-sized* Virgin Mary beside his bed. How can you fuck with the Virgin staring down at you? Ten-inch serrated knives lying on top of his bible." She giggles. "He reads the bible. Can you believe that?"

I can't help wondering what William is like in bed. He's so thoughtful and considerate, but strong too. He seems attuned to my every vibration. The thought sends nerves shooting through my skin. *Casual* sex. How can giving yourself to another person ever be casual? Opening, letting them in? I've walked this earth for almost two centuries and I still don't understand the ease with which women offer themselves up to men who are utterly unworthy.

Of course, Professor Hardcastle is worthy.

Perhaps I don't know what I'm missing. *Clearly*, I don't know what I'm missing. After all the killing and maiming I've seen, sex seems like a rather innocent pastime. Except when unwanted babies are born, or when it injects you with disease, or breaks your heart, or degrades your self-respect, or rips families apart. I squeeze my eyes closed, trying to shut down my archaic righteousness. As a Night Walker, sex with William is free from all those possibilities save one—a broken heart.

And that is more frightening than anything.

"I need more coffee," Dana says, already looking wired.

What I need is nourishment, and as if my blessed angel has heard me a call comes out over the radio.

"Rescue 1," dispatch says, drawing out every syllable.

"Amen," I whisper.

"Respond to person down."

This is it! No excuses. No fear. No mercy.

"Officer on scene."

Dana waits for the address, thrumming her fingers against the steering wheel. "Christ, when is this dispatcher going to retire? Out with it, lady!"

But it doesn't matter to me where we're going or who will be there. I *will* feed. Some way, somehow, I will make it happen. Even if I have to take a 300-pound man down by the throat.

Chapter 24

We've parked on a narrow dirt road and descended by foot through the forest. Now we stand beneath trees, our boots forming a crescent around the lifeless form. Santos hovers like a clenched fist over the corpse and Dana has gone snow white. A teenage girl lies before us, light blonde hair strewn about her round face in a gossamer halo. Dead. The flashing lights of Santos' cruiser seep through the forest. Soon deputies will begin showing up on scene.

A sacrilege. It is a sacrilege.

Santos stares grimly at the body. He has not made eye contact with me once. "I need you to confirm death," he says.

I look at him. The girl's death is painfully obvious but humans take comfort in protocol and apparently Santos is human after all. Dana doesn't move. She stands frozen and silent by my side. I have carried the monitor down with us and carefully I place an electrode above each plump wrist and ankle then turn the monitor on. Flat line.

"She's gone," I say.

"Any idea how long?"

"Rigor hasn't set in. There's still warmth to her. I'd say no more than twenty minutes."

"Son of a bitch. That fucker was right here." He gets on the radio and calls out a search, establishing perimeters, requesting dogs, but I know he doesn't have the resources to corner this predator. I turn to Dana. In our time together, she's seemed unnaturally resilient to the trauma of our profession, an advantage I've always suspected of scant empathy, but not tonight. Tonight, she's shaken.

"Are you okay?" I ask.

"She's dead," she says, sounding dazed. "I'll be in the truck."

I bend to take a closer look at the girl. She's dressed warmly in a bright red parka. A small gold cross lies against her cheek. Below it, her neck is sliced cleanly from one side of her jaw to the other. The snow is pure white, free of blood. How did Santos find her?

I edge a gloved finger beneath her collar and ease it open, leaning in for a closer look. Santos' gaze catches on me, his voice rising, telling me not to disturb the scene. Her throat is delicate. Tender. Her collar falls open letting out a warm pocket of scent and I recoil in horror, twisting, slipping in the snow, scrambling to my feet.

An *Alpha!* An Alpha did this. I lunge for the truck.

Santos grabs me by the arm, yanking me back. "Hey! What is it?"

"Nothing." I gasp, surprised at his strength.

He spins me to face him. "Bullshit. If you know something about this, you better tell me."

I yank my arm out of his grip. "Don't threaten me." My fear coalesces to anger. I'm sick of his hostility. Sick of brutal, violent men. "How did you find her? How is it you found both bodies?"

"What the fuck is that supposed to mean? Do you think I did this?"

"It seems odd you're always around when dead virgins show up."

"How do you know she's a virgin?"

"She has that look about her," I say lamely. The truth is I can smell it on her like an early spring.

"What look is that?"

"Young, country, religious."

"That don't mean shit. These country girls start fucking early."

I give him a disgusted look but he doesn't notice. He's staring intently at the body. "Someone killed her somewhere else and carried her body here." Without touching her, he crouches and peers at her hands. They are small, covered in handmade grey mittens. "Doesn't look like she put up a fight. All her clothes are intact."

"You never answered my question. How did you find her?"

"Her daddy's a hunting buddy. Said she was going out with a black boy tonight and he didn't like it. He tried to stop her, but she had a fit and ran out of the house. He asked me to keep an eye out for her, so I drove here to take a look around."

A black boy? Oh dear God.

"And you found her down here off the road?" I look at him in disbelief.

"Figured she couldn't go far on foot and was heading up the road to meet her date. I drove the roads but something didn't feel right." He stops short.

"What didn't feel right?"

He presses his lips together, squinting off into the forest.

"Tell me," I say, softening my voice. "I want to understand."

He takes a deep breath. "It's this feeling I get when there's killing going on. It puts out a vibration I sense under my skin. It's like a shock wave of evil or something. I don't know how to describe it."

Is that what he feels around me? Evil?

"Anyways, I had a hunch. This fucker's gonna be lucky if he don't get lynched."

"Wait a minute! You don't know he did this. Just because he's black—"

"They had a date. She didn't put up a fight, which suggests she was killed by someone she knows. Unless he has a rock solid alibi, he's a prime suspect."

"That's profiling."

"That's detective work. It'd be the same if he was white. Who else did she run off to see? Her grandmother? If so, the wolf got her first."

My hands clench with rage. I want to grab him by the throat and crush the light out of him. My hunger is rising, splintering into pieces like sharp teeth. I won't let him hurt innocent Lucien. He's off-limits.

Santos senses a change in me and tenses. His fingers twitch. We stare at each other across the snow. He is all lean, hard muscle I long to tear apart.

My phone rings, a blessed distraction. I answer it, expecting it to be Dana in the truck ready to leave, but it's not her.

It's Lucien.

"I'm on my way to Claire's and I saw your truck and the sheriff. Is everything okay?" His voice is small.

"Where are you now?"

"I pulled over. I can see your lights from here. Just got a bad feeling. 'Fraid her dad maybe went Appalachian on her ass."

"See where the truck is? There's a dirt path down the mountain just behind it. You'll see our footprints. I need you to come down here. But brace yourself. You're not going to like what you see."

I hate to thrust this upon him, but I'm sure his reaction will prove his innocence. And if Santos is going to interrogate him, I want to be there. I'm breaking my rules and getting involved, but Lucien is not equipped to handle Santos, a man who has spent a decade questioning terrorists.

"Lucien was this poor girl's date."

"Lucien?" Santos says, surprised. His eyes darken to black points. Already, he has convicted him. How can he not see the light coursing through that boy's veins? The pure shining potential in his eyes?

"He was arriving to pick her up when he saw our lights. He's heading this way now. Unless you're blind, I'm sure his innocence will be obvious."

"This is a crime scene. He can't come down here." Santos, impervious to his knee, stomps through the trees up the mountain to head him off. Reluctantly, I follow, leaving the fallen girl alone. It feels wrong to abandon her, but Lucien is alive and he's the one who needs protection now.

He appears as the darkest of shadows against the snow-dusted trees. He's wearing a black, puffy North Face parka that makes him look bigger than he really is. He halts when he sees the look on Santos' face. I pause, giving them space and watch while Lucien looks for me with a worried expression.

"Is someone hurt?" he asks.

"Fuck yeah, someone's hurt," Santos says. "Where were you 20 minutes ago?"

"On my way here."

"Do you have an alibi?"

"No. I was on my way here, by myself."

"You talk to anyone on the phone?"

"No. What's going on? Is it Claire? Is she okay?" He cranes his head to look past us. The whites of his eyes flash and I smell fear. He tries to walk by Santos, but Santos roughly blocks him. "Hey!" Lucien says. "What the fuck, man?"

In one deft move, Santos has Lucien's arm, twisting it behind his back to cuff him. Lucien spins like a running back, breaking out of the hold and Santos slams a fist into his stomach, then his temple, taking him down. With a savage kick, he knocks Lucien onto his back and falls on him, hitting hard and fast, pinning him to the ground with a laser-like ferocity.

I grab Santos and throw him off. He flies, slamming against a tree and landing on his knees. Stunned, he climbs to his feet and looks at me in recognition and fury. With a roar, he flies at me and I slam him back against the tree. I hold him by the throat and pin him there.

"Stop," I order. "Stop. He didn't do it. It wasn't him. You've got the wrong guy."

"Get off me, you fucking bitch," he shouts and tries to push me away, but I don't budge. I squeeze his throat tighter.

"Don't make me hurt you," I whisper. "I don't want to hurt you." My mouth is inches from his throat. His smooth brown skin smells like sun. And islands. I can smell the blood in him and feel it throb beneath my fingers. Hunger wrenches me. I want to sink my teeth into his neck. If he fights, I will take him.

Please fight. Please. Fight.

His eyes blaze but he freezes and very slowly I loosen my grip, keeping my hand around his throat, reluctant to relinquish him fully.

"I knew it. I fucking *knew* it," he spits.

"Pull yourself together," I hiss. "If you want to know who really did this, get your head together."

He falls silent and still. Carefully, I release him. He breaks away and looks at me in the half moonlight, breathing hard. My cap is lying in the snow and in frustration, I throw my glasses to the ground. I lift my face to the moonlight and close my eyes.

It's done. After all these years, I am exposed. It's a relief actually, to finally reveal myself to someone.

"You know who did this?" he asks, shaking out his fist.

"I know it wasn't him." I motion to Lucien, who is crawling to his knees, dazed, trying to wipe the blood from his face.

"How do you know?"

"Because I can smell it on her. And it isn't him."

"*It?*" Santos' voice comes out a hoarse rasp. "It's true. I'm not fucking crazy." He's whispering, his eyes glittering in the dark, glazing with tears. He begins to collapse on himself and grabs my shoulder to steady himself.

I look from Lucien to Santos, unsure who is most wounded.

Furiously, Santos swipes at his tears.

"I'm not crazy?" He grabs me close, boring into my eyes, down into the soft, wild parts of me. "You're . . . *it* . . . *it's* not normal, is it?"

"You're not crazy." I twist out of his grip, unable to bear it. I must leave, but I will tell him the truth. Ancient lies are driving him insane. "An Alpha did this. A Night Walker male. They are extremely dangerous. Whatever you think I am, he's nothing like me. The males are different. Dominant, vile, ruthless. They detest the weak and are far stronger than I can ever be."

"What are you?"

"I don't know." My voice cracks. "I have been asking myself that for a long time." I stare down at my boots, my voice dropping. "I don't know what I am or where I come from or why I'm here. All I know" — my voice is barely a whisper— "is that I'm a creature of the night and . . ." I take a great breath, "I need blood to survive."

I wait for Santos to reach for his gun. To hold it against my chest and pull the trigger. To feel the piercing relief of annihilation. I won't stop him.

Oh, Father! Father! Let me rest! And call my soul to thee!

"But the first girl was killed in daylight," he says, puzzling out our peculiar existence. I gaze at him. He appears utterly unfazed by my confession.

"I don't understand it," I admit. "I've never known any of my kind to live long in the light."

"To live *long*? But you have heard of them surviving?"

I think back to my early days after my first kill. A thirteen-year-old girl. She gave me such strength I lived for weeks in the sun, but in time the night wrapped its grip around me and gathered me back in. My sun-strength faded, never to return.

I do not wish to tell Santos about my first victim. "I know little of it. There are few of us and we don't compare notes."

A moan reaches my ears. Lucien is struggling to his feet. "Anne?" His left eye is closing and he holds snow to his face. I doubt he's heard our conversation, but if he has I will convince him he is confused from concussion.

"Go to the truck, Lucien," I say. "I'll meet you there in a minute."

"I knew that girl was trouble." He turns and makes his way slowly to the road.

I glare at Santos. "So much for innocent until proven guilty. This isn't Cuba. You just broke every law in the book."

"Fuck the law. Sometimes the law isn't enough. But you know all about that, don't you? You've been living outside the law for how long?"

"I've been running these mountains ten years, helping these people. And starving in the process," I mutter under my breath.

"You've got to find this guy and make him stop."

I look at him in shock. "I can no more stop him than Dana could stop you if you were a rampaging murderer. If he finds me, he will take me and keep me until my last days. Alphas collect females and hold them like slaves. Their appetites are strong and we don't break like human women. I'll go nowhere near him. No one can. He'll finish with this place and move on."

"When?"

"When he gets bored."

"How many girls will it take for that to happen?"

"I don't know. Not many more. He won't want to attract enormous attention. It makes survival difficult. None of us wants to fight a village."

Santos steps up to me with a hard look. "You're going to stand by and let this monster take down our girls? You're going to let innocent girls get drained by a psychopath and do *nothing*? You call yourself a paramedic? You're fucking pathetic."

I turn away, shaking my head. "There's nothing I can do. I wish it were different. I do. But it would be like you trying to take down the Taliban entirely on your own. It's not possible. You would be there if it were, but you're not, you're *here*. Because *here* you can make a difference. If I go after him, I'll end up dead or enslaved. I can't help anyone then."

"Then I would die. I would die before I turn my back on anyone too weak to protect themselves. You're like that murdering Alpha. An animal incapable of selfless courage."

Fear tightens my belly.

Fear for Santos.

"Let him be," I demand. "You can't stop him."

"Then I'll die trying."

"No!"

Sirens swell through the night. Officers are arriving. "What am I supposed to tell them?" he shouts.

"Tell them a psycho is loose. Tell them you questioned Lucien and he's not a suspect. Based on his injuries, he's coming with me."

I turn my back on him and stalk up the mountain, moving too fast for Santos to catch.

Chapter 25

Inside the truck, Lucien slouches on the stretcher, cradling his ribs while I clean his wounds. A two-inch laceration gapes above his eye and there is another ugly gash on his cheek. I bite my lip in frustration. Santos has proven his instability. He is too emotional to deal with this. I long for William's cool calm and suddenly the memory of his hot kiss comes, unbidden and disorienting.

It feels like that was weeks ago.

"What am I going to do?" Lucien asks.

"Wait and let things die down."

"They're going to throw my ass in jail. If they don't find who did this, they're going to blame me. Even if I get off, I'll never live it down. It will follow me my entire life."

I throw a wad of bloody gauze in the trash and pull out my suture kit. Lucien will scar without stitches. Lucky for him I'm the best plastic surgeon in town.

They won't find the person who did this. They will never get near him, and there is nothing I can do about it. Too many know what I am. Santos and possibly William and Lucien. But more dangerous than that is the Alpha. He is the greatest danger of all. It's possible he doesn't yet know I'm here, but if he finds me, I'm done for. I will not live as another's slave, a degraded addition to a madman's harem. I should be in my car, fleeing as quickly as I can this very minute. But there's Lucien to deal with. He needs stitches. There's Ivanhoe, my home. It will take time to make arrangements. I can't abandon my library, my notebooks.

And William.

When I'm done suturing Lucien, I ask him if he's okay to drive his car. I don't want to deliver him to the hospital and expose him to an audience.

"Keep a low profile. Stay calm and tell the truth. Hopefully, Santos will run interference for you. He's a bit unhinged, but he isn't a liar. He won't want an innocent man locked up for this."

Lucien looks unconvinced.

"You've done nothing wrong," I say.

"You think that matters? That don't matter. Claire is *dead*. I could get the chair for this."

"That's not going to happen. They have no evidence. You didn't touch her. Have a little faith, Lucien. Santos and I won't let you take the fall for this."

Gravely, Lucien steps out. I climb in front with Dana, who sits frozen, staring out the window. She's in the passenger seat, normally my place. The heat is off, and I'm surprised she's not shivering in the cold. I turn it up, put us back in service, and head toward town.

"You okay?" I ask. "That was disturbing. It's perfectly natural to be upset by it. If you weren't, I'd worry."

She stares out the window. I get back on the radio. "Rescue 1 to dispatch. Show me out of service for decon." We don't need to decontaminate anything but Dana can't work like this. I drive to the station, which is thankfully empty, and pull into the dimly lit bay. Most of the lights are off, but a single overhead bulb flickers, casting shadows across steel lockers and the concrete floor. Dana doesn't move. Inside, I make a pot of coffee and bring two cups out to the truck for us.

"Dana. Talk to me. Don't lock your feelings away."

Silence.

"Do you want to go home?"

"No!" she says. "I don't want to be alone. I don't want to think about it. That poor girl. Only a monster would do that."

Is that what we are? Monsters? What about the hunter or soldier? Why are they absolved? Is a deer so different from a girl? Does it not feel pain or fear? Have a soul? Gasp and twitch as it fights for its final breath?

If only I could believe some souls are expendable, how much easier the killing would be.

The thought of Claire's father's grief sends pain ripping through my chest. I rub it with my hand as if that will ease it, even though I know nothing will relieve his pain. Ever.

Time heals all wounds—what a fantastic lie.

In the darkness of the truck, Dana and I sip cheap coffee or at least I pretend to.

"Is this how Anne felt?" she asks.

"Anne who?"

"That Brontë chick. Surrounded by death. Watching it come for everyone she loved. Seeing all those dead bodies. No wonder she died so young. She probably just gave up, too tired to go on anymore. Their lives were so sad. I don't want to write about it or think about it."

"That was life then, Dana. It *is* life. Death will come for us all. True, the Brontës had a greater share than most, but they had more love than most too."

"More love? Anne didn't love. Or Emily. Charlotte was barely married when she died. What did they know of love?"

"There was more love in that family than most people experience in their entire lives."

"But they never had a man's love. They never held their own children in their arms. Each one of them was so alone."

I think of Emily and Branwell and the ways they've hurt me. I should hate them for it, but I don't. Despite all the betrayal and brutality, I love them more deeply than ever.

"There are all kinds of love. They may not have experienced romantic love, but they had each other, even if they weren't living in the same place. Their love connected them all like a steel thread, impossible to sever."

"Until they started dying. Then each one fell like dominoes." Dana begins to cry, and I'm moved by her feeling. I didn't know it was there. Then it dawns on me. She isn't crying for the Brontës; she's crying for the golden girl on the mountain.

Dana puts her head in her hands and sobs. I let her. This is good. Far better than silence. She must let out the pain or it will consume her. After a few minutes of hearty sobbing, she wipes the tears from her face.

"Okay," she sniffs. "Enough of that. Let's get back in service."

Her mascara is smeared. I reach over and wipe it away with a finger, surprised at the deep coolness of her skin.

Chapter 26

D ana wants to drive so she climbs behind the wheel and peels out of the station. We roam the town in fast, aimless circles. She's burning off steam and diesel fuel, but I don't say anything. Tonight she gets a pass. She jumps on any call that comes over the radio, which unfortunately is not many. The cold is keeping everyone in. Eventually, we run a few calls but despite my hunger I cannot justify transporting any of our patients. Even my creative writing skills cannot convert a fleabite or bad dream into a trip to the hospital.

My hunger is so acute it overrides my fear of the Alpha. It's my only sensation, growing, gnawing at me. I'm surrounded by predators—the Alpha, Santos—and yet I am oblivious, attuned solely to my ravenous thirst.

At last we respond to the Grangers for a call about the pretty red-haired girl, Savannah. I find her curled up on her bed beneath a worn handmade quilt with a small stuffed giraffe clutched to her chest. She's been complaining of abdominal pain all day. Her abdomen is tender and tiny spots of blood stain her panties. I can smell it. Her first blood is near. In a day or so it will be here. I want to tell Savannah her moontime is being born, ushering her into womanhood, granting her the gift of creation. It is a time for celebration, not fear. But her brothers huddle about and her father watches suspiciously as I palpate her abdomen and bite my tongue. Even her mother looks bewildered.

The Grangers don't understand the signs.

Their ignorance irritates me. My temper is stretched taut. Although it's well within my protocols to transport Savannah for abdominal pain, I know she's perfectly fine. Even so, I advise the Grangers she should get checked out and they concede to transport. They trust me and I easily sweep aside my guilt. After all I've done for this family, why should they begrudge me a little blood? They don't pay their hospital bills anyway and a medical checkup won't hurt Savannah.

Mr. Granger rides with us, unwilling to stay shut up with the children any longer in their suffocating home. In the back of the truck, he fidgets on the bench seat and glances sullenly around. He looks old. He is wearing a sagging pair of blue jeans and a worn-out red flannel shirt that has faded almost to pink. Cat hair sticks to it. He smells like dog and smoke and baby vomit. The bright overhead lights reveal dirt in the creases of his skin and I wonder if they have indoor plumbing. When I take Savannah's arm in my hand to begin the IV, he stops me.

"What ya need that for?"

"So they can do blood work at the hospital."

"What they need that for?"

"Tests. To make sure she doesn't have an infection," I snap. I've had it with him. For a man with libertarian slogans splashed across the back of his pickup truck, he sure calls 911 a lot. My sisters ministered to the dying with no more than boiling water and iron hearts, yet today grown men can't drive their own children to the hospital.

He shifts forward on the seat. "You don't need her blood. I don't give you permission to take it. That blood is mine. Not nobody else's."

"Then why did you call? If you don't want me to do my job, why did you call?"

"Just wanted to make sure she ain't dying or nothin'. That everything was alright with her woman parts. Didn't plan on you stickin' her. Don't give you permission."

"Then I suggest, Mr. Granger, you start doing a better job taking care of your own."

His eyes go black and his calloused hand balls into a fist on his thigh. He wants to strike me. I can feel it sure as I feel the hunger gnawing inside me. A part of me longs for it. Let him dare try. I'll rip him to shreds.

Savannah reaches out, placing her small hand over his fist. Her fingernails are painted in blue glitter. Under the truck's fluorescent lights, her hair flares red as a lit flame. That such beauty issued from this man astonishes me.

"Daddy," she says. "Don't be mad, Daddy. I'm sorry to cause trouble. It's not her fault, it's me." His eyes shift from mine to hers and I see them go soft. Deep. His fist loosens, opens and gently he squeezes her hand.

"Ain't your fault, pumpkin. Not one damn thing in this world your fault."

Suddenly, I remember my sister Maria. When she died, she was almost Savannah's age and had that same look of sacred innocence. Eyes luminous with kindness, always more worried about everyone else than herself, even on her deathbed. Maria was kissed by an angel, Charlotte said, infused with a loftier nature than the rest of us.

How God loves the good.

Together, Branwell and I watched Maria die. And a little while later, we bore witness to Elizabeth's death as well. Papa had sent his children away to school, keeping only Bran and me behind. At six, I was considered too young, and at nine, Bran too wayward to be allowed outside Papa's reach. But the rest of us he sent to Cowan Bridge, believing there is no greater legacy a parent can leave a child, even a girl, than an education.

When Maria was finally released from school, wasted with whooping cough, it was too late to save her. How shocked Papa looked when he carried her into the house. How *furious*. His rage could be a horrible thing. And when soon Elizabeth followed Maria home and then to heaven, he yanked Charlotte and Emily out of school faster than an angel can fall.

Branwell never seemed to recover. Maria haunted him his whole life. And Papa. *Poor* Papa. Only four years before he'd lost his beloved wife and now his two little girls were gone, back-to-back. It wasn't uncommon then and his faith endured, but his heart was shattered.

We all knew Maria was his favorite. She was our favorite too.

Looking down, I find the empty blood tubes crushed to shards in my palm. Before anyone can see, I toss them in the trash then lean back against the seat and stare out the small back window. Every muscle in my body is clenched. I force myself to sit and breathe. And when the tears threaten I breathe them in and hold them, while I gaze unmoving at the empty road unfurling behind me into the cold, dark night.

⌘

At the hospital, I plan to stay in the truck while Dana makes the patient transfer. I have no desire to see Dr. Webb again. Soon I will be gone. But as Dana begins to pull out the stretcher, Savannah grasps fast to my hand, startling me.

Her eyes are wide. "Aren't you coming?"

"Dana will take care of you." I force a smile.

She gives Dana a doubtful look. "But you're my doctor. I want you to come."

"I'm not a doctor. Just a paramedic. So is Dana. You'll be okay." Mr. Granger glares at me and shakes his head in disgust. Savannah holds tightly to my hand with a fierce strength I didn't expect. Her flesh is cool with fear.

"Is this your first time to the hospital?" I ask.

She gives me a worried nod.

With a sigh, I climb out of the truck. Tonight the ER is busy and I keep my head down as we roll the stretcher to an available room while Dana gives the patient report. I pray we don't see Dr. Webb. At least he can't accuse me of breaking protocol tonight. I give a quick glance around but he's nowhere in sight and I'm hoping we'll be on the road before he ever knows we were here.

As we transfer Savannah to the hospital bed, Dana slips away. Damn! No doubt, she's looking for Webb to ply him with her charms. I raise her on the radio. "We're leaving, Dana." As usual, she ignores me.

Savannah casts a worried look my way. "Do you have to go?"

"Yes, darling. Be brave. You have nothing to fear." Now is my chance to talk to her. Mr. Granger is filling out paperwork and we're finally alone. How do I find the words? What was it Aunt Elizabeth said to me when my time came?

"Savannah, I have something special to tell you." She sits up straight in anticipation. "In a few days, your moontime will come. Do you know what that means?"

She shakes her head.

"When a girl becomes a woman, her body syncs with the moon and her blood comes every month. This is your moontime. A time of heightened feeling and sensitivity. It grants you self-awareness and reminds you every month that you have the gift of life." Her little brow crinkles and I long to stroke it smooth with my fingers. "Blood is a blessing. Now you can create life as God does. You must be careful, but don't be scared."

She looks at me in awe, confusion drifting across her face. "I can create life?"

Why hasn't Mrs. Granger told her this? That's her job, not mine. "Yes, but only if you have sex."

Her shoulders slump in relief and it occurs to me I might have convinced her of the Immaculate Conception. "Do you understand what sex is?" I ask.

She stares at me. "I have five brothers and sisters, three dogs, two cats and seven kittens. I may be a hillbilly, but I ain't blind."

I laugh out loud. "Of course you're not." How long has it been since I laughed? I can't even remember. I brush a strand of hair behind her ear. If I had a daughter like this, I'd never want another single thing. She pats my hand as if she's comforting me. "Be brave and take care of your daddy," I say.

"I will. I always do."

I turn to go and pull up short to stop from careening into Dr. Webb. How long has he been standing here? How did I not hear him?

I nod coldly. He acknowledges me with a look before moving to Savannah. I don't want him anywhere near her, but his demeanor suddenly shifts to harmless helper and she smiles at him sweetly.

"Hello . . ." he studies my neatly written report ". . . Savannah. How are you feeling?"

"I'm better now."

"Glad to hear it." There's a tenderness in his voice I wouldn't have suspected. His edge drops away, revealing a nice, normal-looking guy. He might as well be the neighborhood mailman or the guy next door, so innocuous he looks when he stops waving his authority around like a bright, shiny badge.

Savannah relaxes a notch, which helps me relax, and as I start to slip away, she grasps my hand again. She presses it and smiles, and it's like a luminous moon has slid free from a cloud on a black night.

For a moment there is only her and me and Dr. Webb in a close circle around her bed and I can't help thinking what a beautiful family we all would make.

⬡

When Dana and I pull into the station Lucien is there, looking frightened and tired. Less than ten hours ago he was telling me about Claire, how she looked like a princess. Now she's dead and death has become intimate, personal. No longer is it a stranger lying in the truck. Now it's a girl he dreamed about touching, kissing. Perhaps even loving.

Murder is nothing new to me, and I try not to dwell on it. Claire is not my problem. There is nothing I can do for the girls of these cold, blue mountains. I am barely surviving myself.

It's time to make plans for my own survival. I must regain my strength. With an Alpha so near and travel imminent, my weakness is no longer tenable.

Tomorrow I will hunt.

Tomorrow I will kill.

At home, I drop my clothes and collapse into bed, locking myself in like a prisoner. Anyone could come upon me and where could I run? Nowhere. And yet I fall asleep immediately. The sun rises and bathes the world in light, while I slumber in a blacked out room, dreaming of a beautiful Alpha. I feel his fingers hard against my flesh. He's holding me by the back of the neck, pushing my face into the throat of a sweet young child, ordering me to make my first kill.

Chapter 27

Darkness has fallen and I'm dressed for the hunt. I stare out my living room window into the night, scanning the street, bracing for an ambush. Death doesn't frighten me, but slavery is not an option. It's unlikely the Alpha would kill me. He'd use me until he grew bored. And when he was done with me? I don't know.

There is so much I don't know.

What is it about the turning that triggers our basest instincts? And why do I call it the turning when really it is a wrenching, a rape?

Tonight my house is strangely silent. Not even a creak. I wait for Ivanhoe to greet me like a lamp in the darkness as he does whenever I wake. I sniff. Nothing. Worry begins to well in me. This is not like him. For nine years he's been my only companion and in that time I've grown dangerously attached. I shake my head at myself. How can I continue to love after so much heartbreak? Why do I still feel?

I take a long look about my lifeless living room. My books rest quietly, like a thousand slumbering souls waiting to be awakened. My piano rests patiently, ready to sound its music that opens the door to my heart. The room now feels empty without William. His warmth and energy pulsed inside this space, making it feel alive. Awake. I remember his tall form standing before me like a shield, there if I needed it. The casual strength of him.

I imagine for a moment having a life with him. What that would mean for me. Touches. Kisses. Warmth and laughter. The companionship of an equal. Sex. My heart squeezes. But no babies. Never any babies for me. Quickly, I shove the delusional images aside. A life with me is death and darkness, blood and cold. If I truly cared for William, I would do anything to protect him from such a fate.

My eyes fall upon his manuscript. I've read it twice and written neat, small notes in the margins. I will abandon the idea of William but not his work. It's too valuable. His literary confidence right now is an ember in need of a gentle breath to coax it into flame. He must not quit. Even if rejections roll in like an onslaught of Tiger tanks, he must persevere.

I drape the black hood of my sweatshirt over my head, pick up William's manuscript and walk to his house. The street shines wet with snow and the stars spark like fireflies. At his mailbox, I am slipping the manuscript inside when William walks around the side of the house, an enormous pile of wood in his arms. He stops at the sight of me.

"Anne," he says, surprised. The sound of my name against his tongue makes my stomach flutter. It clouds my thoughts. I close the mailbox, shutting his manuscript safely inside. "What's that?" he asks.

"Your novel," I manage to say. "I've taken some notes."

"You read fast."

I nod and begin to back away.

"Wait. Where are you going?" I don't answer and he drops the pile of firewood on the porch then strides to the mailbox to retrieve his soul. My back is turned. I'm walking away with a rudeness that breaks my heart, but I can't stay. A hand falls on my shoulder, stopping me. I sigh.

"Please, Anne," he says. "Wait." He steps in front of me, a shield again, but this time more obstacle than protection. "Please come in for a moment and have a cup of tea."

Please, please, please. Never has a man wanted the presence of my company like this. The power of that simple word—*please*—is astonishing. I shake my head, no. "I can't. I've got to get home." *And hunt. And pack.* I gauge the moon in the sky. I have about nine hours of night left.

William doesn't move. "I don't want you to go."

My heart skips a beat. I search for my breath, but it has been sucked out of me like air yanked through a chimney. "You don't want me to go home?" I say, breathless.

"Anywhere." I stare at him. He rubs a hand over his face, raking his hair back. "I know I'm being frighteningly bold, but I have the distinct sensation you're about to slip away and I'll never see you again. You have the look of a caged animal about to bolt."

"Why would I do that?"

"I don't know."

"I have a job, a house, a cat. Where would I go?"

"I don't know, Anne. It's hard to know where someone will go when you don't know where they came from. Please, come inside for a short while. Indulge me." Then with an air of desperation, he says, "I have a question about my manuscript. It won't take long." He turns me toward his house, guiding me up the steps. I'm acquiescing as if hypnotized. *Please.* He said please again. How many times is that?

As always, he is gentle with me, so different than Santos who looks at me and handles me as if I am dangerous. William treats me carefully, concealing his strength as if coaxing in a wild creature he is afraid of frightening off. I feel like a dove he's caught in his hands and wishes to keep, precious beneath the weight of his palm, when in reality I'm as hard as stone.

With a light hand upon my back, he eases me over the threshold into his home. It is Arts and Crafts style, at least a hundred years old. There is brick and wood and deep stained glass. Stacks of books rise from the floor like teetering towers of Babylon. A heavy desk is engulfed in loose sheaves of paper, notebooks, yellow index cards, and antique silver cups of red, sharpened pencils. Woody snoozes before a crackling fire, oblivious to my presence.

In the center of the room is a large oxblood sofa, leather worn and cracking, with books strewn across its cushions and onto the coffee table. Polidori, Byron, and the Brontës.

I blink, trying to absorb it all.

Brontëana is everywhere. All our novels are here, creased and under-lined and broken in from repeated scrutiny. There are multiple volumes of poetry, mostly out of print from the looks of them. Biographies of Patrick and Branwell. Charlotte's letters. List after crinkled list of our belongings (a comb, a sheet of music, a tin box), or books we read, pictures we drew. Family trees tracing Mama's and Papa's lineage back centuries. An index of possessions Aunt Elizabeth left her nieces. Copies of paintings and drawings done by us all, some hanging or tacked upon the wall, others stacked against it in a leaning pile.

On William's desk, in an etched silver frame, is an ethereal draw-ing that Charlotte sketched when I was on the brink of womanhood. It's one of the few pictures of me that exists and is uncharacteristically pretty, capturing a long graceful neck, delicate curls, and a whimsical femininity that hardly resembles me. Above the fireplace is a reproduc-tion of the Gun Group, a singular portrait Branwell made of his three remaining sisters and himself. He holds a rifle in his hand and has placed us all before a table upon which lies a dead pheasant. I smile at the memory. Such effort he exerted in corralling Emily in with Charlotte and me, and then convincing her to stand still for the family portrait. How distasteful we found gazing upon a dead bird for hours while Bran

attempted to capture the scene. And in the end how we howled in horror at the poor renderings of us all. Years later, we wondered if our cruel
reception of his work was the reason he abandoned his audition with
the Academy of Art, confidence shot, and absconded with the money
we had painfully scraped together for him. As the single son of the family, he was our great hope. But the mind that blazed so brightly as a boy,
eventually blackened and sputtered out beneath alcohol and opium.

Lord, he smashed our hearts to dust.

Suddenly the room howls with ineradicable memories and closes
upon me like damp soil raining down upon a grave. Suffocating! I am
smothering beneath the weight of it all, pain descending, filling my
mind and heart with dread.

William is obsessed.

"I'm sorry about the mess," he says. "I've been so focused on my
book I'm afraid I've let housekeeping slip a bit. You must think I'm an
incurable slob." He begins gathering books and papers, placing them
in semi-neat arrangements.

I'm frightened, but not by William's housekeeping. Now I understand why his novel is so incandescently brilliant. There is a touch of
madness about Professor Hardcastle. I've seen the hook of obsession
too many times not to recognize it. Branwell, Emily, and Charlotte
suffered from it. With Branwell, it devolved into insanity but with
Emily and Charlotte it transcended the physical plane to manifest in
Heathcliff and Mr. Rochester. Although I haven't experienced such
intensity of idolization, I've borne witness to the way it gnaws at reason, ripping out chunks along with blood and nerves. I tried to minister to the gaping wound it leaves behind until I discovered the hard
way that obsession is a wound that will never fully heal.

One must learn to live with it.

William's obsession encompasses my entire family, but I can tell
that it alights most brightly upon me.

He hands me a cup of tea and clears a space for me on the couch. When I hesitate, he stands before me, as if to physically block my exit. The only way I can leave is to make a scene, and that's the last thing I want. My exits are silent, invisible acts, not loud, explosive fights. I sit and sip my tea. English Breakfast after dark. Maybe William accepts the night more readily than I imagine.

He sits in a wingback chair and watches me. His eyes are a deep blue luminosity, ringed in black. Every time I look at them I feel adrift in the universe, on the edge of a bottomless black hole. What's inside?

He sips his tea. "Sugar? Milk?" he asks.

"No, thank you."

"I didn't think so," he says.

Why this fascination with me? Anne *Bell*. He cannot possibly recognize Anne Brontë in the uniform of a paramedic or the black garb of a hunter, across all these crimson, death-drenched years. And if he did, if by some miracle of intuition born from decades of immersion into my former life, he saw some spark of familiarity, why wouldn't he be afraid? Any sane man would be terrified.

I can't believe he recognizes me. It's impossible. Little, gentle Anne is now a rescuer, with the posture and confidence that comes along with such a role. More likely he's just lonely. Obsession isolates and exiles in its own way. Perhaps he has simply met a young woman who reminds him of his obsession and shares his great love of literature. Surely that is all.

"What is it," I ask, "you would like to know about your novel?"

His forehead creases as if trying to remember. He shrugs. "Nothing. I'm sure it's all there in your notes."

"So that was a pretext for getting me inside."

"Yes."

I feel like a squirrel is thrashing in my belly, clawing up my chest, snaking its head up into my throat.

"I'm sorry," he says. "I didn't mean to scare you."

"You don't scare me." I swallow. *You're the one who should be afraid. Not me. I could take you right here before the fire and you could not stop me.*

William is quiet. Flames cast their glow upon him, flickering across his skin, lighting his brow, slashing his cheek. He watches me but doesn't speak. A few times he opens his mouth as if to say something but then closes it, as if at a loss for words. Guilt nips at me. I'm not making this easy on him. Our earlier fluid conversations are gone, and the old Anne is back, remote and reticent.

She is not entirely dead after all.

I let my eyes rest on him and soak him in. All of him. The shape of his shoulders, the rise of his chest. His large pale hands resting on his thighs. The way he goes gentle when he is with me, as if he is setting his strength aside, out of my sight.

I feel my heart reaching out to him, but I yank it back. I don't trust him. I do not believe he is the benevolent professor, seeker of knowledge, man of civilization he claims to be. That may be a part of him but it is not all of him. I have known men too long, watched them die and heal, fight and rest, not to recognize a capacity for force when I see one.

He is only a mortal, I remind myself, and I am a Night Walker. *I am a Night Walker.*

After all these years, I still can't believe it.

He stares at me and my eyes shy away and roam the room again. It teems with ghosts and trembles with remnants of the past. Milton, Shakespeare, Dante. Edgar Allen Poe. My entire family. Everyone in his house is dead and William will die too. Tonight or forty years from now, it doesn't matter, because I won't be around to see it. I've seen enough men die. I've lost enough people. I cannot take any more. I'm not that strong.

I stand.

He follows immediately, but I make it to the door before he can stop me.

"Wait," he says, barring the door with an arm. My breasts graze his bicep and I fall back, embarrassed, fighting to master my breath. "I have one question."

I look up and breathe him in. The scent of him, pine and fire and the subtle touch of sweat. Drink him in, I think. This will be the last time you ever see him.

"Have I . . ." His voice catches and he clears his throat. He takes a breath. ". . . offended you?" We both think of Malaprop's, I am sure, and my face goes hot. His has too. I can see the blood rushing to it. How I long to place my hand against his cheek and feel the flush there. Or perhaps my lips.

"The kiss," he whispers, and a rich warmth blooms over my chest and down my belly. "I pray I didn't insult you."

"Actually, Professor" —I draw myself up like a merciless princess, like the coldest governess you ever did see— "you offended and insulted me. You knew me only two nights before you thrust yourself upon me like a drunken frat boy. Hardly appropriate behavior for the gentleman you profess to be with your fancy aristocratic accent and your high noble education. Tell me, Professor, does that work on your schoolgirls?" He pales and draws back. "And you think Dana has a thing or two to learn about manners?" I give a haughty glance around the room, taking in the professor's life, the cracked leather couch, the clatter of disarray. Then I look him straight in the eye. "I assume your mother raised you better than this. I have no doubt she is *gravely* disappointed."

He flinches and I brush past, letting the door slam behind me like a loud slap to the face.

Chapter 28

It takes all my strength not to race down the street, and the tears burst forth as soon as I make it home. From the hall closet, I grab an old duffel and backpack and slide money in the bottom hidden pockets of both. In my bedroom, I shove clothes inside, a blanket and pillow, the small painted box upon my dresser. My little, wretched life in a bag. Upstairs, I thumb through notebooks, reading through a haze of tears, trying to determine what to keep and what to leave. My hands roam over my bookshelves, grasping at everything, wanting it all. I'm crying and calling for Ivanhoe, but he's nowhere to be found.

I'm leaving. *Now.* While I'm afraid enough to run. Danger is here, upon my doorstep, I can feel it. After two centuries of exile, one learns to read the signs. If I leave this instant, I can feed and still make it to Savannah, Georgia, before sunrise. Dimly, it occurs to me that is south, closer to the sun, but it's familiar, a place of dim basements and crumbling mansions, haunted houses and sprawling graveyards. Perfect sanctuary for a Night Walker, and I know it well enough to survive another day.

I'm not afraid to die, but I will do it on my own terms. But how to leave William? He *wants* me. A man *wants* me. And I want him and I can never have him and the cruelty of it is unbearable. As soon as he makes love to me, he'll know I'm an abomination. Unnatural. Abnormal.

A frigid corpse.

Outside I call for Ivanhoe, my voice rising, breaking into desperation. Where is that goddamned cat? Such sneaky conniving creatures they are. Emily never trusted them and now I understand perfectly! Always hiding when you need them most. Sauntering away with a flick of the tail when you want them to remain.

I stare vainly into the night. Ivanhoe will have to stay behind. It's for the best. I won't drag him place to place, abandoning him amongst strangers in a foreign town. My hands fly to my head and try to hold back the aching pain. The thought of him returning home to an empty house, waiting and waiting for me, hungry and confused, makes my head throb. Who will take care of him? Lucien? Dana? I shake my head against the thought. Then it occurs to me and I slump in relief.

William. William will take care of him.

An image comes. Woody sleeping before the fire. William writing furiously at his desk. And Ivanhoe curled upon the couch against a pillow, surrounded by my poems and pictures, glowing like a ball of sunshine.

With a trembling hand, I wipe tears from my face. I want to say goodbye. I want to kiss Ivanhoe softly on the nose and tell him I love him. No more do I wish to leave a love behind without saying farewell. And yet, it's not always possible. Which is why we must love fiercely, as if every day will be our last. I have loved Ivanhoe well and he knows it.

Inside, I shoulder my bags and take a long, last lingering look. Then I turn off the lights and step over the threshold for the final time. Goodbye, my sweet Victorian. Goodbye, my darling Ivanhoe.

A shriek of misery tears open the night.
I freeze.
It is broken backs and bleeding brains and screaming babies.
It is wrongness ripping its way into the world.
It's Woody!

Chapter 29

I fly down the block toward the sound. Every yelp feels like a 10-gauge needle stabbed in my heart. Sound leads me to scent which leads to the cemetery. I flash past trees and graves, surprised by my own speed until I find the little lamb shaking near a man felled upon a gravestone.

William!

Falling to my knees, I gather Woody in one arm and crouch above William like a dark shade, looking, listening, scenting. His breath comes ragged but thank God his heart beats fast and strong. I tense. The scent of a Night Walker hovers about him, different from the one before. Woody is violently trembling in my arms. A low howl escapes his throat. He's panicked.

"Shhhhh, it's okay my darling, hush."

Silent as smoke, a woman glides from behind a crypt. Her jeans are ripped at the knee, faded from black to grey. They fit like skin and disappear into scuffed leather boots with thick straps crawling up her calves. She wears a tattered t-shirt and leather jacket, both dimly black. Her hair is a dark, tangled catastrophe and glimpses of flesh glow like moonlight from beneath her torn clothes. Her eyes are star blue. They shine in the dark like a lion's and take my breath away.

"Emily," I gasp. My sister.

Chapter 30

She steps toward me, tensed as if waiting for a blow, and for a moment I wonder if I'm hallucinating. Is she a ghost? A haunting? Emily is different than I remember, more animal now than woman, but I feel our shared blood pulsing between us like an electric wire. There is a feral grace to her posture. A wildness that was always there and has finally come into full bloom, erupting into the light of darkness.

God, how I love her.

I bear my fangs and hiss, "He's *mine*."

A shocked look crosses her face. "Since when is anyone *yours*, sister?"

"Since now."

"As you wish. I didn't realize I was hunting your boyfriend."

"He's not my boyfriend." She raises an eyebrow. My hood has fallen back and my bare face, no doubt, reveals all my uncertainty. "He's . . . um, he's a writer," I say, as if this will elicit sympathy.

"Just what the world needs, another vampire book."

"He's not writing about vampires."

"Zombies? The end of the world? The fiction today is utterly detached from reality."

"Some would question your sense of reality."

She smiles. "Touché'"

Bewildered, I look at William. He is unconscious. Gently, I run my hand across his forehead and brush the hair off his face. "What did you do?" I demand.

"I was waiting for the right moment when suddenly that little blind fellow darted in front of him, entangling him in the lead. The man stumbled back and fell, dashing his head against the gravestone of Thomas Wolfe, no less. I must say he's not as strong as I thought, to be felled by such a small creature."

"Why didn't you kill him?"

"That ungodly howling caused me to hesitate. I would have silenced the noisy fox, but I never kill canines. I heard you coming and didn't want our reunion to take place over a corpse. I knew it would offend your delicate sensibility."

"How did you know it was me?"

She looks away. "I've been here a while."

"How long? Have you been *watching* me?"

"So many questions, sister, for a graveyard and a fallen man. I'll make it short. I've been looking for you and Branwell and the trail led me here."

"Branwell?" Unease crawls up my spine. And guilt. I haven't seen my brother since I was newly turned and we didn't part under the best of circumstances.

"Yes, well his trail has gone cold, but I smelled you in the woods and knew I was close."

"Did you kill those girls?" I am afraid of her answer.

She looks at me perplexed. "I only hunt males. I like my blood strong."

"No one is stronger than a mother."

"Oh, Anne," she says in a sad whisper.

Carefully, I move William off the cold gravestone to a soft bed of grass away from her. He is heavier than I would have thought. There's a density to his bones I didn't expect. Rage wells up in me and the sudden urge to rip out my sister's throat hits. So much havoc she's wreaked and so little shame.

I cradle him in my arms. Woody is glued to his side, still trembling, but less so. My presence comforts him. I long to stroke William's skin, to feel its warmth beneath my fingers. I want to run my tongue up his neck and know his taste, but Emily is watching.

"Anne," she says, regaining my attention. "It was my hope that you would be happy to see me. With such an exceptional heart as yours, I thought you might . . ." She tries to finish, then gives up, turns and peers into the darkness. Her white neck is a taut curve. I fear she will vanish as she did before, and I'm not sure what is worse: condemned to kill in darkness by the one I love or abandoned to walk in darkness *alone*.

She frightens me, but I don't want to lose her again.

Though Emily was a year ahead of me, as girls we were like twins. How I worshipped and loved her, as much as my own flesh—nay, more. Far more. She could read my thoughts without my speaking. She knew them by the turn of my chin or the glint of my eye. When we looked out upon the world, we saw the same things: raw beauty and mystery, stories, and clouds, and moors. It was as if our every thought and feeling hummed along an invisible current, experienced by us both, connecting us like soul mates.

We grew into young women and I took her place at Roe Head when she, the strong one, could not physically survive being away from home. Then I, the fragile one, went on to Blake Hall and Thorpe Green in search of independence, refusing to cave to my loneliness and despair. Striving to win my employer's approval, and failing, always failing, but still refusing to return home vanquished.

Emily called me a martyr. Claiming I wanted to die on the cross of my sacrifice in the service of soft, rich imbeciles. Would that make God happy? she asked. Is that the God you believe in? He's not *my* god, she said. My god is freedom and strength, not chains and misery. *My* god is power, not castration.

Needless to say, it was a painful separation.

While I worked as a governess, Emily stayed behind, roaming the moors for hours each day, attuned to every tremor in the air, every shade of grey in the sky, all the while sinking deeper into fantasy, lost in her tales of beloved Gondal—an obsession as tough to quit as Bran's alcohol. As I spent years amidst strangers and wealth, with barely a moment to myself, she spent years swallowed by solitude and freedom, disappearing for great lengths of time into the moors, protected we hoped by her faithful mastiff Keeper and her own indomitable strength. In time, her will turned akin to the landscape, not above or beside it, but within it—fierce and implacable.

Her Gondal stories became increasingly violent. Brutal. Full of vengeance, betrayal, and torture. But as they increased in harshness, she showed them to me less and less, until my creative confidante became an utter mystery and shut the door on me once and for all.

I lost her before she ever died.

"Emily . . ." I search for the right words. Such masters we once were and yet how they fail us! I'm dizzy with anger and love. She was my best friend in all the world, but as I grew warmer, she grew cold. As I grew kinder, she grew hard. She grew toward darkness as I grew toward light, and then she turned me, punishing me for some wrong I still don't understand!

My own sister sentenced me to darkness. She tried to kill William. Finally, I have found someone, been kissed, and my sister tries to kill him. I don't know whether to take her in my arms or strike her.

Not a single person have I ever loved more than her.

How could she leave me?

"You caught me off guard, but believe me when I say I'm glad to see you," I say. "I didn't know if you were dead or alive. To see you is an immense relief." She frowns ever so slightly, and I inwardly cringe at my choice of words. *Relief?* It's so much more than that. "However" —I look at her directly, wanting her to understand— "that doesn't erase the fact you tried to kill my friend. He's an honorable man. Why would you choose him?"

"He's clean. I like clean blood."

Strong, clean, male blood. My stomach tightens.

"Did you attack those hunters? The night before last?"

A slow smile spreads across her face. "The young one was a fighter. Lucky for him I'd had my fill." Her smile fades. "You interrupted me that night as well. You are a bit of a killjoy."

"There is no joy in killing. Especially people in their prime." I place my hand on William's chest and stare at her. His heart throbs against my palm. With each beat, my anger grows. "If you hurt him, I will *never* forgive you. It is a vow I make with the dead as my witness."

"So little forgiveness in your heart for such a devout girl."

"A great deal of time has passed since you abandoned me to the night." She turns her head in denial. "We are both altered. You must leave, Emily. An Alpha is here, hunting girls. One of them was killed in daylight."

Her body goes rigid. "A Day Walker! Have you seen him?"

"Only his handiwork."

"Why in God's name are you still here?"

"I'm leaving soon."

"An Alpha cares nothing for your version of 'soon.' The only way for you to escape is to run immediately. God, Anne, you're an Alpha's dream. You must leave. *Now.*"

I feel the heat of William's body beneath my hand. The rise and fall of his chest. I won't leave him like this. "I'm not going anywhere," I say, suddenly defiant. "I was here first."

"Since when have you become so territorial?"

This takes me aback. Since I came to this town. Since Dana and Lucien and William. Since William kissed me.

Emily looks at me with glittering eyes. "I won't hurt your pet, but I'm going to stay around for a while. You need my protection."

"I've survived this long without you. You weren't worried about that when you left me alone with Branwell."

"He's our brother. I didn't think he would hurt you."

"You didn't think about much, did you?" Disgusted, I pull out my phone and call 911.

"What are you doing?"

"Calling an ambulance."

"You have a phone?"

"Of course I have a phone. I have a job. When you have a job, you need a phone."

"A job?" She wrinkles her nose in distaste. "Our kind doesn't work. We're *free*. What is this persistent fascination you have with work? I would have thought you'd be over it by now. Really, Anne, you don't let go, do you?"

I gaze at her in disbelief. She stands beneath the moonlight, glowing like a nocturnal goddess. If I am the gentle doe, she is the jaguar, strong and proud. All her awkwardness is gone and with a wrenching heart I realize there is the Emily of *before* and the Emily of *now* and they are not the same. My sister has taken to the night as a wave takes to the shore. For her, there is no great struggle. No moral dilemma. Merely the inevitability of nature taking its predestined course. She's shed her human skin and with it the precepts of humanity to be reborn into a perfect, shining animal.

They were right all along.

I remember like yesterday when Emily released her masterpiece to the world. So much trust she placed in tiny Charlotte, who, with the stamina of a gladiator and the will of an emperor, finally convinced Emily to relinquish her work. The reviews were damning. Emily had bared her heart and soul, poured out her innermost desire onto the page, only to be met with outrage and shock. They said she was godless. Barbaric. *Savage.* Oh. how I defended her, even though *Wuthering Heights* filled me with dread. How ignorant they all were, I declared. What small, frightened minds they had.

Wuthering Heights was hellish, I knew, but not Emily. It had nothing to do with Emily.

But now I see it. She is savage. It was there all along, *abiding.* Coursing like a subterranean current beneath the skin, emerging for moments in stories and poems and Heathcliff until the turning set it free. Branwell did this to her. He claimed he couldn't allow the world to lose such a genius. Even then, I knew he was lying. He didn't care about the world. Only himself. *He* just couldn't bear to lose his sister.

How has our love caused so much damage?

I tear my gaze off her, back to William. He should be waking by now. Gently, I palpate his skull, feeling for deformity and searching for the sense of blood welling beneath the scalp. This loss of consciousness is beyond concussion. A bleed must exist in some part of his brilliant mind. The thought is terrifying. Instinctually I sink my teeth into his wrist and drink, oblivious to my sister, aware only of the thick, pulsing life that coats my tongue with warmth.

Through a fog of want, I hear Emily whisper my words:

I have flown to waken thee, for if thou wilt not arise,
then my soul can drink no peace from these holy
moonlight skies.

I'm starving and his blood is strong and clean and beautiful. I feel the heat of it streaking down my core. I suck desperately, my body clenching and warming, wanting more, needing more, when an image of Christ rises up, burning white hot like a nuclear blast. I pull away, panting.

I will put others before myself. *I* will sacrifice.

Emily watches silently. William rests in my arms like a fallen prince. Pale and still as the *Pietà*. I bite into my lip hard, so that our blood may mingle in my mouth, and kiss him deeply so that he may know our blood together on his tongue, down his throat, healing his flesh, erasing all injury.

Sirens howl across the night like lonesome wolves, yet my lips linger. I want more. More blood and flesh. More heat. Life. He's healing and I'm falling into sensation, foreign and utterly forceful.

"If you're not careful," Emily says, "you're going to turn him."

With a start, William wakes to find me kissing him.

Chapter 31

I pull back, embarrassed, while Emily smirks. William gazes at me in amazement, then starts when he sees Emily. Woody is still trembling, and I swoop him up in my arms and hide my face in his wiry curls.

A somewhat dazed William climbs to his feet, struggling to regain his composure. He brushes a thick strand of hair off his face and stands up straight. "What in God's name just happened?" He looks to me, then back to my sister.

"You slipped," I say, "and fell. How do you feel?"

His hand moves to the back of his head and he flinches. "Fine. Just fine." His eyes fall back on Emily.

"Forgive me," I say. "This is my sister, Emily. Emily, may I introduce Professor William Hardcastle."

He stares at her and for a moment I think he may go down again. I reach out a hand to steady him. He looks from her to me, eyes wide but clear midnight blue. Emily and I are standing in full moonlight with faces bare. If there was ever any doubt that I was different, there is surely none now. I bite my lip, waiting for him to run screaming into the night.

"Emily," he says slowly. "How do you do?"

She gazes at him with startled eyes and gives him a nod. A splash of red and white light hits us. We turn to see an ambulance winding its way through the cemetery and when we turn back, she's gone.

"Emily," I whisper, wanting her to stay, yet fearing it as well.

Lucien steps out of the truck and threads his way between headstones toward us. I slide deeper into a shadow and drape my hood over my head. He looks perplexed when he sees William and me, standing unharmed.

"You okay?" he asks.

"False alarm. Sorry to call you out," I say.

William brushes the snow off his warm wool coat. "I took a bit of a tumble, but I'm perfectly fine now, if only rather embarrassed."

Lucien shakes his head. "Weird times. Dana never showed up for her shift tonight. Jimmy gave me the overtime. He's threatening to fire her. Says he's tired of her princess attitude. Maybe you should give her a call."

William frowns. "She never showed up for class today either. I'm afraid I'm going to have to fail her."

"But she finished her paper. I read it over. It actually wasn't that bad."

"I hope the killer didn't get her. Though she doesn't really fit the profile," Lucien says.

"What profile is that?" William asks.

"Sweet, innocent virgin."

Lucien's partner for the night, Chewi, walks up, hands shoved deep in his pockets for warmth. His beard's a profusion of chaos and his shirt's out. When he sees me, he makes a too-late effort to tuck it in. "What's going on?"

"Nothing. No complaint," Lucien says.

"Well, let's get the hell out here. This place gives me the creeps." Without a word, Lucien turns and slouches toward the truck.

I am afraid to look at William so instead I kiss the top of Woody's head. His trembling has subsided and he's calming in my arms. Ivanhoe jumps upon a crypt and looks at us with shining green eyes. *Now he shows up, the little brat.*

"Anne," William says. "Look at me."

Reluctantly, I obey. William grasps me gently above the elbow and guides me into a beam of moonlight. Carefully, he eases my hood back.

My hair is down, tousled from my run to the graveyard. I try to hide my face beneath it, but slowly he brushes a strand of hair off my face. His fingers leave a trail of warmth across my skin and I close my eyes, reveling in the sensation. This, I want to remember. My body is tingling, whether from blood or desire I'm not sure. Maybe they are the same.

He slides his hand beneath my chin and tilts my face up to his, into the moonlight. He *sees* me and he is not pulling away.

"There's something I want to show you. Will you come with me?"

I can taste him in my mouth. Strong and beautiful.

Silently, I nod. He is impossible to refuse.

Chapter 32

As we walk toward his home, I rock Woody in my arms like a babe. William appears deep in thought and doesn't say a word. Does he recognize Emily? Me? We look so altered from the turning, he couldn't possibly know. Few artistic renderings of us ever existed and even then, they hardly did us justice. What reason would he have for believing Anne and Emily Brontë are here in Asheville almost two centuries after their deaths? Only a madman would consider such a thing. Then I remember, William *is* slightly mad, although it is hard to reconcile his appearance with the thought.

We come upon his green and burgundy home. I didn't really see it earlier, so dazed was I by his *pleases* as he led me inside. Now I take a closer look. It's in need of a new roof and paint job, but nonetheless appears sturdy. Two reading chairs and a lamp snuggle on his front porch, which is strung with tiny, twinkling amber lights. Ivy spills over a pot down a wall and a Montford neighborhood flag hangs beside his door. For a moment, the ridiculous hope flares that he's taking me to his porch to sit and talk about literature with Woody at our feet, Ivanhoe upon the rail.

Instead, he opens the protesting passenger door to a boxy gold
Mercedes. The door sticks and he gives it a yank. I slip in over the
duct-taped leather seat holding Woody in my arms. William shuts the
door behind us.

I'm supposed to be leaving. *What in the world am I doing?* But I
can't leave Emily. Not when I just found her. And yet if I'm so worried
about my sister, why am I in the car with William?

Self-awareness can be such a burden.

It takes a while for the car to start. William presses his lips
together as the engine struggles to turn over. I remember my earlier
words, *your mother would be gravely disappointed,* and shame stings
my cheeks. I can see embarrassment at his recalcitrant vehicle rising
in his face, filling him with blood. He smells delicious. "It's in need of
restoration," he says with a worried glance my way. "As is the house,
also. Something I plan to do if any of my books ever become profit-
able, which I expect to happen about the time hell freezes over," he
murmurs under his breath.

The car is old, but classic. Finally, its engine rumbles to life, and
William turns the heat all the way to high. The radio wells up, a
slow blues song. "Strange Love." And I am back in New Orleans,
pressing into a dark corner, transfixed, boots sticking to a beer-slick
floor, while Slim Harpo seduces the room with his harmonica. I was
especially vulnerable in New Orleans. The smoke-drenched bars full
of howling horns and whiskey-soaked voices continually lured me
out of hiding. All rhythm and blood. Swamp blues and heartache.
Music like I had never heard before, roaring, hollering with life.
The Big Easy, full of easy kills. I never partook, but many Night
Walkers did, slipping through bars and alleys feasting upon drunks
and whores. They have always liked New Orleans. Especially Alphas.
I didn't want to leave, but I couldn't stay. It was impossible to remain
invisible.

William pulls onto the road and drives through town. My chest grows tight. Dawn is eight hours away, and I don't know where he's taking me. To travel without control like this is a ridiculous risk. Yet for some reason I trust him when only earlier tonight I thought I didn't. God, I'm so confused. Emily and Day Walkers and William Hardcastle. It's utterly overwhelming.

"Don't worry," he says. "I'll have you home at a respectable hour." He gives me a reassuring nod. When his eyes catch mine, the knots in my stomach tighten.

"I'm sorry," I say, "for my horrid words earlier."

"I forgive you." He stares out the windshield. "I think I could forgive you anything."

He doesn't know what he's saying. He doesn't know what I've done.

As we drive through Biltmore Village my curiosity grows, and when we turn onto Vanderbilt Drive in Biltmore Forest it begins to rage. Where could he possibly be taking me?

Eventually, William turns onto a narrow dirt road that seems to run along the eight-thousand-acre Biltmore Estate. High, graceful trees hang over the drive, their bare branches in Gothic relief against the sky. I've lived here almost ten years and never seen this particular road before. After a mile or so of driving through dense forest, we arrive before an iron gate, tall and steel grey.

I suddenly grow cold.

William leans over me and pulls a remote out of the glove box, pressing it. The gate glides open. I cast him a look of astonishment as he drives through a back entrance to the Biltmore Estate.

He smiles at me and I am warm again. "Have you ever been here before? Outside of work, I mean. Have you seen the full grounds?"

I shake my head no.

"They were designed by landscape architect, Frederick Olmsted. He designed Central Park as well. Together, he and Vanderbilt reshaped the very earth itself, the swell of hills, the lay of water, yet I find it absolutely astounding how natural and harmonious it all appears. Vanderbilt had quite an artistic instinct."

"Well, he could afford to, couldn't he? You make them sound like gods, fashioning the earth, directing the waters."

"Not gods. Visionaries. Many people have money, but few have any aesthetic vision. Money wasn't Vanderbilt's passion. It was beauty. He drained most of his family fortune creating what you see here. I imagine some of the heirs never quite forgave him."

There is an inviolable sense of sanctity to the land I can't deny. A hush. The trees rise about us, enormous and grand while snow dusts the earth like crushed pearls. Who could not find peace here? In the distance, the chateau looms out of the night like an enchanted castle. All the lights are out. It looks empty and dead.

We circle the house in a wide loop and I lose sight of it behind a hill. William follows a road through never-ending trees and when he slows I see the great house rising once again over the crest of a far hill beyond a lake. Nothing lies before us except more quiet road and swelling hillside. Confused, I look around, wondering why he has stopped, feeling my breath turn shallow.

Again he reaches into the glove compartment and presses a remote. "Last time," he says. To my surprise the very ground before us shifts, then drops away, revealing a broad tunnel lined with thick stone pavers descending deep into the earth. Dim, spectral lights illuminate the way. William pulls the Mercedes forward and we roll into the depths, down and down and down, while the earth rises behind us, sealing us in.

Fear rushes my heart. My vision sharpens and the volume of the world wells up. I can hear everything. The tires turning over the thick pavers, *click clack, click clack*. William's breath. The sound of Woody's heart beating against my palm.

I do not know this man. This is only the third night of our acquaintance. I am stronger than him, but not infallible. I can be trapped and held. Tricked. What a fool I've been! To follow like a lamb to the slaughter the first man who kisses me. Am I so *desperate* for affection? All the questions I have never asked come rising up. What is he doing here? Why has he accepted me so readily? Why so few questions as to my strange habits? Waking up with my blood in his mouth.

It hits me like a blow: William Hardcastle is not all he claims to be.

Santos. Afghanistan. For three days, William interrogated the Night Walker. Watched him die. What did he learn?

Chapter 33

"Easy, Anne," William says. "I give you my word, I shan't let any harm come to you. You are perfectly safe."

Woody stirs, looking around, unseeing and blinking. He sniffs the air. I place him on the car seat and William reaches a hand out, grasping my arm to stop me from bolting. "Trust me. You are under my protection." His heart beats so smoothly I can't believe he is lying.

William steps out of the car with Woody, whom he places on the ground. He comes to my door, but I don't wait for him to open it. I step out and give him a dark look. My heart is racing while his beats calm and steady. *He* should be afraid, not me, and with a shaky breath I try to keep that in mind.

Woody and I follow him to a pair of enormous hand-carved doors. They swing inward, seemingly of their own accord, and I am presented with a grand, expansive dome-shaped room with cathedral-like ceilings. Chandeliers of Murano crystal illuminate the room in shades of lavender and pink. An immense Persian rug covers thirty feet of floor, embroidered in tight silk stitches with trees and birds and fruit. Across the room are walls of books and scrolls vanishing up toward the ceiling. I follow them with my eyes, tilting my head back to see. Epictetus in Latin, Aeschylus in Greek, the Torah in Hebrew, Sanskrit, Coptic, Russian, Old English fairy tales, Gaelic and Icelandic myth. Everyone is there: Dickens and Dostoyevsky, the Rosettis and David Vann.

Delicate ladders on wheels are placed before the ascending souls and halfway up, a narrow ledge circles the books. In the center of the dome, stained glass glows from the light of the moon. Stars and a crescent moon are emblazoned upon it and in one corner a crimson sun is just beginning to rise.

A fire blazes beneath a carved marble mantle, reminding me of Savannah's long bright hair. Its heat licks out toward me in sparking tendrils. An endless library table resides some distance away where an elegant man sits at one end. A manuscript is open before him. With a start, I recognize the Biltmore's night watchman, Old Man Vander. Tonight his hair is down, silvery white. Instead of his park ranger uniform, he wears a velvet smoking jacket and black silk trousers. He smells of tobacco and *blood*.

A Night Walker! It's a trap. William has betrayed me.

I spin for the door, but it shuts behind me with a heavy thud. There are no windows, only the skylight high above. In fury, I turn on William but he's sauntered away closer to his ally.

Vander stands and gives me a deep bow.

"Anne," William says, "may I present to you George Washington Vanderbilt. And to you, sir, I present, Miss Anne Brontë."

I recoil in surprise.

With a liquid wave of his hand, Vanderbilt says, "I have outgrown formalities. Please call me Vander, my dear. I know exactly how you're feeling, Miss Brontë. It appears the erudite professor has a knack for tracking. He has found me out as well. But after all these years of solitude, I believe you'll find it rather pleasurable having a friend and enlightening conversation. I'm sure you will come to appreciate his talents as much as I do."

"I won't be staying around to appreciate anyone's talents," I snap. "And the name is Bell. Anne Brontë is dead."

Vanderbilt nods. "I quite understand, my dear. But desperate times call for desperate measures. Someone is killing the young maidens of our fair town and as I do not leave the grounds, it falls to you to bring this predator to justice."

"To me! Are you nuts? I can no more stop an Alpha from killing than end a world war."

"Once you eat properly, your fortitude will be restored. Anorexia has made you frail and given you a greater sense of vulnerability than you really have. Please, my dear, take a seat and let us get caught up on one another's lives."

Vander stands and pulls out a carved, high-backed chair from a circular, more intimately sized table. It is covered in rich brocaded cloth. Gold thread glints beneath the Murano lights. In the center burns a crystal hurricane lamp. I hesitate. There's nowhere to go. Apparently, I'm locked inside this luxuriant crypt. Death clearly has not slackened Vanderbilt's appetite for the accoutrements of wealth. I look at William, who nods confidently.

Reluctantly, I sit. William pushes my chair in for me. I could rip his head off and yet his chivalry remains un-dampened.

"If you'll excuse me for a moment, I'll prepare us some refreshments." In a flash, Vander disappears within the labyrinth of his compound.

William takes a seat across from me, looking flushed. He nervously clears his throat while Woody stretches before the fire.

"How did you know?" I ask.

"Your name, for one. Acton Bell was Anne's pen name."

"That's quite a leap. There are a thousand Anne Bells around."

"Yes, but not with a Haworth accent and identical penmanship that you left on my edited manuscript. You forget I'm well acquainted with the study of linguistics and have spent countless hours studying Anne's eccentric handwriting with a magnifying glass in an attempt to access her soul. There was also the painting above your mantel. The sheet of music at your piano. Your cat's name, Ivanhoe. The Brontës were avid Scott fans. Your sister's name, Emily. And," he smiles, "your unnatural beauty."

A dry, mirthless laugh escapes me. "One thing Anne Brontë was never known for was her beauty."

"That's because no one looked closely enough. It was there all along in her violet-blue eyes and transcendent mind."

I shake my head. "No rational human being would have made such a connection."

"Reason alone does not lead one to truth. Instinct must sometimes be our guide. My curiosity was first aroused years ago when I came across one of your paintings in my mother's parlor. She was a collector of 20th century English landscapes. Immediately, I recognized it as from your hand but the timeframe didn't fit. Still, the signature was a replica of your own, only instead of Anne Brontë, it was signed Agatha Benoir. The name was different but the letters were exactly the same, as were your favorite shades of color upon the canvas. Your light, graceful brush strokes. The iron-grey sea and lavender clouds. But something was new. Death permeated the image as never before. Researching Agatha Benoir, I discovered she had been a field nurse in the First World War, which I assumed would explain the painter's fixation with death. At the time, I brushed it aside as an uncanny coincidence and left it at that. Until I came across another painting in a Boston antique store, this one signed by Ashley Boone, painted 40 years later."

I shrug. "Another coincidence."

"It would seem so. But if you'll forgive my bragging, I must say I have a talent for tracking—records, that is. They whisper to me and I sense which way to turn—what is a dead end, which bolted window to force, or ancient lock to keep prying. Your paintings led me to a slender book of children's stories that happened to be illustrated by Addison Beckman in 1963. I must say, Anne, you are resolutely loyal to your own style."

"Which is why my work no longer sells," I say wryly.

"Unfortunately, people prefer styles less delicate for today's crass times. The idea of vampirism never occurred to me—" I flinch. "I'm sorry. Does the word offend you?"

"I prefer Night Walker. It's less . . . coarse sounding."

"Hmmm. It reminds me of something else. Never mind. The idea of *Night Walkers* never occurred to me. I'm embarrassed to say I was thinking along the lines of spiritualism."

"Spiritualism?"

"An embodiment of the spirit."

"Possession? You thought my spirit was possessing someone?"

William sighs. "I didn't know." He rubs his forehead and takes a deep breath. "Honestly, I was thinking more along the lines that a deep affinity might exist between two souls, below the conscious level. A linking perhaps of spirit. Maybe some rare creatures have a consciousness so bright and powerful that it continues on after the body has passed to touch other living beings." He runs his hands through his hair, leaving it even more disheveled than before. "I didn't know. I had no idea really. Then I went to Afghanistan and my entire world was blown open."

"Jadallah."

He nods.

It's as I suspected. This is the problem with Alphas. They are too bold and reckless, endangering the rest of us with their disregard for caution and their outrageous appetites.

"While Santos raved of demons, I expanded my research into paranormal literature. Bram Stoker was onto something, but his imagination ran away with him. Legends exist all over the world, from all different ages. The idea took root in my mind that there was an element of truth to them. Nothing so fantastical as fiction can lead us to believe, but something rooted in science. What if" —William taps the table in thought with a strong, graceful finger— "when Neanderthal and Cro-Magnon evolved beside each other, a third species of human was born as well?"

"I'd hardly call us human."

"You bleed, do you not? You breathe. Your heart beats. You are simply harder to kill, but you are mortal." He looks at me intently. In the soft light, his eyes have turned a Prussian blue, rendering me faintly dizzy. "Are you alright, Anne? You look especially pale tonight."

"I'm fine," I say, but it's not true. Hunger and the shock of seeing my sister have depleted my reserves.

He studies me for a moment, then continues. "Cro-Magnon had a far superior intelligence than Neanderthal and as a result, to his lower-minded cousins, he might have appeared a god."

"Are you comparing us to gods?"

"Of course not, though Vander has his theories about Jesus and Night Walkers."

I look around. "And where is Vander? Draining a virgin chained in his dungeon?"

William smiles, dismissing the idea. "As I was saying, there are significant differences in physical power between Neanderthal and Cro-Magnon, and it isn't beyond the realm of science to believe that the Night Walker is simply another offshoot of man, a nocturnal variant that somewhere along the way broke off from the evolutionary chain."

"Our superior strength has not helped us ward off the brink of extinction."

"Neither did Neanderthal's. With every strength comes an equal vulnerability."

"So you think we have existed from prehistory?"

"It's possible. Only detailed DNA analysis could prove it and I'm not a scientist nor do I have access to such equipment."

My eyes grow startled.

"Don't worry, Anne. No one has plans for making you a test subject. Origins have never mattered much to me. Who is our creator?" He throws up his hands. "What difference does it make? How or why, who will ever know?" He slaps the table passionately. "The point is *we are here* and what we do now is up to us!"

"And here I thought we were star children."

"You look like one," he says, his voice going soft, and I glance away, embarrassed. My hand moves to my throat, as if I can hide my pulse pounding there. Why isn't he repulsed by me? It would be easier if he were. I must admit his ideas are comforting. It's nice to imagine I am simply an evolutionary variant and not a demonic abomination.

"Why aren't you afraid?" I ask.

He stares at me in disbelief. "Afraid of Anne Brontë, child of God? Are you kidding? I was delirious with joy. You're one of the gentlest souls to ever grace this earth. I, more than anyone alive, know your character. Anne Brontë would never harm an innocent. That's not who you are."

I'm stunned into silence. How does he think I've survived all this time? On water? On wine?

"And Vander," he continues. "Once I discovered him—an entire adventure in itself—accustomed and educated me to your kind."

"Vander does *not* represent my kind. We are anomalies, I assure you."

"And yet you are the only ones I know. Both learned and civilized. Disciplined and restrained." He looks at me warmly, eyes brimming with trust.

It's true, I've never seen a Night Walker like Vander. With a library. Manners. A beautiful home. Branwell was learned and civilized once too, but later even he took shelter in ruins and feasted upon children like a rabid dog.

"Did you ever share these ideas with Santos?" I ask.

William shakes his head. "No. I had to be sure. Santos isn't interested in reason. He sees the world in black and white, good and evil. He isn't comfortable with the complexities of human character, the endless variety of motivation. It's easier to believe that our enemies are one-dimensional. Evil. They are easier to kill that way, and Santos has done his share of killing."

Then why didn't Santos kill me? I still don't get it. Maybe it wasn't the right time, with Lucien nearby. Maybe he's waiting for the perfect moment. Fear crawls up my spine.

"You need not worry about him, Anne. Santos would never hurt a woman like you."

"To him, I'm not a woman. You underestimate the fear our presence can evoke. Furthermore, your theory doesn't explain the change: why we are born one way and then turn into something else."

"I don't know all the answers. It may be a rapid evolutionary sequence that is transmitted from one to another. Death is the chrysalis. Like a caterpillar turning into a butterfly."

"You make it sound so beautiful. It's not. It's blood and death and fear. Screaming and tears and constant darkness. Burning to death in the sun while your heart explodes from the pain."

Suddenly, the sharp scent of blood hits me and Old Man Vander boldly strides back into the room.

Chapter 34

"On that note," Vander says, holding a silver tray lightly aloft like a waiter from Café de Flore, "let us have a touch of sustenance." A large, heavy chalice and a dusty bottle of wine rests on the tray Vander places upon the table. Opening a great cabinet, he pulls out crystal glasses, dusts off the wine bottle with an embroidered cloth draped over his arm, and proceeds to pour William some wine. Then he turns to me.

From the silver chalice, he fills my glass with hot crimson blood. It shimmers in the light, still steaming with warmth, like a newly fallen doe in the snow.

"Don't be alarmed, my dear. There are no virgins chained in my dungeon. This comes from rabbits I lovingly raise and painlessly kill myself. I promise you they live a life of luxury and ease and" —he gives me a wicked wink— "it's true what they say about their breeding habits. I can't dispatch them fast enough."

My mouth waters. Vander slides the glass before me and I almost faint. My hands clench the seat of my chair to steady myself and I glance at William, ashamed of my hunger.

"It's okay, Anne," he says, with a grave blue gaze. "I'm quite used to it. Drink so that you may live. You were put here for a reason, but you will never decipher it if you are too weak to think straight."

Trembling, I reach for the glass and, holding it with both hands, sip. The blood touches my tongue, jolting me. It's fresh and hot. I taste grass and wildflowers. Sunlight. It's free of pain and fear, those remnants of stress that taint hunted blood. It's so sweet I could cry.

"All of it," Vander says sternly.

Eagerly I drain my glass, then set it down, chagrined while warmth flows over my skin and across my chest.

William watches, amazed. "Already, there is color in your face. Your lips are turning pink as I speak." I blush and Vander smiles.

"It will give you strength," he says, refilling my glass.

This is more sustenance than I've had in weeks. I fear I may get sick if I drink too much. Gingerly, I take a small sip, relishing the sweetness on my tongue. Not so delicious as William's blood, but enjoyable nevertheless.

Vanderbilt fills his glass then says, "Now that we have refreshment before us and a council of three, let us begin."

"These are the facts," William says. "Two young girls have been killed. One 12-years-old. The second, 18. Both had their throats cut and were exsanguinated. I had the opportunity to examine the first body and saw no evidence of bite, but it could be that the cutting was designed to camouflage the teeth marks."

"That was the case with the girl I saw," I say, newly energized. "No evidence of a bite, but her throat was cut in such a way as to erase evidence. I did distinctly smell the scent of an Alpha."

"Did you ever see the first body?" Vander asks me. I shake my head. "Well, it would not be unreasonable to assume that she is the victim of the predator who killed the second. So what can we do?"

"Alphas are too dangerous to fight, unless you" —I look at Vander— "think you can take him. But if he was turned in his prime, I don't see how it's possible at your age. No offense."

"No offense taken. Also, I do not leave these grounds."

"Surely," William says, "for this, you would make an exception."

"Biltmore is my creation and my world. She is my raison d'être and I am her guardian. My leaving renders her vulnerable. I will only do so if her protection requires it."

"Then it's up to Anne?" William says. "You expect a small female to go up against a deadly, psychotic male?"

"If not, then why did you bring her here?" asks Vander.

"So we could talk, formulate a plan. Perhaps Santos and I—"

"Even in her weakened state, Anne is stronger than both you and Sergeant Santos."

"But not strong enough to take on an Alpha," I say.

"Exactly," William agrees. "So what do we do?"

"Wait for him to pass through," I say. "He'll get tired of this place and move on."

William gives me a shocked look. "The Anne Brontë I know and respect would never say such a thing. She wouldn't silently stand by while the powerful obliterate those most vulnerable."

"Anne Brontë is dead. And she was a quiet witness, not a fighter. I know too well what an Alpha can do and I wish never to experience it again."

"So we give up?" says William. "Do nothing? While he moves from town to town killing girls on the verge of womanhood? Evil exists when good men do nothing. I am not that man."

"You sound like Santos. Sacrificing yourself in vain will accomplish nothing."

Vander takes a sip of blood. "William brings up an interesting point. Girls on the verge of womanhood. Both virgins, according to the medical examiner. What's the point in that? Is it merely some psychological fixation or could there be some physiological element?"

For a moment, William seems lost in thought then he studies me. "Throughout time and myth, virginity has been seen as having power. Joan of Arc. Artemis and Athena. Queen Elizabeth. Virginity is perceived to contain purity, a closeness to divinity."

"That implies that sex is bad," I say. "Aren't we beyond that by now?"

"There are physical ramifications to virginity as well," William says. "Freedom from disease. No births, no miscarriages, no injury."

"And emotional ramifications," Vander says. "No broken hearts or shattered expectations. Less bitterness to stain the blood. As you know, Anne, blood takes on the taint of its owner."

I try to hide the sadness in my voice. "A virgin is perfectly capable of having her heart broken."

"But less likely," William says, his gaze going dark. "The pain is more acute when not only your heart has been rejected after giving it, but your body as well."

"Virgins of a particular age are pure potential," says Vander. "The potential to create life undiluted by disappointment or compromised by disease. But how to explain the first kill in the light?"

"Blood is the life," I say, thinking aloud. Lightly, I caress the stem of my glass. "Is it possible that some girls, once they reach puberty, contain a greater 'potential' for life?" The memory of my first feed comes rushing up and shame breaks over me.

"What is it?" William asks. Mutely, I shake my head. I've pushed this memory down so deep that I can't speak of it.

Vander gazes at me, concerned. "Anne, are you alright?"

I stand and walk to the fire, turning my back on them, staring at the flames. That is where I belong. In the flames of hell.

Eventually, I find my voice. "I might know how the Alpha did it. Survived the sunlight, that is. But I will have to tell you about my first kill. It's an experience I hoped never to think about again."

"If it can save a life, then you must," William says.

I turn to him. "You will not like it. You will not like it at all."

"I have seen my share of killing, Anne. I am not as sensitive as you imagine."

I look at him fully. God, he is beautiful. He has a nobility all too rare in men today. He kissed me. And I have tasted his blood. Strong, pure blood. After my story, I doubt I will ever taste him again.

I gaze into the fire. Savannah's face comes floating up to me out of the flames. She is only 13, the same age as my first kill. It is too young to die.

Sacrifice. I am willing to sacrifice so that others may live.

A grandfather clock chimes twelve times, filling the room with sound as I gauge the moon shining through Vander's skylight. Midnight is here. The witching hour. I take a deep breath and look down. In the fire's glow, my boots gleam from the richest cream I can find, but now with the light thrown upon them I see the deep cracks in the dark brown leather and the small stains of blood like damp raindrops I can't ever get out. It's easier to forget they are there in the dark, but here in the light I see everything.

I was buried in these boots.

"It was after my sister Emily turned me."

Chapter 35

Only months before, I had lost my closest friend in the world: Emily. And months before her Branwell had died a sudden death, shocking us to the core. Nothing was left for me. No love or friendship. Only endless service amongst people who cared nothing for me and valued me even less. Or maybe more novels, in which I poured out my deepest thoughts to have them scorned and derided by those who read them.

I was ready to go. I felt no fear, only love. My greatest worry was for Charlotte and my father. For them to lose us all so rapidly would be a grievous blow from which I knew they would never recover.

I journeyed to Scarborough to see the sea once more. On my final night, Charlotte stayed by my side. "Have courage, Charlotte," I whispered, as she grasped my burning hand. She was so pale with fear and grief. Stoic, yes, but I could see the horror swimming beneath her facade. All of her creative confidants, Branwell, Emily and now me, dying within one year. It was too much. There wasn't enough courage in the world to shield her from this loss. Poised on the edge of death, I forgave her then, all her judgment. Her damnation of my work. So much pain was coming for her and my poor father, whom she begged not to come, afraid the sight of me would kill him, that I could feel nothing for her but pity.

And transcendent love.

Fever dragged me into a dreadful darkness. Steaming delirium. The heat felt like hell and in desperation I hacked off my long hot hair with a pair of my sister's sewing shears. Charlotte, at the insistence of her friends, had retired for a few hours to take some much-needed rest, and in those moments Emily appeared by my side. She glowed in the darkness like a beacon. I remember the feel of her cool hand against my forehead. So soothing. So settling. "Don't be afraid, my love," she said. "I'm here now."

The vision gave me immense comfort. I thought my dead sister was waiting for me at heaven's door. All of it was true! God. Heaven. Serenity. I would be reunited with all my loves. My mother would hold me in her arms. My sisters Maria and Elizabeth. And I would finally know the existence of God. Bathe in His divine light. Be one with Him. In that feverish apparition, all my faith was restored. "Take me, my Lord," I prayed. "I am yours."

I survived the night, beset by wild dreams and apparitions. Branwell's ghost murmured in my ear. A dark form loomed over me, trying to kiss me. The blessed sun arose one final time as I rested upon the couch, listening to the waves outside our window, Charlotte speaking softly to Ellen in the background.

I closed my eyes against the day and called my willing soul away, from earth, and air, and sky.

I was leaving her, leaving this world behind. And I was ready. Inwardly, I recited my poem like a prayer:

I know that my Redeemer lives; I do not fear to die;
Full sure that I shall rise again to immortality.

I long to view that bliss divine, which eye hath never seen,
Like Moses I will see His face, without the veil between.

Then was all blackness and cold.

I awoke in a frigid grave, buried deep. It smelled like wet earth and worms and fresh pine. I don't know how much time had passed, but possibly days. I was so ravaged by disease, it took time for me to heal and turn. All the fears you can imagine upon waking in a grave came rushing at me. Absolute horror at the knowledge I had been buried alive. Thirst so fierce it tore my throat. Cold so deep my limbs felt frozen. I could hardly move. I screamed and scratched and clawed at the wood. Panic welled and broke in brutal waves over my ravaged mind. In a frenzied blur of terror, I smashed through the coffin and dug my way up out of the earth into the warm night air.

Branwell was waiting. My supposedly dead brother stood at the foot of my grave, shining beneath the stars like a dark Apollo. His blazing red hair shone in the starlight, warming me. "Welcome to the night, Anne," he said. His first words, as if the night were a blessing.

I fell into his arms and he held me, and never had I felt such comfort from a man. He brought me to his abode, plying me all the way with soft, careful words. I clung to him. His ravaged dissipation was gone. Never before had I noticed his beauty, the thrilling brilliant energy of him. It intoxicated and frightened me. Every touch of his flesh sent heat sparking toward my core. My own brother was stirring new and overwhelming sensations in me.

But then came the hunger. It howled at me. Ripped and tore at my flesh like a fiend. I thought it was a nightmare from which I couldn't awake. Impossible for it to be real. *Impossible.* I'd gone insane from fever, broken from reality, or perhaps this was a vision of hell worse than any I'd ever imagined.

Branwell had brought me to a secluded manor, abandoned and crumbling upon the moors. Emily and I had wandered far and wide, yet never seen it. It was something out of Gondal, so Gothic and dreary looking. He led me deep into its bowels and I followed like a dazed lamb after her shepherd. *Don't leave me,* I begged. He locked me in, for my safety he said, and then vanished.

And where was Emily? She had run, abandoning me to my fate, apparently unable to bear the destiny she'd thrust upon me in her moment of grief. And yet, I couldn't hate her. I understood. I knew too well the pain that came from losing her. When she died, I died too, and I would have done anything to have her back.

Anything.

Emily and Branwell took to the night in a way I never did. It was like they were born for it, their souls akin to darkness, carved from the moon like the owl or the wolf, whereas I was made for the light. Long before the turning, Emily worshipped nightfall. She'd been a tormented sleeper, haunted by guilt-filled nightmares I never understood and visions of the dead I didn't see. And still she longed for the sun to set. She once wrote:

> *O Stars and Dreams and Gentle Night; O Night and Stars return!*
> *And hide me from the hostile light that does not warm, but burn—*
> *That drains the blood of suffering men; drinks tears, instead of dew:*
> *Let me sleep through his blinding reign and only wake with you!*

Emily wanted to be a Night Walker before she knew what one was. Sometimes I think she summoned it. She was made for this world, and maybe Branwell too, but not me. I've always craved the sun. My poems are threaded with its metaphor. Light is God. The darkness,

His absence. I believe Emily knew this, and fled from the shame of stealing my eternal peace.

But Branwell would not desert me. He would be my protector. The only son, the elder brother, he would guard me in death as he never had in life.

His philosophy was simple: embrace my nature completely. For him, it was all or nothing. A great leap into the void. He wanted me to learn to feed, and only human life would suffice. That's what we were made for. That is from where our strength comes, he said. Animals were for the weak, the soft. Human blood was for the strong.

Of course, I refused. Bring me death, please, it would be a salvation, but I would not skulk upon the earth like a beast, tearing open the throats of men, lapping at their blood like a devil.

William said that I was the brave one. This is not true. What's true was that I had no fear of death. That was my greatest strength.

For weeks, Branwell kept me locked away in that dungeon. I grew weaker and wilder as the nights passed. My discipline for this new life hadn't been forged and memory of our human life still pierced me. All I wanted was death. Oblivion. A long, dreamless sleep. I no longer believed in God. This hell had shattered my faith. What God would create creatures like us? Demons must rule the world. The angels had fallen and Satan had gained dominion.

Was this the apocalypse?

Branwell brought me boys, hoping I would feed. He thought males would be more amenable to me and the younger they were, the more manageable. He wished to spare me a great, bloody fight. But I refused to eat, so he consumed them in front of me with as much pleasure as he took in his opium, instructing as he went along, oblivious to any fear and pain he would bring their families.

We knew pain. The Brontës *know* pain. I didn't understand how he could inflict such suffering on others. The boys quivered in horror, stinking with terror, the most horrible odor I'd ever breathed, and more than feeling for them, I felt for their mothers. Their sisters. The wives they would never love. The children they would never sire. It wasn't just one life Branwell stole, it was a line of lives stretching into infinity. It was a wake of pain that would only end when every single person who had ever loved these boys was dead.

I wouldn't do it, yet he refused to give me an animal. As far as he was concerned, no doe or rabbit was worthy. He felt that once I crossed that undead threshold and made my first kill, all the pieces would fall into place. My nature would be complete. I would know my true self. He truly believed killing could bring self-knowledge and purpose.

He rambled on and on, saying, "Blood is the life. God tells us this. If God would give His own child to you, do you think He'd withhold a peasant in order for you to have eternal life? Jesus rose from the dead. He is one of us. Embrace this life. Embrace your destiny."

Starvation confused me. Branwell could be so persuasive and now his burning beauty clouded my mind. His reborn intellect shone like a sword, sharper edged and brighter despite his bizarre rantings about Jesus and Lazarus. *The Resurrection.* Even as a man, his mind blazed with intelligence until he snuffed it out with opium and alcohol. But those addictions were born from constant craving. His maker, a soul thief, was to blame. He had feasted upon Bran for years, taunting him with a promise of eternal life. Seducing and using him. Branwell told me everything and promised he would take care of me in a way his Alpha never did him. He would love me in a way he had never been loved. Gently. Softly. Sweetly.

It was a lie.

One night he brought me a young girl, warm and soft as a kitten. Camilla. Her eyes were doe brown. Freckles sprinkled her nose and trailed off her cheeks. Her nails were torn. One was ripped clear off her thumb, leaving a small oval of raw flesh gaping at the air. He tossed her in my cell like a rat to an anaconda, leaving her there, still and silent in the corner.

She stayed with me for three days. The moon was dark. I learned all about her. From what village she came, who her father was. The names of her brothers. I thought if I knew her, she would be impossible to kill. When the moon returned, a slender shining crescent, it brought Camilla's moontime. She began to bleed her first woman's blood and then to quietly cry at the shock of it.

The aroma hit me like a mortar. An uncontrollable instinct rose up, and I struggled to control myself. "Don't cry, child," I whispered. "Your first blood is a gift." I edged closer, trying to soothe her, but she recoiled from me, pressing deep into the wall. I could hear her heart pattering like endless rain. "It is a moment for rejoicing," I soothed, trembling like a hyena as I crawled toward her on my hands and knees.

"No," she said with conviction. "Stop." I could imagine her speaking to her brothers, giving them orders to which they yielded. *Pick this up. Put that down. Stop fighting.* She spoke as if she were used to being listened to. Cherished. "No," she repeated, like a little mother scolding me.

Blood touched her thighs, drenching the room in its smell. Starvation overtook me. I fell on her like an animal. She began to fight, furiously, and I only wanted her more. The hunger rose up, pure as God, and I was on top of her laying her into the ground, sinking my teeth into her throat.

I drank her dry while she squirmed and squealed beneath me. It was like pure heaven coursing down my throat. I felt the blood healing me. Sanctifying me. Her final moment rushed up like a hand that gripped my heart. It was the life force, beating fast and fierce, clinging to existence with that indomitable will of the young. I felt it fight and pull, and greedily I yanked and drank it down and swallowed it all.

Branwell had known what he was doing. But he hadn't known how powerful I'd become. When he returned and saw with satisfaction that I had drunk and was standing strong and still beneath a shard of moonlight, he unlocked the chamber door and opened his arms wide.

"Come to me, love. Now we are true equals."

But he was wrong.

I was stronger.

I swept past him. When he caught my wrist, I flung him so hard against the wall he fell broken and stiff. I was momentarily afraid I'd killed him but then I could hear his heart, his breath, even the blood coursing through his veins. I heard the grass outside. An owl call. The stars shine. I heard the night.

And I flew to it like a flame falling back into the fire.

Chapter 36

Vander and William are silent. I search William's face, but he is looking into the fire, and I cannot read his gaze.

So much for his captive dove. Vulture is more like it.

"At first, I was free from the sun's harm," I say. "I survived an entire rotation of the moon moving about in full sunlight. A Day Walker. But as time passed, dawn came on brighter and more harshly until eventually it was stolen from me entirely."

Vander looks shocked.

"I thought my initial light tolerance was because I was new. My tolerance has grown weaker and weaker with time. I knew no other of my kind to share my experience with. I ran far and fast from Branwell and he never found me. It was perfect exile, absolute isolation. But now I wonder if my solar tolerance came not from my youth, but from the girl. I had taken her at the very moment of menarche, when the potential for life is quickening, manifesting itself in a physical way. Perhaps this is from where my strength came."

"Your solar intolerance stems partly from your weakness," Vander says. "You have not taken a life in years and your immunity is low.

The more life we take, the stronger we are, but still I thought there was not enough blood in the world to make one a . . . what did you call it . . . Day Walker? *My God.*" Vander stands from the table and begins pacing. "But, you, Anne are proof! A month is an outrageous time for our kind to experience the sun. I have never known anyone to survive more than a few hours and that was at their strongest and they were scarred and ravaged for the rest of their days, which is the price one pays for *crossing a Vanderbilt!*"

William and I both tense.

Vander catches himself. "Forgive me. It was a long time ago, but I too have had a trying experience with my maker. I may not be a great fighter, but I have other means. Needless to say, he paid for his ignorance." Vander wags a finger in the air to no one in particular. "Don't ever fuck with a Vanderbilt."

"Maybe this Night Walker unknowingly stumbled upon the mystery as Anne did," William says. "He's trying to reenact the kill by choosing young, virgin females."

"Yes," said Anne. "But it's not their virginity that grants him immunity and makes him a Day Walker. It's their quickening."

"And how would he know when that time would come unless he captured young children and held them for months or for years?"

"And even then, how would he know when to feed? He may not have put the puzzle together. I never would have if we hadn't had this discussion. On the rare occasions I've seen others of my kind, deep conversation wasn't on the agenda. Especially not with the Alphas. They're too territorial. Dominant. There is room only for one."

Vander gives me an arch look. "For someone who has known few vampires, you certainly have entrenched ideas about them."

"Please don't use that word," I say. "It's so distasteful."

"'Vampire'?"

I nod with a grimace.

"Would you prefer Nosferatu?"

"That sounds like a bad movie."

"Yet we have more in common with the vampire bat than any other creature in nature."

"We don't have wings and hang upside down to sleep, nor do we live in colonies."

"And yet we both survive exclusively on blood."

"Perhaps," William interrupts, "our killer is just as in the dark as you were all these years, Anne."

"Well, if this is the case he will keep feeding upon young women," Vander says. "There will be no end. He must be stopped."

"But how?" I throw my hands up in frustration.

Vander stands and stokes the fire, musing. "He has his weakness. Stoker got some of it right. We may not turn into animals or mist or control the weather, but we are not without resources. We heal faster and live longer, but, thank God, we are not immortal. These days, enough firepower exists in the world to fatally wound him. We need no longer fight with swords and clubs."

"Santos," I say. "He might have the firepower to stop him."

"Yes," says Vander, "but not the speed or strength."

"Or the patience." William suddenly stands. "Swords, however old fashioned, are not a bad place to begin. Vander, didn't you say once that every civilized man should be proficient in at least one weapon, regardless of his occupation?"

"I do believe I did." Vander smiles and with a glint in his eye, turns to me. "Anne, my dear, what is your weapon of choice?"

I give him an incredulous look. He raises an eyebrow, as if to say, *Yes? I am waiting.* "I am a healer. A nurse and paramedic. I strive to curtail injury, not create it. After all the wars I've witnessed . . ." I wave my hand, as if I can bat away the entire idea. "Fighting is not in my nature."

"A weakness we must remedy," Vander says.

"What need do I have for it? You don't honestly imagine I'll get into a sword fight with a Day Walker?" I laugh at the thought.

"One never knows, my dear, and at the very least, training will help build your strength and confidence. Only the strong can protect the weak. I have an extensive collection of weapons. You may take your choice. Katanas, naginatas, tantos, sai, Malaysian throwing knives, German daggers, AR15s, Uzis . . ." I wrinkle my nose in distaste. "Yes, too crude," Vander agrees. "What am I thinking?" He stills, illuminated by an idea. "How about the bow and arrow? You can be Asheville's Katniss Everdeen."

"Who?" I ask, bewildered.

William comes close to me and places a finger on my chin, tilting my face up to his. His eyes are the color of a darkened dawn, that time of greatest longing for me, when I sense the sun slowly coming, feel its softening of the world, the orange and lavender of the sky about to bloom, yet am forced to retreat before I can steal even a glimpse. He is that glimpse. His pupils expand as he looks at me as if they are soaking me in. For a second I fear he'll kiss me right here before Vander. I feel my face grow hot and almost wish for my anemic coolness.

"I know the perfect weapon," he whispers. "Elegant *and* deadly." His voice transfixes me, unfastening my resistance. William still wants me. I feel it. I killed a girl and he still *wants* me. He releases me, but not before quickly running his eyes down my body as if gauging my suitability. Then he pivots and strides toward the bookshelves. Reaching out, his finger alights on *Les Trois Mousquetaires* and tilts it back.

A broad segment of bookcase glides away, revealing a hidden room. Instead of books, weapons line the walls, gleaming and glinting in silver and steel and gunmetal grey, carved and etched, handles wrapped in leather, or, waiting to be held bare and cool in one's hand.

William picks one up. With a flourish, he whisks a slender sword into the air and takes a fencing stance. A graceful aggression. His body holds the posture as if he's done this all his life. "With your superior speed and strength, Anne, this might one day come in handy."

"My strength is nothing compared to an Alpha's," I say.

"Then we must work on your skill."

Chapter 37

William presents me an exceedingly slender sword. "This is a saber capable of piercing and slashing."

I don't move. "It's utterly unnatural to me. I abhor violence."

"Anne," says Vander, "purity of heart will not slay this monster. Some beasts must be conquered through force."

"But then I will be just like him."

"Only if you enjoy it."

"Trust me, my reluctant warrior." William reaches for my hand and guides it to the weapon's hilt, wrapping his fingers over mine, closing them upon the weapon. An intricately engraved guard curls over my hand and wrist for protection. I try to breathe. It feels as if William is bending me to his will, but I'm not entirely sure I mind. He draws his thumb across my wrist and fingers, adjusting my grip. "For one night, allow yourself the pure pleasure of movement. Fencing is an extremely refined art, and I suspect with your creative temperament, you may quite enjoy it." He releases me, leaving me awash in longing.

I look down at the floor to hide my fresh warmth beneath my hair. Vander is smiling. He is, no doubt, enjoying my discomfort, reclining in his chair as if watching a play upon his personally designed stage.

"Be careful, William," he says. "Anne is stronger and faster than she looks. Go slow and easy, my man."

"I shall never underestimate Anne's strength," he says, pulling me into the center of the room. "For *He that dares not grasp the thorn should never crave the rose.*" I smile at the sound of my words on his tongue. Grabbing his own saber, he confidently demonstrates the proper stance.

I attempt to mirror him but I am certain that I'm failing miserably. This will be the perfect opportunity to show off my athletic ineptitude and humiliate myself in the process. At least I have one thing going for me. I'm wearing my sleek black hunting gear, and although it is not the traditional all-white garb of a fencer, I'm dressed somewhat appropriately for exercise. William squints slightly as he sizes up my stance, then comes back to me. His hands move to my hips, shoulders and grip, making minute adjustments, refusing to linger. Cool and professional, he is all seriousness but I feel shaky. The tip of my saber trembles. In 165 years, I have not been touched this much. I take a deep breath, willing myself to concentrate on his words and ignore the distraction of his physical presence.

"Where did you learn to fence?" I ask.

"My mother was a traditionalist with strong Romantic tendencies. When I was a young boy, she insisted I learn Latin, Greek and fencing. Later I continued my training at Oxford."

Vander takes a sip of blood. "Your advantage, Anne, comes in being underestimated. The Alpha believes you are gentle and passive. You will win through misdirection and skill. Most Alphas don't know how to fight with any technique. They have never needed to. Always his strength has been enough, and no one uses swords anymore. The flesh, no matter how strong, cannot withstand steel."

"But I can't kill a Night Walker with one night's training."

"Surprise trumps training," says Vander. "I speak from experience. I used a blade myself once, having never trained with it, only watching and waiting."

"On whom?"

"My maker."

"You killed your maker?"

"I was not made to be a slave."

William momentarily pauses, not seeming to have heard this story.

Vander gives a flourish of his hand, as if it's all past. "He turned me for my fortune, then kept me prisoner so he could milk me dry. He took great pride in being a 'working man' and believed that my wealth had made me soft, when in reality the *creation* of my dream had made me quite hard indeed. He built barns. I built this." He waves his hand as if to take in not only his underground castle and the outside estate, but the mountains and forest and all of Asheville itself. "With a bit of seductive maneuvering, I lured him to Blood Mountain. We made love beneath the waxing moon and at the peak of his pleasure, I drove a saber through his flesh."

A look of amazement crosses William's face followed by a flicker of wariness. *Yes, William. Vander is dangerous. We are* all *dangerous.*

"I struck beneath the clavicle, driving down through the lung, avoiding the heart, jamming the blade deep into the earth. He was pinned as thoroughly as a butterfly to a corkboard. I left him, fully expecting him to escape. I didn't want him to die. I simply wanted him to suffer. But apparently he was too injured in spirit and flesh to free himself. At sunrise his screams began, hysterical and horrifying, until he somehow managed to escape. Needless to say, he was the Master no longer." Vander raises a finger to capture our attention, as if by some bizarre circumstance he had lost it. "Never underestimate your opponent, Anne, but pray they underestimate you. Enough talk-ing." He gives a quick clap. "Begin."

William and I make eye contact across the length of our blades. "Nice and slow," he says. "Follow me." He feints and parries, for-ward and back, carefully. The blade dips and swoops like a flash of light, its presence in time and space as fleeting as a shooting star. Shining and brilliant. The blade itself reminds me of William. Graceful. Surprising. And entirely capable of hurting me if I'm not cautious.

Along the way, he names the moves: attack, feint, lunge, dis-engage, remise, flick, parry. Then it is circle parry, riposte, counter attack, point in line. The words draw me in. There is something romantic and adventurous about them. Perhaps it's time to reread my Dumas, this time in French.

I follow with astonishing ease, my body moving naturally as if I have fenced all my life. William quickens his pace. His speed surprises me. He is fast for a mortal. And strong. The tip of the blade is cov-ered, but I am careful not to let loose the full extent of my strength.

I don't want to scare him away.

❧

We fence for hours and, to my great surprise, I learn surprisingly fast. William begins to gleam with the sheen of sweat while I remain cool and dry. His hair grows wilder with every lunge. He moves faster and attacks harder, yet I handle it all with a skill it took him years to attain. Finally, after I have beaten him yet another time, he throws the saber down in a fit of frustration.

"This is ridiculous! She learns in a few hours what I have trained all my life to do."

"I'm sure if you were like me you would beat me with ease."

William frowns. "I don't understand. You seem a genetically superior being in all manners: physically and mentally. If our antagonist is the same, it will be very hard to beat him indeed."

I laugh. "Despite my preternatural strength, I am hardly superior mentally, I assure you. The turning does not make one more intelligent. If anything, it hijacks our reason, enslaving it to instinct and impulse. Why else would we hide in the shadows like fugitives and contribute so little to humanity?"

"It is true, William," Vander says. "Remember who you have across from you. All the Brontës had brilliant minds. Do not confuse Anne with the rest of her kind."

"And remember," I say, "Santos and his men took down Jadallah. You handled him yourself in interrogation. We are not gods. I think I am just especially invigorated by a good meal and friendly companionship." I smile. "Both, I have not enjoyed in a very long time."

"Well, I throw in the towel." William re-sheathes the saber and returns it to its home. "You, Miss Bell" —he bows— "have quite vanquished me."

Suddenly, I feel shy. "I assure you, Professor Hardcastle, you are the first."

I hand him my saber but Vander says, "No, Anne. Keep it. Take it home and practice. Tomorrow night, if you're free, we will train again."

"Very well," I say, wondering if I'm holding the very blade that killed Vander's maker. My brow knits as the thought flits across my mind.

"That is a fine saber," he says. "It strikes straight and true, but you must use it with absolute commitment."

I sigh. One night is not enough to reconcile me with the thought of killing after I have spent so much time and effort trying to free myself from that necessity. As a girl, the death of a sparrow *crushed* me, and now William and Vander expect me to kill coolly, dispassionately. Regardless,

I do not wish to argue with Vander. He seems as stubborn as any Brontë I've known, and I certainly don't wish to disappoint William.

"Sunrise is a few hours off," Vander says to William. "I think it's time to show Anne home."

"Certainly." He nods and takes a sip of chilled water. "Thank you for the refreshments." William strides over to Woody and, bending down, gently places a hand on his softly breathing chest. "Time to go, Woodrow. Wake up."

Woody issues a low growl, apparently not wanting to be disturbed, but William slides his large hands underneath and picks him up, cradling him in one arm. "He's cantankerous when he's tired." He moves for the door and pauses, waiting for me to precede him.

"Give us one moment, William," Vander says. Somewhat reluctantly, William steps out of the room.

"Anne, I have something for you."

In a flash Vander vanishes and just as quickly reappears, with a plump calico-colored rabbit in his arms. It is a docile thing, calm against his chest as he strokes it.

"If you are to have enough strength to protect your friends, it's time you fed for real, Anne. This fellow has had a charmed life. Take him fast before he has time to be afraid."

He holds him out to me. Tears are welling hot behind my eyes. So silly, I know. Life comes from death and this fellow has his part to play. It's all life rising and dying, a great circle that I don't want to be a part of. I want to step off the wheel of bloodshed. Why can't I be like the monks or yogis who live free from killing? I've met them. Such enlightened beings, thrumming to a higher frequency, in harmony with the universe while I constantly struggle to survive, contrary to nature and humanity. Why can't I be like them?

"Someone must protect this town, Anne, and you are the only one with half a chance."

I shake my head in disbelief. What can I possibly do? Why do they overestimate me so?

The rabbit is warm and soft in my hand. His tiny heart beats against my palm, a pitter-patter against my skin. I stroke his fur and run my fingers over his long, elegant ears and I remember Lucien's mountain girl, drained of blood in the snow, left bare to the sky for Santos to find; and with her held fast in my mind, I sink my teeth into the rabbit's velveteen neck and drink.

He doesn't fight. I pull hard and fast to end it quickly, yet he relaxes like a willing victim. Within seconds, he falls unconscious and I perch on the precipice of the final pull. The pulse of life clings, clutches, and claws for continuance, and with an easy yank, I pull it free.

Chapter 38

On the way home Woody curls up on my lap, a soft bundle of warmth, while William drives the long way, quiet with thought. I keep the window rolled up for his sake, and gaze out at the ghostly night. The stars burn like flames in the sky, throwing their light upon the river, drenching her slow, cold curves in their glow. The town, snow-dusted and moonlit, shimmers beneath the streetlamps.

Saturated in color amid blankets of white, the night is beautiful. Through the stars and the moon, the sky sparks midnight blue and iridescent, not black as mortal eyes would see it. It is a deep, dark ocean of galaxies flung above us. The trees gleam evergreen and rich taupe. In town, brick buildings of Art Deco red rise from the snow as pale steam streams from their chimneys like mist.

Deep colors. Quiet colors.

A new, glorious vision of the night grips me, ripping away the veil of darkness.

The Kingdom of Heaven is here upon Earth, yet men do not see.

Has the night been heaven all along and I blind to the beauty? By ignoring midnight's call and denying the mystery, what miracles have I missed? What wisdom?

I feel more alive than I have in decades. My fingers itch with want of a paintbrush or pen. Scenes drift by the window and I drink them in, even while my awareness stays keenly on William. He's only inches away, bombarding me with his scent and warmth. I can sense his heartbeat. The lambent pulse of him. That throb of energy that every living being radiates out to the world. I wonder how he can take this world of Night Walkers so calmly. All his known beliefs and suppositions have been thoroughly upended. Time and death modified and extended. Stretched. Yet none of it seems to have shaken him.

His endless quest for knowledge ignites me. He is a seeker. A hunter of truth, not blood, and this, I realize, is the most powerful hunter of all.

I'm humming with energy. The usual shame that comes from eating is absent, and I wonder why. Is it because now I intuit a purpose for myself? William wants me to be strong. He believes that I am, and I feel myself surrendering to his view, wanting it to be true so as not to let him down. It's not lost on me that he has studied my work and words for years. I hope that in knowing this current incarnation of Anne Bell his image of "the bravest one of all" has not been entirely shattered.

What if I am a grave disappointment?

As we pull into my drive, Ivanhoe hops onto the porch to examine the strange car sliding up beneath our Great Oak. His emerald eyes peer through the darkness. The headlights sweep him and he squints, but his fur lights like flame, reminding me of a candle in a window awaiting my safe return. Until now, he's been my only friend and tenderness washes over me, catching my breath in my throat. To think I almost left him! Never again! I love this cat. And my home too. In a different way, but still, I feel great affection for this old Victorian that has sheltered and soothed me. My books and artist's studio. The violet of the paint appears deep plum at night, which is the only way I have ever seen it. Now I wonder how it looks in the day. I miss the light. To see William's face in the sun, the lit blue of his eyes, his hair streaked in a thousand different shades of cognac.

The greatest theft of all is the sun.

I know that I shouldn't . . . mustn't reveal my vulnerability, but I can't stop myself from saying it. "I hope you're not too disappointed."

"In what?" he asks, surprised.

I hesitate. "In me. In this . . . Anne Brontë. Bell. The one that hides and runs and drinks the blood of velveteen rabbits."

Slowly, he reaches out and slides a loose strand of hair behind my ear. His touch is pure heat dragged across my skin. He looks at me as if staring directly into my soul. I wonder why he hasn't run in horror. I long to lean into his hand, but don't move. He traces his finger over the line of my cheek, caressing the bone. "I've been dreaming of you for a very long time, and now that I've found you, you are even more than I ever imagined."

I bite my lip and look down. I have been touched so much tonight it makes me dizzy. As if I have drunk too much wine and the world is spinning. The feel of William's fingers against my skin quickens my breath. He doesn't withdraw, only watches. I'm sure he can see my chest heaving in the dark. With a shuddering breath, I struggle to compose myself.

He slides his hand down to the pulse in my throat, where my heart surges against his fingers. He pauses before drifting to my clavicle, running his fingers lightly along the curve of bone toward my shoulder. He appears mesmerized by the act of touching me, as if I am a dream that at any moment may vanish. As if in touching me, he proves that I am real. He traces a line of fire over my skin, sparking a trail of electricity across my flesh. Despite my cool hardness, I feel delicate beneath his hand.

Fragile.

Precious.

I'm trembling now, entangled with fear and desire. My breath shakes, torn free from my control. I don't know whether to run or surrender. I am awake. *Alive.* Aware of his every move and breath. I want to feel his pulse against my lips. I want to climb into his lap and wrap my legs around him, press my chest against his so that our hearts beat as one while my face is buried against his throat. I want his hand on the back of my neck, pressing me into him, closer and closer, fingers wrapping in my hair, pulling my head back to kiss me. His hands on me everywhere. His tongue in my mouth. His breath.

I want all of him. *Now.*

But I can't look up. I'm as awkward as ever. All I can do is stare down at my hands, unable to speak or move as if I'm still that shy mortal girl imprisoned in the turmoil of her desire.

William places both hands firmly on the steering wheel and stares out the front, into the darkness. He takes a great, deep breath. "It has been quite a night for you, Anne. You have found your sister, met another of your kind, fed properly, and practiced the art of fencing. I'm afraid of overwhelming you. I don't want you to flee." He swallows. "Now that I've found you, I am not prepared to let you go."

His words dazzle me. They cannot be real. None of this is possible. It's only a dream, a slipping into fantasy, always a risk when you live so long in your imagination.

He turns, and his eyes fall on me like a violation. His body is taut with restraint, yet he edges toward me while simultaneously gripping the wheel, holding himself back. "You said your time here was coming to an end, but I entreat you to stay a while longer. Promise me you won't vanish, Anne. Promise me!" It's a demand, not a request.

I find my courage and look back at him. His eyes are the color of gloaming, blue gliding into black, a color I have dreamed of but never felt against my skin. And suddenly I know that all the stories we ever told are true. Angria and Glass Town. Gondal. *Jane Eyre* and *Wuthering Heights* and *Wildfell Hall*. All the souls we ever imagined are real, somewhere, waiting to be found.

"I promise. I will not vanish without a warning."

He grabs me by the forearm. "You will not vanish at all. Promise me!"

Without a word, I extricate myself and place Woody on the seat between us. I want to promise with a passion he can never know, but my word is sacred and I will not give it unless I know I can keep it. My word is the one part of myself I refuse to relinquish.

As I reach for the car door, he stops me. "Let me, please." He gets out, comes around to my side, opening it. When I step out, he looms above me like an officer in his high-collared coat. "Don't forget this," he says, handing me the saber. He gives me a wicked smile. "I assure you, tomorrow night I shall not be so gentle."

On impulse, I reach up and graze my lips against his, light as a ghost, then turn and run for home.

I feel his eyes on me the entire way, and when I close the door behind me, leaning back against it, trying to catch my breath, I feel his eyes on me still, piercing through the oak, hot as a fired rifle pressed against my flesh.

All separation of spirit gone.

Chapter 39

Inside, I find Emily sitting at my desk, looking through my notebooks. A flare of anger ignites. We had always respected each other's privacy. Well, except Charlotte, the snoop. Emily's regard for propriety was tenuous before, but since the turning it seems to have been eradicated. There is a feral quality to her now that unnerves me. However, I say nothing.

I set my saber by the door and spin a dimmer switch so that the chandelier lights softly. Next, I turn on a Tiffany lamp and it wells up in rich shades of amber and blue. Ivanhoe is at my legs, slipping through them like liquid gold.

"How'd you get in?"

"The key beneath the pot on your porch. So obvious, Anne. How can you be so careless?"

I build a low, slow fire. In the kitchen, I heat water for tea, keeping an eye on Emily, afraid she might slip away again, leaving me for another century. Ivanhoe howls at me and I pour him dry food, then place a small bowl of cream beside it.

"I can't believe you have a cat," Emily says. "What do you do when you have to run from here?"

"Since I've had him, that hasn't happened, but I will take him with me when I leave," I say, inwardly vowing I will never panic and leave him behind again.

"I've missed our animals," says Emily "Keeper especially."

I smile at the thought of the big Mastiff mongrel. "Did you know he was at your funeral?"

She tilts her head in surprise.

"He walked beside your casket as it was carried to church, and during the ceremony he sat quietly with us in the pew." Her eyes glaze and she looks away.

"I didn't know," she said.

Then the scroungy mongrel refused to move from her bedroom door, waiting and waiting for her to come home. But I don't say this. I can see her pain is fresh enough. Even near death, wasted and starving, Emily had gone to Keeper on teetering legs, rebuffing all help while Charlotte and I watched from the shadows, ready to catch her if she fell as she fed him from her own hands. Emily showed more tenderness to Keeper and Flossie than she did her own sisters, refusing our care, armoring herself in steel stoicism until her very death.

She spurned our love, but it didn't matter. We gave it to her anyway.

Emily turns a page of my notebook and begins to read, "*Noah lived 930 years. But we are more ephemeral, risen and walking, made of dust but filled with thirst. Dust that will not rest. And this is god's will, but his cruelty was to make the dust think, so that it would know its thirst as it walked.*" She looks at me, curiosity lighting her eyes.

"David Vann. He's an extraordinary writer."

"Is he writing of us?"

"No, only mere mortals."

"Do you think he could be one of us?"

"It seems unlikely. He's a professor at university."

"You are the only one of our kind I have ever known to work. Is that how you have afforded all this?" She glances around the room with an air of disdain.

"I've worked since the Crimean War. Over the years I spent little and put the rest in savings. It's grown considerably. In the 80s, I began to invest and to my surprise did extremely well."

I walk to my bookshelf and finding *Goat Mountain*, hand it to her. "Keep it," I say. "I've read it a dozen times. Although beware. It's a bit bleak."

"I'm not afraid of bleak." She smiles sardonically. "Your library is astonishing. Can you imagine if we had this before? We would have thought we were in heaven."

"I have not once mistaken this room for heaven. Heaven would contain more light, more warmth."

"The night is full of light and warmth. It is subtle and hidden, more powerful for its concealment. You always believed, Anne, that the more exposed something was the less mystery it contained. The night is gentler than the day. Quiet. I much prefer it."

"And more dangerous too."

"No. It simply requires more awareness."

A tendril of anger flickers within. Did Emily ever ask herself what *I* would prefer before she condemned me to this prison? How readily she embraces the darkness with all its blood and death. Does killing not bother her at all? The night *is* more dangerous because *we* are in it.

I force myself to cool. My sister is here. Emily is in my home before the fire, talking of books. How I have dreamed of this moment! I must be grateful.

"Do you mind stoking the fire?" I ask, indicating the heavy iron poker near her. "A little light can't hurt. It's been a long time since I've gazed upon your face. I'd like to see you clearly while we speak."

"Is your vision so weak you need fire to see by? You are starving yourself, sister. This is not how we are meant to live."

"It's ironic you would say so. No one had such mastery over her appetites as you."

"Now that I am free, I enjoy sustenance."

"Do you really call this freedom? Killing? Draining little girls dry. Stalking brilliant professors in the moonlight to end their contributions to the world?"

"I don't kill children and I was not stalking your professor. I was just teasing you. I enjoy cemeteries. They remind me of home. I was merely gazing at the tomb of Thomas Wolfe when that half blind terrier started at the sense of me and tripped up his master. I would not have harmed a blind dog's master. Who would take care of the poor little fellow then?"

"You have more compassion for an animal than for the professor, who happens to be a Brontë scholar."

"Animals are innocent. Humans are not, and anyone who devotes his studies to our legacy surely has a touch of madness about him."

Her hands drift to a volume of the *Luminous Gospels*.

I cannot contain my excitement. "Those are newfound gospels of Thomas, Philip, and Mary Magdalene." Emily's eyes spark in surprise at Mary's name. "Scholars say Mary was Christ's greatest disciple. She wasn't a prostitute at all. That was a false claim made by the early church to weaken her role—"

Emily cuts me off. "Why aren't I surprised?"

If only I'd known earlier these gospels existed, how comforted I would have been! I remember my spiritual breakdown at 17. I almost died from loss of faith until Minister La Trobe visited my bedside and guided me toward the light. Yes, there is the Father, and He is harsh, but there is also the Son, and *oh my*, He is beautiful. My vision of God had been steeped in the Old Testament, forged in its laws and duties, condemnation and punishments, but Reverend La Trobe showed me a new vision of a New Testament. He pulled me back from the brink. I lived 12 more years.

Emily tosses aside the gospels, looking bored. "You are tenacious in your beliefs, Anne. I'll give you that. Even death cannot destroy your faith." She shakes her head, confounded, as if I am an imbecile. Hurt wells. Why did I say anything? Her contempt for my beliefs was strong before, one more reason we grew apart. Why should she feel differently now, condemned to walk the earth like a fiend?

"How do you survive?" I ask abruptly.

"By constantly moving. Never staying in one place longer than a few months at the most."

"For all these years?"

"Yes, Anne. What you have done here is pure suicide. You've been lucky, that's all. It's obvious you don't value your life much."

"Do you really call that a life: moving constantly for a century and a half? Never having a home or making connections."

"I enjoy it. The earth is beautiful. Especially the New World. There is still so much to see."

"But no one loved their home more than you. Every time you left, you almost died."

"It was the confinement of society that injured me, not movement. My soul requires solitude, wilderness, freedom. The wide-open earth. It is society I cannot bear and the imprisonment insignificant minds press upon us, with their petty concerns and inane small talk. As if others could know how I should live? Who can know that better than myself?"

"How do you feed?" I brace myself for the answer. How many humans has she killed in all her years? Thousands? Her jacket is off, thrown over the couch and I see her more clearly now in the firelight.

Beneath her torn t-shirt and long, tangled hair, she glows. Her eyes are blue and luminous, her limbs sleek and strong.

I feel weak and pale in comparison.

"I hunt the strong. Males mostly. Occasionally I take a female prostitute." I must look shocked because Emily says, "If she so little values her dignity, why should I? Sometimes I take the evil, but it leaves a bad taste in my mouth, so I have come to avoid it."

"Who are the evil?"

"Pimps, dealers, rapists, murderers. You'd be surprised at the never-ending supply of targets, especially in cities, which I detest and enter only to hunt."

"Too bad you couldn't take out some of the world's dictators and spare us a few wars. Hitler or Pol Pot sound like appropriate marks."

"I don't involve myself in politics, although I did hunt for Bin Laden, but I could never find him. Generally, I avoid cities."

"So why are you here?"

"As I said, I was looking for you and Branwell."

"Is Branwell here? Is he alive?" My heart leaps with excitement and a trace of fear. With all his flaws, I still desperately love my brother, even as the mere thought of seeing him unnerves me. Still, Branwell is impossible not to love. Oh, how he tried and tested all of us, me especially. I wonder what the years have done to him. Has his soul gone dark, as his days once had?

"Yes, he's alive, but he's very tricky and paranoid. I've been on his trail for years, but always a step behind. I don't understand why he wishes to avoid me, unless it is out of guilt. That's something I understand." She looks at my seascape above the fire. "Like you, he has continued his art. I see it on walls and buildings all over the world—Palermo, New York, London and Cape Town—incredible graffiti, like markers taunting me, pointing me in a certain direction with their ancient obscure symbols and allusions to Horace. But when I arrive, he's always gone. The last time I saw evidence of him was in Miami, but the trail went cold. No vampire stays in one place long. How in God's name have you survived with boyfriends and partners and jobs?"

"I don't have a boyfriend," I say indignantly.

"Then why are you glowing?"

Mercifully, the teapot begins to squeal and I escape to the kitchen, where I prepare our ginger tea. I bring out a tray with a china pot and two delicate cups, placing them on the table before us. Emily wrinkles her nose. "Tea? Really?"

"Have you tried it?"

"Not in about a hundred years and it was horrible."

"Try this. It's organic gingerroot from Burma. Just sip to warm the tongue. I make it mostly for the scent. The Hawaiian Blue is wonderful too. It smells like spring."

Emily takes a sip. "It isn't bad, but I prefer blood."

I press my lips together to refrain from chastisement. After so much time apart, now is not the time for judgment but Emily notices my expression anyway. I could never conceal much from her. So little has changed between us and yet *everything* has.

"We are animal creatures," Emily says.

"We are spiritual beings."

"You deny your nature, Anne."

"As do you. By surrendering to your basest impulses, you deny your higher self."

"By denying your animal instincts, you betray yourself."

We fall silent, both of us staring into the fire. I see red flames of hell warning me of what's in store for both of us. I wonder what Emily sees reflected back at her.

"Perhaps we are both, animal and angel," I finally say. "The aim is learning how to find the middle way, or maybe making a choice between the two."

"Why choose one or the other when we can be both? The world is not so black and white, Anne. We do not all stand on one side or the other. You are an Angel of Darkness, sister, and the world is a brighter place for having you in it."

My heart cracks. "If only it were true."

"It's true if you choose it to be so."

With envy, I look at her. She leans back in the chair, legs crossed like a man in her black leather boots, sparking with energy, clear in her nature like a jungle cat or a hawk on the moors, free from morality and shame. Oh, how good it must feel to be at one with yourself!

I take a sip of tea when suddenly her whole body goes rigid. Her head whips to the door. "Someone's coming." She stands and darts to the shadows. In a flash, I am beside her, my hand on her arm.

"Wait, sister. You're safe here. Let me see who it is."

Her muscles tense beneath my hand and she pulls away. "Emily. Wait. Trust me. I'm not as clueless as you think." She stares at me with flashing eyes. "I need you, sister. Don't leave me yet." Her eyes soften and I release her. She backs further into the shadows and hovers there, watching, waiting.

At the window, I sweep aside the thick curtain. The sky is shifting from black to lavender and grey. Dawn is coming and with it Santos, stepping out of his squad car.

Great.

With a hand on his holster, he takes a determined step to the front door and I pray that I am not mistaken in placing my trust in him when it is all too clear he has so little trust in me.

Chapter 40

"It's Atticus Santos," I say to Emily. "I know him." I open the front door before Santos can knock, staying back from the newborn light. He looks at me, frowning, and peers into the room over my shoulder as if he senses something, but Emily is frozen in the shadows, invisible.

"Can I come in?" he asks. "It's about Dana."

"How nice of you to ask permission this time." I bar the door. He glowers at me while looking slightly uncomfortable and I can't help smiling in satisfaction. I glance behind me for Emily, who is increasingly curious.

I take a leap of faith and trust him. If Santos meant me harm, surely I would know by now. "I have company. My sister. I expect you to act civilized or I'll throw you out before you can blink."

He glares at me, clearly unaccustomed to being threatened by a woman. I step back, holding the door open and cautiously he walks inside. His hand is still at his hip. I grab and remove his Taser and firearm, setting them on the piano while his eyes blaze in outrage.

"You can have them back when you leave," I say.

Emily chuckles in the dark and Santos stiffens.

"Show yourself, Emily. Don't taunt him. He knows what we are."

"For God's sake, Anne." She steps into the room. "Tell me you're jesting."

"Jesus fucking Christ." Santos squeezes his forehead as if warding off a headache. "I wish this were all a fucking joke."

"Do you *mind*?" I say.

"What?" he asks bewildered.

"Your language."

"You drink blood and I can't say 'fuck'? Really?"

I glare at him, but he doesn't notice. Emily has stepped before the fire, drawing his attention as the light hits her eyes. They shine like an animal's.

With a sharp intake of breath, he moves for his weapons but I block him.

"You're safe here. Everyone in my home is safe. You are each under my protection."

Emily smirks, taking pleasure in his fear. "Like you could stop me if I wanted him."

"This is my home, Emily, and if you can't respect that, you can leave this instant." Reluctantly, she drags her eyes off him and takes a seat in a great wingback chair. Santos doesn't sit. His body is taut, ready for retreat, but his eyes are riveted on my sister, as if trapped by gravity.

The fire flickers, casting licks of savage light about her. She gleams with the wild glint of a dark goddess. A Kali or Anat or perhaps Artemis as she watches Actaeon being ripped apart by his own dogs. I wonder if she has been following the wars. Has she seen Santos before? Her eyes are locked on his and they stare at each other like lions circling in a forest.

Look away Santos. Look away.

"Please have a seat," I offer, but he ignores me, and finally, to my relief, wrenches away his gaze.

"How many of there are you?" His voice sounds breathless, a sound I've never heard from him before. "Is your entire family . . .?"

"No," I say. "There are not many of us. Emily was turned on the edge of death and then turned me before mine."

She cocks her head at me, but doesn't speak.

"You're so young," he says.

She shakes her head in contempt. "This is the delusion of the modern world. You think death a great anomaly and are outraged when it strikes anyone but the old. Such denial is childishly ignorant."

"Are you calling me stupid?" Santos flares.

"If you think we're too young to die, then yes, you are stupid."

"Emily," I warn. "Santos has lost many brothers. Be cautious with your words."

She falls silent.

"What's this about Dana?" I ask.

"She didn't show up for her shift and I can't find her."

"Lucien told me. She's been overwhelmed lately with school and work. She probably needed a break."

"She's been acting strange lately. Nervous and edgy, like she's hitting meth or something. How can you be her partner and not notice?"

"I have noticed, but she's going through a lot right now and she was just faced with the corpse of a murdered girl. Dana may appear unfeeling at times, but she's not completely callous." I squint at Santos. "I thought you two weren't seeing each other anymore."

"We're not. She's seeing that ER doc. Another strange figure. He only works at night." He gives me a pointed look. "And he signs on at various hospitals for just months at time. What kind of doctor is that?"

"He's a traveling M.D. He fills in when other doctors are on vacation." *If I were smart, I'd do the same thing.*

"I don't like him. Ever since he showed up, Dana's been acting edgy. Can you just give her a call? Check in on her? She won't pick up for me."

"I'm not her keeper. It's not my job to keep tabs on her, and I assure you she won't appreciate it."

His eyes burn me and I want to recoil, but I force myself not to move. *He can't hurt me.* "You're a real piece of work," he says through gritted teeth.

"What does that mean?"

"You think you're so superior, all compassionate and noble, but it's fake as fuck. You won't do anything to help those murdered girls and now you won't even go out of your way for your own *partner.*" His voice is tense with restrained fury. He opens his mouth to hurl another insult, but then grits his teeth and chokes his words back.

My throat thickens with shame. *What do you want me to do!* I want to yell. *Dana's not my friend,* and immediately I am awash with guilt for thinking it. I don't have friends. I can't afford to.

"Get out," Emily whispers in a low voice. "You have no idea what you're asking." Her hands are clenching the armrests so hard I fear she'll break my chair.

"Just call her!" Santos yells.

I turn away. This is what he thinks of me. This is how he has always seen me. False. Dishonorable. Selfish.

I find my phone and call Dana to appease Santos so he'll leave. Why did I ever trust him? How stupid of me to think he could feel anything but abhorrence for me. And now I've exposed Emily. What a fool I am! Tears of frustration threaten, but I turn toward a dark corner so no one can see. Just as I suspected, Dana doesn't answer and I leave a message, letting her know I'm checking in. When I hang up,

I turn to Santos with perfectly concealed anguish raging beneath a calm facade.

No one was ever better at hiding their pain than me.

With an even voice, I say, "She does this, you know, when she meets someone new. She disappears for days, sometimes weeks, but she always comes back around."

"When she's done with them," he finishes for me.

"That's not what I said."

"You didn't have to. Look, this isn't personal. This isn't about me and Dana. I'm here as a deputy. Two girls have been killed and now Dana goes missing."

"She doesn't fit the profile and she's a lot more street smart than those little girls."

"She's in trouble, I can feel it. The only reason I'm alive is 'cause I trust my instincts, and my gut is telling me something's wrong. Keep trying to reach her and if you hear from her, let me know. Here's my number." He throws a card on the piano, then gives Emily a hard look. "This is my town. If anyone else goes missing and I find out you had anything to do with it, I will hunt you down and kill you. I don't care whose sister you are."

In a flash, Emily moves on Santos. Reflexively his hand goes to his hip, but his weapon isn't there. She stops mere inches from him, but he holds his ground.

"If you threaten me again," she hisses, "I will rip out your throat before you finish speaking."

Santos doesn't flinch, just stares her down with eyes of black fire. His courage is preternatural and I see her hunger flare up, reaching out toward him.

I shove them away from each other. Santos slams against the piano, but Emily has always been strangely strong and it takes all my strength to edge her back.

"Enough," I demand. She looks at me then glides away. Why am I protecting Santos when he hates me? And Emily. If he knew she killed that hunter . . . Suddenly the ramifications of my trust in each of them comes crashing down. What was I thinking in letting them meet? Since when have I placed my faith in the nobler nature of humanity? My naiveté has endangered everyone. My head begins to throb with despair and I place a hand on the piano to steady myself.

The sun is rising, hot and bright, and all of a sudden I am bone-tired. William is right. A lot has happened in just one night, and I long for his calm, steady reason. I want his presence beside me. I know I mustn't trust him, either, but the thought of him is a comfort. Santos and Emily are like volcanoes of violence tilting toward eruption. They exhaust me.

Santos grabs his gun and Taser, slamming them into their holsters. "I'm going to find Dana and that bloodsucking Alpha parasite and I'm going to kill him and cut off his head." He turns to glare at me. "I should have known better than to ask a *girl* for help."

Emily bristles. Before she can reply, he yanks open the door, flooding the room with dawning light and we fall back into the darkness fast as we can.

The door slams behind him and the sound of an engine roars to life, then tires squeal and he speeds away.

I collapse limply into the nearest chair. Ivanhoe peeks his head around a corner making sure the coast is clear before trotting over to me and jumping onto my lap. Gratefully, I gather him to me. "That," I say wearily, "is our sheriff's deputy. You couldn't have made yourself more welcome if you were an outlaw riding into town on his stolen horse. Really, Emily! What were you thinking?"

"What was *I* thinking? What in God's name were *you* thinking, letting a man of the law into your home! If he had his way, he'd burn us all at the stake. I don't understand you, Anne. You were always so rational and now you seem entirely devoid of common sense. It's as if you have a death wish."

"Well, it seems we all had a death wish, didn't we?" I snap. "Apparently, some things never change."

Emily crosses her arms. "Except Charlotte. She was the only one with the stomach for living."

"Why didn't you turn her?"

"I would never!" she says with indignation, then more sadly, "So she could fuss at us for eternity?"

"I miss her."

"Me too." Emily falls into a chair and stares darkly into the fire. "You know, I've seen him before. In Afghanistan. He's one savage son of a bitch. You have no idea what he's capable of. He has a cruelty . . ." She falls silent, unable to speak, lost in memory. I wonder what she sees, sure it is an unspeakable act of brutality that only war can breed. Finally, she looks at me. "A professor and a soldier know what you are, Anne. If that professor figures out *who* you are and discovers your age . . ."

I bite my lip.

"Anne! No! For the love of God!" she roars. "The world cannot know this. They will never leave us alone. They will hunt us down and study us. Weaponize us. Experiment on us like lab rats to unlock the secrets of eternal youth and health. Wars will start over this. *No one* can know. You absolutely must leave now. Forget all this." She motions around. "It's nothing but chains, holding you back. This is the prison, Anne. You don't own it. It owns you. The darkness is freedom. Secrecy is our *shield*. You are going to get us all killed."

I steel myself against her paranoia. "Humans are not the enemy. Our greatest threat has always come from each other. Our kind is far too dangerous for them to contain, and besides" —I glance toward

the front door where sunlight is leaking beneath it like a toxic cloud—
"no one is going anywhere for now."

"When night falls, I'm leaving with you or without you."

Pain wells up, deep and sharp, but I squeeze my eyes closed and
force it back. Do I mean nothing to her? My *blood* sister twice over—
how easily she abandons me.

But though, poor solitary dove, must make, unheard, thy joyless
moan;

The heart that Nature formed to love, must pine, neglected and alone.

Ivanhoe purrs beneath my hand, reminding me I have one loyal
friend. To hide my grief, I bend and kiss him softly on the forehead.

Emily falls silent, brooding before the fire with a blackened brow.
She has taken to this rebirth as if it were a blessing. And why shouldn't
she? It has given her what she always wanted. Freedom. The power to
throw off the chains of society and death. Draped in the night she can
live without judgment, free from the expectations that hold us captive. Even here, in my home, her wildness burns with a fierce grace.

Her eyes slide to the door. She was my closest friend, and yet I
have no idea what she wants now. To stay with me or to run again?
How cold and impenetrable she is. Where did all her thrumming,
sea-deep passion go? Her undying loyalty? I'm too tired to argue with
her, but I know I can never live like Emily does, running and hiding
from humanity, living like an animal. It's not my nature.

I would rather die.

Perhaps I shall.

Chapter 41

I lead Emily downstairs to my room, but before I allow her to climb into my bed and sleep, I force her to strip and take a shower. This isn't easy. She has dirt beneath her nails, a leaf in her hair, and traces of blood in her clothes, and yet she acts like a little girl again, back from the moors, refusing to bathe before bed. When she drops her clothes to the floor, I take them to the washer and throw them in along with mine. "Those are my favorite jeans," she warns.

I raise an eyebrow. They're worn through at the knee and there's a horizontal tear below the back pocket, which holds a slender volume of Shelley's poems that once belonged to William. He must have dropped it at the graveyard. Perplexed, I set it aside.

"They're not going anywhere," I say.

"Isn't that one of the best inventions ever?"

"Jeans?"

"Absolutely. And motorcycles. And washing machines."

I can't help but laugh and some of the tension between us ebbs. We get in the shower together, just as we used to bathe when we were young. "You always were the pretty one," she says, "but look how beautiful you've become. Your eyes are more violet than ever. Like amethysts."

"You too, Emily. You're lean as a blade."

"My form is better suited for today's age."

"Ah, but don't you miss the 19ᵗʰ century?" I ask.

"Hell no."

"Isn't it ironic that the very transformation which has made us fairer has thrust us even further from love?"

She turns toward the hot water, letting it run over her face as I drizzle shampoo in her hair and work it into her scalp and mane with my fingers. The aroma of wildflowers fills the space. Her smooth white back is to me when she asks, "Have you ever had a lover?"

"No." I pause, astonished at the question. "Have you?"

She doesn't answer.

"Emily!"

Silence unspools, then she finally says, "That is a story for another day, sister."

"You can't ask a question like that and then go silent. That is entirely against the rules of sisterhood. Tell me!" I try to turn her to face me but she refuses. Her strength is greater than mine and she's impossible to budge. I know if I push too hard she'll fall into an intractable silence which I have always been powerless to break. Only when she's ready will she confide in me. Still I beg, "Was he a man or a Night Walker?"

"Not a *human*," she says indignantly, then falls quiet, leaving me more curious than ever.

A Night Walker then.

My mind is swirling with questions. Emily had a *lover?* A *Night Walker!* Was he an Alpha? Of course—she would never tolerate any-thing else. Not all male Night Walkers are Alphas but they are the ones who tend to survive. Our lives are brutal and the gentler souls tend to perish. But how did Emily manage him? Did he subjugate her? Impossible! I have so many questions, but I know they will only cause her to withdraw further. When Emily declines conversation, she's as implacable as Heathcliff and every futile cry for mercy only serves to harden her more.

We towel off and slip into pajamas. Emily crinkles her nose as I slip a long white nightgown over her head. "I certainly don't miss dresses," she grumbles. She barely tolerates my combing out her long, thick hair.

"Don't you ever use a brush?" I ask in wonder.

She shrugs. "What for?" Then she squirms and shifts as I manage with the patience of Job to comb out the mass of tangles. Fortunately, her pain tolerance is high, as I can't help tugging at an especially tenacious knot now and then.

When Emily's hair is smooth and her clothes are drying, I bolt the bedroom door and set the saber beside it with an embarrassed glance toward her. She doesn't say anything, but there's a look of approbation in her eye. I can just hear her thinking, *at least Anne's doing something toward self-preservation.* Ivanhoe has leaped upon the bed, given Emily a delicate sniff, and begins purring as she gathers him in her arms and gently pets him.

"What a beautiful color he is," she says, stroking his back. "Like the sun."

I shut and lock us into pitch dark and we curl up together in our snug abode and drift toward sleep. All is quiet. Emily wraps her arms around me like when we were motherless little girls, and for the first time in years, despite Alphas and danger and death, I feel that I am home.

❧

I sleep far too long and when I awake alone in my room, night has thoroughly fallen. It is my second shift off from work, and I'm determined to call in and give my two weeks' notice. My fear from last night has eased. Emily and Vander and *William* have soothed it. This time I shall plan my escape, not run off in a frenzied panic. I run my hand over the soft silk comforter and think of William—the first man who has kissed me. It's hard now to imagine I died without experiencing a single heated kiss. A deep ache throbs within that I've never felt before. Pure lust. William is a force pulling on my flesh, opening my body to the light.

I can still feel his touch waking me from a dark sleep, but Emily is right; I must leave, make a new life, one that William cannot be a part of. Only sorrow will come from loving me. I cannot expect a professor to move every ten years or flee his life at a moment's notice. My hands fly to my cheeks and I blush at the thought. The *supposition*! As if we could ever be in a relationship. How absurd! Living together while I'm shackled to the night and he works in the day. Feeding in secret so as not to repulse him.

I wrap my arms around myself. Impossible.

We are to meet again tonight at the Biltmore for further training. Vander and William seem intent on preparing me for a great battle which I know I will never fight. Instead, I will flee. This is who I am. The hare not the hound. But I did promise to warn William of my impending departure. What harm can come from a few additional hours of companionship when I may live for centuries more without it?

A nagging doubt tugs at my heart. I know what the harm is . . . it's in the enjoyment of it . . . the fellowship. Wanting it. Growing attached. I should sever the first stirrings of connection right now, before it takes root and grows and I am hooked like a gasping fish.

First, I'll walk to settle myself and gather my thoughts, and if I come across appropriate prey, I will eat. I need strength for my journey. Emily and I can hunt together tonight. Maybe she'll enjoy the blood of a stag, not her usual fare, but variety nonetheless. Just to move through the forest with her under a shining net of stars, like we used to as girls . . . to be together again. I'm sure she will come with me if I ask.

But when I venture upstairs, I don't find her. The dryer is empty and her battered backpack is gone. Abandonment rips through my chest like shrapnel and I rub my heart as if I have a physical wound.

Why didn't she wait? My simmering anger ignites into flame, breaking away from me, spilling into the night.

I will hunt alone.

Chapter 42

The forest flies by me as I drive toward the Black Mountains, where the trees grow thick and wild with life. The bend of a curve looms up reminding me of the "wolf attack" back toward the Smokies. Now I know that Emily was responsible, and that incident had nothing to do with the murdered girls. I wonder if Santos suspects the kills are unrelated. Why did Emily attack *two* grown men? Two *armed* men. It's incredibly bold. How much blood can one woman drink? A human can sustain a Night Walker for weeks or months, depending on the vibrancy of the blood. It's a waste to take more than that.

Beside me on the seat lies the saber Vander lent me. I don't know what I plan to do with it, but since our practice session last night I feel vulnerable heading out in the wild completely bare of arms. Plus, after my walk I'm going to the Biltmore. My hand tingles in anticipation with an itch to hold the weapon again. How natural it felt in my palm. And how glorious to move in perfect harmony with William, as if we were one, connected by an invisible thread. Fencing with him feels like finally dancing at a ball to which I was never invited and could only ever dream of instead.

In consternation, I press my lips together. This is the problem with weapons. Once you take satisfaction in them, you feel exposed and vulnerable when they're gone. I've managed for years without them. Why do I suddenly need forged steel to survive?

Because an Alpha is killing our girls. My stomach tightens. It's risky being out here alone, but I must eat. I cannot rely on Vander for food, and so far, the Alpha has struck before sundown, although his last kill was toward twilight, which suggests his sun-strength may be fading and his desperation growing. However, it's not his pattern to hunt at night and I am not the type of girl he is looking for anyway.

I'm east of Asheville when my phone rings. It's Dana, *thank God.* I've left multiple messages to a silence so sharp it resembles a slap in the face.

"Are you okay?" I ask.

"Never better," she purrs.

"We were worried. Santos has been looking for you. He's concerned."

"He's a psycho stalker. Tell him to get a life. Hey, I know you're off tonight. I thought you might want to grab a beer. Where are you?"

I am flabbergasted. *Grab a beer?* "I'm near Black Mountain. Just taking a drive."

"Perfect. I'm not far. Let's meet at Lookout Point. I'll bring the beer."

"Are you sure, Dana? It's freezing. I'm not sure you should be outside. What's going on?"

"There's something I want to show you, Anne. Believe me, you are going to want to see this."

I gnaw my lip, hit the turbo and fly across the mountain. Within minutes I zoom past downtown Black Mountain, three quaint blocks of galleries and tea shops, all closed. A few bars are open, and as I pass the White Horse jazz seeps through my window. I've always liked this little town with its hippies and hikers, artists and Christians, all living peacefully together. The energy here feels different. Soothing. Although tonight I'm not feeling it. I zip beneath the great stone arch to Montreat College and turn on Lookout Road. The road constricts and I force myself to slow, gliding into the trailhead parking lot as I text Santos: *I've found her. Lookout Point. Heading there now.*

I turn off the engine and am greeted by a violent stillness. Where are the night sounds? The rustlings and ramblings of my nocturnal kin? The trees look lean and grim as if they are starving in the snow. Dana's new Camaro is there, silent but steaming in the cold. It's empty. An eerie feeling comes over me. All of this is so unlike her. She has never shown the slightest interest in seeing me outside of work. In fact, I've always had the distinct impression I bore her to tears.

I slip on a cap and glasses, step out and look around. An opaque darkness stares defiantly back. Before I lock the car, feeling utterly ridiculous, I reach for the saber. I am in my hunting gear again, and I secure it to my leather belt. How preposterous I must look, coming to see Dana with a saber on my hip, but what the hell. She already thinks I'm a complete eccentric anyway.

Silently I thread my way up the narrow path, listening. The moon is hot and burning. Almost full. It trickles through the naked trees, glinting off branches, sparking off the snow beneath my feet. I can smell the snow. It smells like virginity—blameless, waiting to be touched. Since feeding on the rabbit, my sense of smell is sharper. I can barely remember what it felt like after feeding on a human, how strong I must have been, and my weakness is more obvious to me now than ever.

I'm an invalid compared to the rest of my kind.

It is a half-mile trek to the summit and in this weather and dark-ness, the path is abandoned. Dana has always liked drama, but she's never been much of a hiker and this setting seems especially out of character. My senses coalesce to a sharpened edge. With every step, I anticipate the musky scent of an Alpha reaching out to strike me, but all I smell is red spruce and Fraser firs. Rock and snow. I strain to hear something, anything, to indicate life lives here. The silence is unnatural.

I should turn back, but Dana's my partner. She's only a young woman and I'm a Night Walker. What if she needs me? An image of Santos flashes through my mind. He thinks I'm a coward. What if I am?

William thinks you're brave. Be brave for William.

"Over here!" Dana's voice rings out like a disembodied ghost, tinkling in the breeze like glass chimes. "Almost here," she says teasing.

How can she hear me when I cannot hear her? My heart grows cold. Nature has always felt safe to me, but now I feel out of my element. Alone. I shove aside the feeling. Even weak as I am, my strength is far greater than Dana's.

She can't hurt me.

A clearing opens upon a rise of earth, and there she is, atop a slab of rock in a clingy red dress and knee-high, lace-up leather boots with stiletto heels. She stands poised at the peak of the stone swell, like a revenant upon the altar. Behind her, Greybeard Mountain and the Seven Sisters sleep in the shadows. Her heels are high and sharp, pointed like daggers. Not appropriate hiking gear, that much is certain.

She steps into the moonlight and her eyes glitter.

I freeze, speechless.

"What do you think?" She spins like a debutante at her coming-out ball. Her hair flings out, flaxen and shimmering as sunshine. "Aren't I magnificent?"

No! No! No! This can't be happening. Not Dana. Please, not her. She will be a merciless killer unleashed upon the world.

She stops spinning and stalks over to me. "You, Anne, have been a very naughty girl. Keeping so many secrets. I always wondered why you had such flawless skin. Such shiny hair with that horrid diet of yours. Not nice for a girl to keep all her beauty tricks to herself. You have been selfish, Anne. Very selfish indeed. All that talk about serving humanity, and here you are keeping health and immortality all to yourself. Why not share the wealth?"

She is standing inches before me, her eyes glinting like gems. In a flash, she grabs my glasses and crushes them beneath her stiletto.

My voice sounds weak and breathless. "Who did this to you?"

She rolls her eyes. "Who do you think?"

"I have no idea."

Dana shakes her head in disbelief. "You've seen him up close. Are you so blind that you can't even recognize your own kind? All this time I thought you were the strong one, but now I know that you are pathetically freakin' weak. You're so weak you even pass for human. So weak that even he didn't recognize you for what you are. But don't worry, Anne, I didn't reveal your secret. You could never give him what he wants. There's no reason to distract him when I'm all he needs."

Abruptly, she grabs my wrist and twists, forcing me to my knees. Pain shoots up my arm into my shoulder and a cold sweat breaks over my skin. "Dana, what are you doing?" I stammer. "I'm your *partner.*"

She scoffs in disdain. "You don't care about me. You don't care about anyone. You want to keep everything for yourself, you selfish bitch." She twists my wrist until the splintering of bone rings out. I gasp in pain. "See how strong I am? Feel how hot I burn. Soon I will have *my* virgin and he and I will walk together in the sun for all eternity. I love it!" She squeals in delight.

She releases my crumpled form and screams to the night, "I am woman! Hear me roar!" Her bare arms rise above her head in triumph while her face throws back to bathe in the moonlight.

I rise to my feet, shattered wrist forgotten, and drive my saber straight through her heart.

Chapter 43

Her mouth falls open, eyes widening as she stares down at her chest uncomprehendingly. Dana's hands move to the blade but I pull free the saber, the scent of blood slamming me as it shoots from her heart. She looks up at me in horror, trying to speak, her hands pressed over the neat wound, holding back blood streaming through her fingers onto the snow.

Within seconds, she's unconscious. I catch her as she falls and gently place her on the ground, hearing her heart pulse more faintly with every beat. It sounds like rain falling lighter and lighter upon a window until, finally, it is still at last.

I cover my eyes and cave into myself, willing this nightmare away, but when I look again, Dana lies before me in an ever-widening stain of blood. The snow is death-drenched and the night perfectly silent, bearing witness to my crime.

A sob tears out of me. My hand covers my mouth but I can't stop it. I collapse to my knees, shuddering as eons of darkness and fear, murder and exile come rushing upon me. *Pain.* So much pain and grief and shame. I am sick of this life. This endless death. When will

God release me? The longer I live, the further from grace I fall. No matter how hard I try, I can't stop killing and His light dims with every drop of blood I shed.

We are all alone.

Emptiness crashes over me. Without Him, I'm crushed in loneliness. *With* Him, I'm crushed beneath abandonment. It's the same in death as it was in life; I have always forever been alone. William will die, Emily vanish and Ivanhoe rot to dust. It's too much to bear. I'm not strong enough.

I am the weak one.

The sick one.

The unloved one.

I brush the hair off Dana's forehead, lay my head against hers and weep. "I'm sorry. I am so sorry, Dana," I sob.

"Don't cry for her."

My breath catches.

"She really isn't worthy." Standing above me in a beam of the moon is Dr. Webb. I blink, trying to clear my vision from tears. My mind stumbles and all I can think is how inappropriately he's dressed for the weather. His khakis and snug t-shirt reveal a thickly muscled frame. A pit bull, that's what he reminds me of; short, stocky, and strong. His eyes glow glacially out of an impassive face.

I clamber to my feet, fumbling for my saber discarded on the ground, but before I can reach it, he picks it up and examines it in the moonlight. I step away from him.

"You are old-fashioned, aren't you?" He smiles, then tosses it at my feet. "Take it if it makes you more comfortable."

"Why did you do this to her!" I yell. "Why couldn't you let her be?"

"She chased me like a huntress. I only gave her what she wanted. That girl was a whore."

"Then why *turn* her, to spend eternity by your side? If you think so little of her, why did you do this to her?"

"I most certainly had no plans for eternity. Only pleasure. Every Alpha needs a mate and I've been alone a long time. Celibacy is for priests, not vampires, and when it comes to sex, I prefer the willing. Dana was one of the few mortal women strong enough to handle my appetites, but even she had her limits."

I have not seen an Alpha in fifty years, but it's just as I remember: the sense of entitlement to whatever they want, the belief their superior strength preordains them to dominance. It's arrogance born from unchallenged power. They have no compassion for the soft, only contempt.

Where is Santos? I pray he doesn't stumble upon us. Even armed, he's no match for a Day Walker.

My hands are sweaty with fear and I struggle to grip the saber slipping against my palm. The tip trembles when I point it at him. He smiles. He fully takes me in, dragging his gaze across me like a man appraising a potential slave or a horse. It's the first time he's seen me out of uniform and he seems pleasantly surprised.

"Easy, Anne," he says in his doctor's voice, the same tone he used with Savannah: kind and considerate. "There's no reason to be afraid."

"Aren't you angry with me for taking your plaything?"

"Dana was demanding but she led me to you, and for that I thank her. I have always preferred a more gentle girl. We are far more compatible, don't you think?"

I give him an incredulous look. "If you think that, you are no better versed in reading women than in honoring the sanctity of your profession." I sheathe my saber. He is a Day Walker, albeit a waning one, and I will not get into a swordfight with him. The broken bones in my wrist grate and my legs shake beneath me as I edge away from him, hoping to flee toward my car but in a blur he blocks my path.

He's fast. Too fast. My heart races in my chest and I force myself to breathe. I am a woman with the power of intellect on my side. I will stay calm. Composure has always been my greatest strength.

My hand slides to my pocket, where I find my phone and painfully press speed dial for Asheville dispatch. I don't know what I expect them to do. Rescue me? Send police and fire? By the time they arrive, it will be too late.

But Webb crushes my phone to dust in his hand. Like a lightning bolt, he strikes me across the face, knocking me to the ground, dazing me. Stars flare behind my eyes.

"Enough of this." He grabs me by the chin and, crouching, draws my face close to his. Blood runs down my forehead, stinging my eye. His fingers dig into my flesh, holding me like a vise. "I'm trying to be reasonable but you're not responding, so let me be clear." His voice turns whisper soft. "I'm in charge. You will obey."

I push away from him but he sinks his teeth into my throat. I take small, shallow breaths and try to push him off, but I might as well be a newborn fawn clutched in the jaws of a wolf.

He takes a deep pull of blood then releases me and yanks me to my feet. "Fighting is futile," he says. "You only bring pain upon yourself."

I struggle to free myself, even though it's pointless. He hits me again, knocking me back to the ground.

A great wave of black engulfs me and the world goes dark.

Chapter 44

Shadows flicker at the edge of my vision like quivering ghosts as I awake in an expansive room. Heavy wooden beams crisscross the cathedral ceiling. Flames hiss and pop in a great stone fireplace, the only light in the room. Heads of murdered animals line the walls like morbid curiosities, trophies of pain. Nausea rises in my stomach at the sight of them. There are stags and bear, a mountain lion, a zebra—all emblems of death, stuffed and displayed with pride.

The windows are flung open wide and a freezing wind groans through the trees like an abandoned lover. Starlight slips inside, dusting the room with the faintest of glows and I try to sense how much night is left. I am weakened from blood loss. Webb has drained me enough to be a pliant captive, too frail to fight back.

He's wrapped me in the softest of furs and placed me on a couch. My head rests on a leopard-pelted pillow. He sits before me in a leather chair studded with metal nails, looking at me with an expression of deep concern. As I wake, I see him before me, taking slow deep breaths. Although not tall, he must have been immensely strong as a man, with broad shoulders and thick arms and thighs. Built for power, not grace. A swinger of clubs, not dancer of sabers.

My heart begins to race in my chest from blood loss and fear. I feel like a child next to a king's champion. He is impossible to fight through physical means. In a haze, I think back to all the stories I have ever read: legends, epics, fairy tales, and myths. How did the hero survive? Odysseus? Persephone? Gretel? But my mind is a swirling vortex, unable to grasp any conscious thought. I can't make it work. Webb compels my attention, sitting still and dangerous, mere feet away.

Head swimming, I pull myself up to a sitting position.

"You are delicate," he says. "I've never seen one of our kind who has lived like you and survived so long in civilization. I thought I was the great anomaly. Why do you starve yourself? Is it a psychological weakness you had as a mortal?"

I shake my head, trying to clear the fog from my mind. "I . . ." My voice comes out a raspy whisper. My wrist is throbbing and I cradle it with my other hand. "I know how it feels to lose people. I don't wish to torment others with despair."

He smiles. "A sensitive soul."

"Loss has taught me compassion. Have you not lost anyone?" I wonder when he was turned.

"Not really. My mother died when I was a small boy. My father died decades ago, but he hasn't been missed."

"Did he love you?"

"No. He was a surgeon. A son was the least of his priorities. That was the fifties when childcare was a woman's domain."

"Love and protection of a child is a father's domain as well."

Webb smiles sadly. "Who can protect us from this? No mortal. Did your father protect you?"

I look away to hide my grief.

"There's no room for mortals in our life, Anne. They will never be able to protect you. But I can."

"Like you protected Dana?"

His eyes grow hard. "She belonged to me and was not for you to take, but you are far more my type."

"Tractable."

"Pure."

"I'm a vampire. How can you call me pure?"

"It's all over you. I smell it on you. I taste it in your blood. You're a virgin."

"That doesn't make me pure. What one holds in her heart grants purity, not sexual experience. I'm a killer."

"But you're really not much of one, are you? Come with me, Anne, and I'll do the killing for you. I'll protect and provide for you. You'll be safe with me and appreciated. I will cherish you."

"I will be owned and controlled."

"Is it not the way of men and women? Security in exchange for beauty and sex."

My breath catches.

"There's no rush, Anne. We have all the time in the world. Time for you to come to know me. Trust me. We can be partners and work together. We can have our own practice or travel the world and minister to the most vulnerable. The forgotten. Think of how many lives we could save together."

"You kill people. You kill girls." I say, outraged. "How could I ever trust you?"

"Because I will not kill *you*. I kill girls because they give me strength. A virgin at menarche grants me immunity to the sun but sadly it only lasts so long, and the timing is difficult to orchestrate unless I hold the girls hostage." He frowns. "I am not a maniac."

"Why Claire? She was 18, well past menarche."

"My immunity is slipping. One can only remain a Day Walker for so long. Virgin blood is pure. Pure blood is strong blood. Full of life and power. It allows me to move at sunrise and sunset. This makes it possible for me to do my work, and if I occasionally show myself in the daytime a few times a year, no one will ever suspect me. You and I are the same, Anne." My eyes widen in disbelief. "We work the night shift when everyone is at their weakest. We are the strong. Awake and alert. Never tired. The night is full of trauma and injury, but we are ready. By feeding on a few girls a year, I save countless others. It's the price they pay so that others may live."

"It's wrong."

He smiles. "Because they are female? Would it be less morally offensive to you if I killed boys?"

"No," I say, disgusted. "That's wrong too."

"Then adults? Only adult males are worthy of sacrifice?"

Numbly, I shake my head.

"Must we starve to death, Anne? Were we put here to starve? Should we never go to war because killing is wrong? Because mothers or daughters will die in the crossfire? Do we let tyrants reign because we don't have the stomach for killing?"

"*You* are a tyrant. Killing little girls. Cutting their throats open."

"They felt no pain, I *promise* you. No one kills as humanely as I do. A deer gunned down in the forest stinks with fear. My girls die free of it. So fast they don't know what's coming. They are holy sacrifices upon the altar of medicine. I am far more compassionate than others of our kind."

"It's wrong to kill like that."

"But can you explain why? Hunters kill."

"To eat."

"That's what I'm doing. Eating. Humans murder billions of animals a year for the pure pleasure of meat when they want it. Not for survival. For *pleasure*. A thousand boys are trained every year to kill in the military. Are they psychopaths? The world sanctions killing because it knows that to kill is human. We are animals. We are killers."

"That's not what Jesus taught. That's not what God wants."

Webb throws his head back and laughs. "That's how God made us! In His image! God is the greatest predator of all. The Bible's replete with tales of God's murders. He killed thousands when he was angry or disappointed. Entire tribes and towns. Think of Noah's flood! The greatest genocide. He murdered all humanity except for one select family. We are created in God's image and God is the greatest killer of all."

"Not my God."

"So you can create the God you want? I didn't realize that was an option. Throw out what makes no sense and fashion your own version of divinity. *Hmmm*. I wonder what my God would look like. I think he'd have horns." He smiles, showing sharp white teeth.

"Life is sacred."

"Yes, it is. And that is why I've dedicated the past fifty years practicing medicine and saving lives. You are a beautiful soul, Anne. It's why I find you so lovely. Your discomfort with my victims comes from your sense of their vulnerability. Girls are more vulnerable than men, especially compared to me, and this makes your heart reach out to them. But it's our way to survive on the backs of the vulnerable. The wolf hunts the doe. The lion consumes the lamb. Civilization is built upon this principle."

"There's always an excuse for killing, but that's all it is: an excuse. You must feel the discord in your soul when you kill those girls."

"I feel nothing of the sort. They die so I may live. You'll come to see in time, Anne, that I am not a bad man. But how long can anyone live in the darkness and not feel his soul shrivel within him?

Don't you long for the sunlight? That golden warmth upon your face at early dawn, when the entire world begins to glow from within to remind you of hope. The sky pink and gold and palest blue. Don't you miss it?"

"Of course, but I will not kill for it."

"What will you kill for?"

My brow creases.

He waits and, after a moment, smiles. "You don't know, do you? That's something you must decide." His gaze is soft and full of warmth and I'm utterly thrown off balance.

He disappears and I attempt to stand but am so weak I must lean against the couch. My breath comes in tiny, shallow pants. I step toward the door, and see my saber resting there. Slowly, I am making my way across the room, leaning on furniture all the way, when Webb reappears. He's at my side, sweeping me up in his arms as if I am a princess, light as a sunbeam.

"You are weak. Rest." His voice is tender and my eyes fill with tears. He's confusing me. I wish he'd stay mean. His cruelty is easier to fight than his kindness. A small, soft part of me wants to wrap myself up in his hardness and surrender. I could close my eyes for just a second and rest my head against his chest. I'm so tired and he is strong. He *wants* me. He won't get old and sick. He won't die on me.

He places me on the couch again and sets an old, worn medical bag beside it on the floor. "Your wrist is broken. Let me set it." He kneels and takes my hand in his. He's gentle and careful, and his flesh is warm. A look of anger flashes through his eyes as he feels the bones of my wrist beneath his fingers. I am studying his face and when he glances up to see if I am flinching, his eyes catch mine. Fear sparks in him. He is awash in vulnerability. Suddenly my desire is reaching out toward his loneliness until with a gasp of shame, I yank it back and armor it in disgust. Webb composes himself, but almost imperceptibly his hands begin to tremble as he begins manipulating my wrist.

"It's shattered," he growls. "Dana was careless, due to jealousy no doubt. It's becoming more evident that you did me a favor. I would never have chosen her as a companion had I not been alone for so long and had she not such . . ." he searches for the right word "... powerful appetites." He heaves a great sigh. "I'm not sure what is worse: the darkness or the forced loneliness of our existence. The women of our kind are so rare and shy, it forces us to mate with humans. Yet their fragility is" —he grimaces— "unappetizing. It disgusts me, quite frankly. To be with someone of my own kind, an equal, to love freely and without restraint, that's what I want. After all I have given to humanity, I deserve it."

"What do you mean we are rare, the women of our kind?"

"Don't you know how few of you there are, compared to us?"

I remain silent, unwilling to reveal the depths of my ignorance. All this talk of love and sex is making me uncomfortable. I look at Dr. Webb, a human turned in his prime. Although paler than your average man, he radiates virility. What must it be like for him to move through eternity alone, without a mate? Or breaking any transient lovers he did find? I was celibate my whole life. It was all I ever knew, so the loss, I suspect, was not so great for me. But even I feel crushed beneath the weight of loneliness.

I am dizzy and disoriented—anemic, no doubt, thanks to Webb, I remind myself. *He is a wolf. He is a wolf. He is a wolf.* He sunk his teeth in my throat. He drank my blood. He hit me. My face still throbs from the blow. I mustn't forget.

Don't forget, Anne. Don't forget.

With perfect care, Webb sets my wrist and wraps it, occasionally glancing up at me to see how I'm faring. The pain retreats to a dull throb when he realigns my broken bones. He's a superb physician, but that should come as no surprise; he's had many years to practice. It's true that he's saved numerous lives in only the few months he has been here, certainly far more lives than he has taken.

I think of William and wonder what he would think of Webb's arguments. I assume he'd reject them all without hesitation, although he is certainly no pacifist. He was at war in Afghanistan, and may well have done things of which I have no inkling. But even if he had, I know it was not with an easy heart. I know he did not casually justify his behavior and shrug off his guilt like an old coat.

He's who I want. Not this psychotic killer. No matter how reasonable Webb's arguments are, I reject them all. Not because I'm entirely certain they are wrong, but because I must make a *choice* about how I live and what I believe and I refuse to let others decide for me. I must choose for myself.

Sartre said we are condemned to choose, but that's not it. We are *free* to choose. This is what the serpent whispered of in the Garden of Eden—freedom. And oh, what a heavy price it exacts.

I choose love. Compassion. I choose to let my heart be my guide, not the cold, sharp blade of reason. And I can't help smiling because I am sounding like Emily. Always I was the rational one, the critical one, while she followed her instinct with wild abandon. I don't know what is right or wrong anymore. I only know that I must be loyal to my own heart, because if God can be heard anywhere, it is there.

For now, I will appear pliant. I will be as Webb wishes: obedient, docile, soft. And then I will escape and find William. I will make love to him, and he will be my first. And then I will let him go, and I will roam through the darkness alone so that he may be safe and find someone else with whom he can make a life.

Chapter 45

When my wrist is firmly wrapped, Webb takes each finger in his and presses. My hands are cold and white and the blood does not rush back to my fingertips as it should. He is kneeling before me, and he places an arm on each side of my thighs, pinning me down with the force of his presence. I feel his desire: aggressive and dominating. My breath comes quick. I need blood. Oxygen. Slowly he takes my chin in his hand and kisses me softly on the mouth. His teeth are sharp. I try to turn away, but his fingers tighten, holding me. He bites the inside of his mouth with his own teeth, so hard blood wells up. Suddenly I'm leaning into him, hungry and desperate, trying to stop myself from kissing him but I can't. I can't stop. He tastes of raw, bright sunlight and I'm wrapped in a bolt of lightning, jolting back to life.

Finally he pulls back with his eyes closed, unbalanced. His chest is heaving and his hands clench the couch so tightly he's torn through the fabric. Mortification sweeps through me. My hand flies to my mouth. In disgust, I wipe the blood away, recoiling from him in horror, kicking out with a boot to his chest, but he refuses to release me.

His hands grip my thighs like iron, pinning me down. "I will prove my loyalty to you," he whispers. "With you by my side, I will be a better man. We will save thousands. You will see that I can be good. I'll take care of Dana's body. Then I will nourish you and give you the sun. When you feel it, you will never want to return to the darkness. I will give you the light, and once you taste it, you will remain with me forever."

Chapter 46

He picks me up and carries me into the basement. A grimmer bridal chamber I have never imagined. It smells of musk and mold. There is a large four-poster bed carved with branches and leaves and covered in white animal furs. The floor is concrete, overthrown with threadbare kilims and old Turkish carpets. A fireplace sits cold and empty. Two smooth sconces glow an insipid yellow on the wall. Webb shows me a dresser and opens a drawer. "There are clothes here for you. They were Dana's but you can find something to wear. Nothing red, please. A bathroom is in there. When I return, I expect to find you bathed and clothed."

"They'll know I'm gone. They'll look for me."

"Who will? All your friends?" He smiles and I can't help recognizing his beauty. "Dana told me how many you have. It doesn't matter anyway. We're leaving soon."

"They'll suspect you."

"They'll think we had a passionate affair and ran off together. Or I'll tell them there was an illness in the family. Either way, great reward requires great risk. You, my love, are worth it." Webb turns and leaves the room. The door closes and bolts slam shut, then all falls silent.

I sit on the bed. There are no windows in either the bedroom or the bathroom. No A/C vents. The only door is the one Webb exited through and it sounded solid when he closed it. Still I know I must escape. Now's my chance, while Webb is gone dealing with Dana's corpse. I cringe at the thought of her, the need to dispose of her body, but I can't think about that now; there will be time later to grieve.

Sliding from the bed, I crawl to the fireplace and peer inside the chimney. It's sealed shut. Next I move to the door and study it. The handle is an ornate iron affair, the kind you see on a front door, not an interior, with a thick deadbolt that can be opened with a key from either side. A second deadbolt has been installed above it, again accessible from outside. Chills run up my arms and I try to clear my thoughts.

In all my time as a paramedic, I've learned a few things from firefighters. Standing by at house fires while they forced entry may now come in handy. My hand slides over the door and I give it a whack. Solid core. It's inward-swinging, with hinges on my side. With the right tools I could remove the hinges or force the door inward, or go through the lock. But I don't have any tools and I'm too weak to use my bare hands. My despair rises. If I were at my peak strength, I could rip the handle right off or kick through the door with my boots but I'm so ridiculously tired. Webb drained me.

What else will he do?

With a roar of resolve, I clamber to my feet and begin searching the room for something to use. I've got to toughen up. Charlotte and I once ran four miles over steep hills in a torrential rainstorm for the sole purpose of clearing our honor, and we were no warriors. Back then, I had my cursed asthma and Charlotte was as small and nearsighted as a squirrel. If we could fight for honor as mortal girls, I can fight for freedom now.

In the bathroom I search for a razor blade or scissors but there's nothing. The bedroom contains only soft, silky things: pillows, blankets, animal throws. There isn't even a table lamp. Frantically, I throw open drawers and rifle through Dana's belongings: slinky panties and bras, clingy crimson dresses, a pair of fishnet stockings. All her clothing is a different shade of blood. I remember her once saying how she despised pink, "a weak color for weak little girls." Red is powerful, she said. Red is for women. I couldn't obey Webb and dress in another color even if I wanted to.

The thought of him spurs me on. I begin throwing her clothes onto the floor in piles of lace and satin. Nothing but softness and beauty. I want something hard, sharp. In despair, I yank out the dresser drawer and, screaming, hurl it across the room. It hits the wall and explodes into a storm of slivers, reminding me that I'm not your normal girl.

I am a Night Walker.

But the effort has exhausted me. My head swims with dizziness and I rest it upon my knees to keep from passing out. Blood pulses through my wrist with each heartbeat, numbing my fingers. I must be stronger. I've been locked in a dungeon by a sociopath who expects me to be bathed, dressed, and yielding upon his return.

My nightmares have come true.

Slowly I raise my head and realize I am kneeling as if in prayer. I clasp my hands before my face, white fingers steepling toward God. What can I ask that I have not already asked a million times before? God, please save me. I have begged Him for almost two hundred years. All he's given me are silence and death.

The room is ice-cold. Frigid concrete seeps through the carpets, into my knees, up my thighs. My bones ache. My wrist throbs and my head hurts, but worse than all of that is my soul.

My soul is shot to hell.

And all of a sudden I hear a voice, clear and deep as a church bell. Papa!

As iron sharpens iron, so one person sharpens another.

I'm a little girl again sitting upon the hard pew of our cold church, listening to Papa's sermon. But this time is different. This time I *hear* what Papa's really trying to say for I'm no longer a child. I'm a woman who knows the shadows and the valleys of death. I've been beaten by the hammer of hell and I've survived. This isn't the first dungeon I've been in. Webb's not the first Alpha to hurt me. All that's come before has sharpened and honed my heart.

I am sharp as iron and I must save myself.

There is one last drawer. I inch it open, afraid it will be empty but hoping it's full of whips and chains and handcuffs—potential weapons. I hold my breath. When I slide it out, I see only shadows inside. Pulling it wider, I wait while my eyes adjust to the dark, yawning hole. Emily's right, my night vision has grown pitifully weak. Blackness swirls then fades to navy. Navy! My heart skips and my hand flies inside, landing upon cotton and polyester. Dana's work uniform has been rolled up and shoved inside. I rifle her pants and pockets, feeling for the knife she always carries. Nothing. My hand sweeps the drawer, fingers running over the grainy wood, alighting upon her canvas belt, desperately searching for what I know should be there.

I find it! A leather case. With my good hand, I pull out Dana's Super Tool Leatherman. She bragged it was the most steroidal multitool around, bequeathed to her by Firefighter Tom. Pure stainless steel with nineteen components: pliers, cutters, crimpers, snippers, and a dozen other superfluous things a paramedic would never need. But now I bless her love of extravagance and fumble open the tool like a starving man ripping open a can of beans.

I spend entirely too long trying every adjunct on it to get through the lock. Screwdrivers, nail files, knives, pliers, the saw, even the can opener. It's useless and I'm making no progress. Time is running out. A master of speed and efficiency, Webb could return any moment.

What I need is an axe and I'd smash my way through like a berserker. In desperation, I abandon the locks and wield the tool as a hammer, slamming it against the bottom hinge again and again, a deranged Bertha beating at an attic door. Pain rips through my wrist, and I relish it. I *deserve* it. If I'd been stronger, this wouldn't have happened. Dana wouldn't have fooled me. Webb wouldn't have found me. When I feed, I'm fast as a cheetah shrouded in invisibility. Untouchable.

I want to tell William that I was never offended; I am enraptured. I want to tell him that he's the most beautiful man in all the lives I've ever known, and I love him.

Nevermore will I lock my words away. Nevermore will I allow myself to grow so weak.

In a frenzy I attack the hinge and strike and strike and strike. "Nevermore!" I yell.

The hinge tears off and clatters to the floor.

I freeze for a second, momentarily stunned, then I'm prying the door open from the bottom, squeezing and kicking myself through like a rat. The top hinge is secure and the hard edge of the door scrapes against my ribs and hips as I push myself through.

I'm up and running, stumbling upon the stairs, crawling up them like an injured beast, dragging myself to my feet and breaking through the first window I see, falling onto the soft powdered snow in a bed of glimmering glass, sliding down a hill into the trees, running for the forest like Atalanta.

Chapter 47

I race through the night, dodging trees and stumbling over stones. The moon has risen in the sky but the night is dark as pitch and I can barely see. Disoriented, I stop to gain my bearings. I must calm myself and think. Momentarily, I close my eyes, straining to hear the sound of Webb's approach, but the woods are deathly silent. I long for the saber I left behind then realize with a start that I'm still gripping the Leatherman. Quickly, I clip it to my belt and begin running toward town, panting for breath, and shooting like a falling star straight into Webb's arms.

I fight as hard as I can to free myself, but he is a Day Walker and compared to him I am little more than a starving girl.

"Fight all you want," he says, grasping my face, forcing me to look at him. "I like to fight. It's so much more fun with you than with mere mortals, though I must say, you're almost as weak."

I try to pull his hands off me, but his arms are thick and unyielding. The wound above my eye is open and bleeding again. Blood trickles down my face, biting at my vision. "I'll never go with you," I hiss. "Kill me here. I will never live with you."

He runs a finger over my lip as if he wants to kiss me. "Killing you is not my intention. With a little sustenance in you, no doubt you'll see things more clearly. I have plans for you. For us." He releases me and holds out a hand. The world tilts to a blur. "I truly don't wish to hurt you, Anne."

"Liar!"

His eyes shift into a softer blue, slightly less arctic, and I sense the desperation concealed beneath their edge, a deep aloneness spilling out to touch me. He kneels like a white prince and takes my hand, his voice a fierce whisper. "You have no idea how I restrain myself for you. I want you to choose me, but you must know I am in charge. In your body, in your bones, you must *know* it so you will never leave me."

I pull away but he gives me a tug and I'm tipping into his arms. He picks me up and sets me on a fallen tree, then takes a knee so that his face is near mine. He leans in and I freeze as he draws his tongue over the flesh above my eye, licking the wound clean like a mother tending her pup. My heart turns to ice. I'm repulsed. He's an animal. How did he ever pass for human?

"Come with me, Anne." He takes my good hand, so pale and small in his. "We are alike. That's why we seek civilization. We're not made to be alone. Give me a chance, Anne. *One* chance, and I promise I'll take care of you."

"You're ruthless." I try to extricate my hand, but he won't let go. "You kill little girls."

"Only so that others may live. I can give you the sun on your face and a million colors you have forgotten. Light. Heat. I can give you a family, whatever you want: animals, children, luxury."

"Children?"

His eyes spark. "Babies." He whispers the word, drawing it out like a blessing.

"You're lying. It's not possible."

"There's no reason it shouldn't be. We're the same species. We are the same, Anne."

I shake my head. "It's impossible. I don't bleed. There are no children of our kind. To do this to a child, condemn them to murder and darkness and blood. It's insane. You're insane."

He grips me by the shoulders, his eyes shine in the blood-red light of the moon. "That's what they always call those who have broken free from their cages. I have a vision others are too afraid to see. Open your mind, Anne. If we have the courage, we can do anything we want. Man's rules don't apply to us. We aren't like other people. We're special. Better. *Ubermen*. We create our own reality."

Numbly, I shake my head, refusing to believe. The bones in my wrist grate from his grip on my arm, stealing my breath. "There are no Night Walker children, ever."

"How do you know? You still have eggs and I ejaculate."

In horror, I try to wrench myself away. "No!" I gasp. "We can't *mate*. We can't live together. You're a monster." My eyes are filling with tears. "I won't be your slave."

"It's not a slave I desire, Anne. It's a lover. A wife."

With a moan, I push him away but my hands only draw him in. Doubt entwines my brain, and suddenly I feel as if Branwell is here, seducing me with his tangled web of words.

"You're so cold, Anne. So pale." Webb carefully takes my broken wrist in his hand and the warmth of him seeps through my skin into my shattered bones. "You are snow white. You are dying, my pet. Let me save you. Let me give you life. Warmth. I can heal you. I can fill you with light."

I am running on the moors beneath a clear vast sky. The sun shines warm upon my face. A barking Keeper tears through the green-gold heath rippling around us. Small violet bluebells quiver in the breeze like gems dropped from heaven. Emily is there and her eyes glow like the sea when the light shines upon it, a deep, incandescent blue. Strands of copper glint her hair, her cheeks flush rose pink from the wind, and I know if the right man were to see her like this, he could not help but fall in love.

Heaven lives in the light. Darkness belongs to hell.

I'm so tired and cold and lonely. What if I could improve Webb, tame him? Together we could save people, travel the world, find the most vulnerable and injured.

For the first time, I allow myself to truly look at him. Webb's brutal strength pulls at me, filling me with shame at my weakness. Everything about him screams power: the thick bones of his wrists, the deftness of his fingers, the talent as a doctor thrumming through his hands. He has saved the unsalvageable, I've seen it.

Temptation whispers of surrender like a soft breath against my throat. How easy to turn one's life over to another. Let someone else take control and surrender to the heat of their strength.

But that is the way of a child and I am a woman.

There's no going back.

"I'd rather be free than safe," I whisper, grasping for conviction.

He touches my mouth with his thumb. "You are not free now, my dove. You're a prisoner to the darkness, held captive by your own fragility. Women crave security, not freedom. You were not made to go your own way, but to hold the world together. That's your strength."

His touch is gentle, the skin of his hands, smooth. It's what I've always wanted—a home of my own with a husband—a doctor!—and children, a little terrier by my feet and Ivanhoe curled up on a chair before the hearth. What good is liberty without love? I would sacrifice freedom for a life like that in a single heartbeat. So many women would.

Not Emily.

Her blue eyes flash through me like starlight. She would laugh in Webb's face, throat-punch him and run like a leopard into the night. She would never trade freedom for dependency. Submission would never even *occur* to her.

With a trembling hand, I yank my wrist free. "I don't want you," I hiss. "You repulse me. If you were the last being on earth, I wouldn't come near you. Fuck off."

His hand flies out and stars scatter behind my eyes.

"What happened to not wanting to hurt me?" I spit blood in his face.

He spins me and throws me over the fallen log. My shirt rides up and rough knobs of wood jab into my belly. He is on me like a rabid dog, teeth sinking into my throat, sucking, pulling, while his hands grasp for my belt and release it, reaching for buttons and ripping them open, yanking at my pants as the icy air slices my back like a whip.

His hands throb with fury.

I twist against his grip like a feral cat, clawing at his fingers upon my flesh, fighting to hinder the consummation of his desire as all my strength ebbs.

I'm fading, drowning in bitter cold. His teeth lock me in place while the world dims and darkens, growing colder and colder. Silence swells. Sensation fades while my heart beats frantically against the force of his will like a trapped bird.

So this is how they feel. All my victims. My first frightened girl, the soldiers, the deer and the rabbit. Frozen beneath the force of another's hunger, aware of impending obliteration, but helpless to fight it. *Wanting* to live.

I'm dying and now it seems too soon.

I'm not ready.

Chapter 48

I drift in a world of emptiness. Fear recedes to a pinprick and there are faces swimming up to me out of the dark. Charlotte, Papa, Elizabeth, Maria. Mama. Is she waiting for me upon the threshold of heaven? Or am I en route to hell?

Sweet oblivion seduces me. It is greater than hunger. To be nothing *forever*—what a gift.

But not yet, Anne. Not yet, a voice inside my head whispers loud as God.

With all my will, I cling to consciousness. My fingers search for the Leatherman at my waist, sliding it off my belt. Webb's teeth are locked in my neck and his stomach clenches against my back as he sucks my blood. One hand claws at my pants while the other gropes for his own and tugs them open.

Blindly, I fumble the multi-tool apart until I feel the sharp edge of a blade. Then I reach back and jam the knife deep between Webb's ribs.

He howls and falls off me, but I turn on him and drive the blade into the crook of his thigh, missing the artery by a hair's breadth.

Incredulous, he kicks me away and climbs to his feet, when a blast of sound crashes through the night, knocking him back.

Shots ring out, louder and louder and I am back in Crimea, bullets flying, mortars falling. I'm scrambling for cover, ears ringing, crawling through the snow. Where, I'm not sure. The world's gone dark and hazy as if I'm a prisoner of the underworld. A doomed Inanna. I try to crawl, but cannot even rise to my knees. All my strength has fled. Another blast rings out then strong arms grab me, jerking me to my feet.

Let me go! I try to scream, but the words don't come.

"Bell, it's me. Santos." At the sound of his voice I stop struggling and wait for my vision to clear. "My God," he says, "you're drained."

"Where's Webb?" I whisper.

"He ran like a little bitch."

Santos throws my arm around his shoulder and we move quickly through the forest. Fast. He's moving too fast. The ground lurches beneath me as I struggle to remain conscious. Everything's a blur and I can't catch my breath. I need to rest but he holds me fast. Then the slick, cool vinyl of a seat catches me and a door is slamming, an engine revving. I am in the backseat of a squad car. We are speeding away.

Tires slide out and the car regains itself.

"Bell, are you okay? Look at me. Open your eyes!"

Santos.

I peer through the wire-meshed window separating us but all I see is a dark blur. Red and blue lights throb across the forest reminding me of flashing fireworks. How America loves her fireworks.

And freedom.

"Stay with me. Hold on."

I close my eyes and drift off. I'm so bone tired all I want is to sleep.

Time to sleep.

A fist slams the window separating the backseat from the front. I open my eyes. "Hold the fuck on, Bell!" Santos yells at me. "William is waiting. He knows what to do."

William? My first kiss. My last kiss. For him, I will stay awake. I roll onto my back and stare at the ceiling. I am panting. It's my hemoglobin, struggling to keep up, but there's too little of it, too much blood loss. I need oxygen, blood. A transfusion. No hospitals! Where's Webb? Did Santos shoot him? I want to ask, but don't have the strength to speak.

The car squeals around a sharp turn, slamming me back against the seat. Nausea rises in my throat. Each turn steals my breath and grates my broken bones against each other. "Slow down," I moan. "You're going to kill us."

We hit the interstate and he punches it. Red and blue lights burn my eyes, and I close them. Santos is on the phone, barking out a stream of questions.

"Why not a hospital? You want me to go where? Will, are you fucking crazy? Yes, I trust you. Okay, Will, okay."

William is waiting. I'll see him soon if I can stay awake, but I'm so sleepy.

A wailing siren startles me from sleep. With a jerk, I open my eyes to see the flash of an intersection and city lights morphing into a wave of light. Then there is only darkness and trees and the thrum of his engine tearing down a forest road. Santos is on the phone, getting directions. Eventually the car slams to a stop, almost throwing me to the floor. I hear him mumble, "I can't fucking believe this," before slowly pulling forward.

I glance out the window and see an iron gate receding into the forest as we drive through it. "Where are we?" I moan and then I remember . . . the secret back entrance to the Biltmore.

"What the fuck?" Santos says. "What the hell is she doing here?"

The back door is yanked open and the hinges groan.

"What happened to her?" It's Emily. She is climbing in, placing my head on her lap, stroking my forehead. "What the hell happened?" she yells to Santos.

"He got her. The Alpha or whatever the fuck you call him. He had her by the throat. Just like fucking Afghanistan."

Emily is here and I relax beneath her touch. "I thought you'd left." My voice comes out a whisper. "What are you doing here?"

"Tracking someone."

"No, Em." I grasp her arm. "Not William. He's mine."

"Hush, sister. It's not him I want."

"Then who?"

She brushes the hair off my face. "Rest, sister." Her voice is soft and soothing and I remember being a little girl, Mama dead, and Emily, herself so small, holding me in her arms, cooing to me.

She does that now. "It's okay, Anne. It's going to be okay."

I smile. Because the last time she said this to me, it all turned out very badly indeed.

Chapter 49

I feel the car winding its way down into the earth. Santos mumbles under his breath and Emily is coiled beneath me.

"Where are we?" she asks Santos.

"The Biltmore. An underground tunnel. William's here. He has . . . what she needs."

"She needs blood," says Emily.

"I know." The door flies open and William is pulling me out of Emily's arms. She reluctantly lets go. He cradles me against his chest and suddenly I feel perfectly safe.

"It's okay, Anne. Hold on, love."

Love. William called me 'love.' To hear that word once before I die. He sweeps me into a great room. "She's been drained. God, she's freezing. Can she die of hypothermia?"

"Yes." It is Vander. "If it's severe enough. Follow me." My head rests against William's chest, and I hear his heart beating strong and fast. He cradles me like a child. The sound of running water rises up. I'm in a copper bathroom, expansive and softly glittering from another chandelier. A chandelier in a bathroom. "Put her in the hot water. I'll get blood."

William sets me on the edge of the tub and begins stripping off my clothes, heedless of my protestations. "Anne, now is not the time for propriety. Your clothes are soaking wet and freezing from the snow."

"I can do it," I say weakly, although I can barely sit up. Water is filling the tub, hot and steaming.

"I've seen a naked woman before." My jacket and slender tank top are pulled off and I wrap my arms around my chest, shielding myself. Since the buttons are gone, he is easily sliding my pants down, leaving me wearing only black lace panties. He picks me up and places me in the warm water. *Ah, heaven.* I lean my head back against the tub, drifting off. "Stay awake," he orders, shaking me roughly. His fingers press into my bones.

"So rough," I mumble, "for a gentleman."

Vander appears and I reach for a towel hanging beside the tub and pull it into the water, covering myself.

Vander looks away. "Give her this."

It is a steaming goblet of blood. William holds it to my lips as if I am a child too weak to hold a cup. "Drink, darling."

Darling.

He called me darling.

I can barely swallow but somehow manage to sip.

"Drink it down, Anne. All of it." His hand is on the back of my head, holding it up.

I obey, sucking the hot, thick fluid down and reviving with each swallow. My hands grasp the goblet like a drunk, desperate for one last swig of whiskey. Ignoring the dull throb in my wrist, I pull the goblet from William and gulp at it, oblivious to his presence.

Vander appears again. "This is what she needs. Fresh life. Take it." He hands William a plump rabbit the size of a small fox. He is the color of marbled topaz. William hesitates only a moment before cradling it in one hand. Thankfully, Vander withdraws.

Through the walls, I hear Emily's voice, high and angry, questioning Santos who, sounding cornered, barks back.

Shaking, I set the empty goblet on the side of the tub and William places it on a table with the pitcher.

"Take him quick," he says, holding out the bunny. It stares at me with warm, wide eyes.

I look at William. "I don't want you to watch . . ." My voice is small. "...and be scared away."

"Scare *me?*" He gives an abrupt laugh. "That's impossible, Anne. I know what you are. I'm not afraid."

"It's ugly."

"Life is ugly and we must face it. I'm in your life now." His voice falters. "I mean . . . that is . . . if you'll let me." He groans in frustration. "God, Anne, how I wish you'd trust me."

The rabbit is squirming in his hand, soaking up William's tension. I take it from him and lay the poor creature against my chest, stroking him and murmuring. I am wet from the bath, but he rests against me and calms. After a quick glance at William, I grasp the rabbit by the ears, exposing his neck, and sink my teeth into the flesh. Already my teeth are sharper than before. With each swallow I take, the pain in my wrist subsides. There is no struggle to contend with, only a soft acceptance, and I am immensely relieved William doesn't have to witness a fight.

When I'm done, William wraps the corpse in a towel and calls for Vander, to whom he gives it at the door. When William turns back to me, my eyes are glazing with tears. "There's something you must know," I say. "Something you won't forgive."

"You underestimate my affection."

Numbly, I shake my head. "Dana is dead. I killed her with . . . the saber. She was turned." The tears come faster now. There is no way he can possibly accept this. "I drove it through her heart."

Surprise swims beneath his gaze. Perched on the side of the tub, he takes a washcloth, gently wiping the blood and tears from my face. "You did the right thing, Anne. She would be a remorseless killer. Without morality or compassion. You spared the world from a demon."

"I killed my partner." I am sobbing now.

"You protected her from a life of killing. You gave her the peace you were never allowed."

"She didn't want it."

"Which is why she did not deserve the darkness. She wasn't worthy."

I'm confused. Dazed. The blood has revived me, yet I feel drained. I have lost too much and what I have finally found has come too late. Tears run down my face and I wipe at them furiously.

He tilts my chin up and kisses me, devouring my sorrow. Heat floods me. His lips are warm, his hand strong on my neck and then I'm kissing him back, wrapping my hands around his shoulders, surrendering to the pull of his body, wanting his heat. I forget the towel and climb into his lap, dripping wet while a hunger rises, seizing me.

I am *alive*.

Civility no longer matters. Those rules are for humans. Not me.

Passion burns away all shame. I am naked in his lap and he kisses me hard, touching me everywhere until I am gasping. He is picking me up, laying me down on the carpet beneath a soft gas chandelier, and I am pulling him to me, wanting him, needing him. Now.

God, yes, yes, yes, please, yes.

A crash sounds in the other room and William freezes, breathing hard against my throat.

"Enough!" Vander bellows, whether to Emily or Santos, I don't know and don't care. All I want is William, his heart pounding against my breast, his heat coursing down my throat, his body hot and hard inside me.

I press my nakedness against him. "Don't stop," I plead. "William, kiss me." I wrap a leg around him, pulling him closer. "I want you. *Now,*" I demand. My voice is hoarse, full of vibrations I've never heard before. It sounds like someone else is speaking. My fingers bruise his skin. I don't know who this woman is but she feels powerfully good.

He takes my hands, pinning them above my head. His fingers wrap around my wrist, sending a delicious pain through my arm. "Not here, Anne. Not like this." His voice is thick as smoke. I lift my body to meet his, to capture him with a kiss, but he resists.

"Anne," he moans, gripping my wrists, hard. Hard enough to break a mortal girl, but not me. "I want our first time to be special, not a frenzied thrash on the floor with people just outside the door."

My breath catches. He *wants* me. I can feel his desire against me and want to flip him onto his back and take him right here on the floor. He couldn't stop me if he tried. I know he wants it, but it would be wrong to use my strength against him. I close my eyes, fighting the impulse, struggling to endure the ache of pain throbbing in my core.

I want to consume him.

He kisses me again, pressing his weight into my hands, his heart heaving in his chest. Then with a groan he pulls away and draws me to my feet.

Disappointment breaks over me in blazing agony. It hurts so much I could cry.

He reaches for another towel, this one the size of a small sheet, and wraps it about me. I blink away tears. His eyes are storm dark. I can feel the heat of his skin in the air between us as if the sun burns beneath his very flesh.

Who needs the light when you have this?

"I apologize." He runs his hands through his hair, leaving it in damp disarray like a mad professor. "I lose all restraint when I'm with you." He takes a heaving breath. "You must put on some clothes before I completely lose my mind."

"I have some here," Vander says from outside the door. William closes his eyes, knowing Vander heard everything. Emily brushes past Vander into the room and stops when she sees me in William's arms, naked and panting.

"I take it you are feeling better," she says.

"Yes." I blush. "Much better."

Emily looks at William. His shirt is translucent with wetness and clings to him like a second skin.

She turns back to me. "You need a human. Not a rabbit."

"It's a start," says William. "Her bruises are already fading." Lightly, he brushes a thumb over my cheek where Webb struck me.

Emily hands me the clothes. "It might help for you to dry off first. William, I think you might want to check on Sergeant Santos, before he turns on your host and impales him with one of his own weapons."

An alarmed look crosses William's face. He gives me a look that screams he wants to stay, but reluctantly leaves me with Emily. Silently, she begins to make me presentable. Vander has lent me a little dress from the 1920s, and as I slide it on I wonder to whom it belonged. His wife? Daughter? My bare arms and legs look startlingly white against the deep violet, and I can't help feeling like a bit of a harlot after my behavior with William.

"The color of night," Emily says.

"Hmm?"

"This dress' violet color suits you. It complements your eyes."

"I find it hard to believe Vander didn't have a pair of slacks around."

Emily scoffs. "Like all aristocrats, he's a slave to his treasure, living in this castle beneath the earth, like a dragon chained to its jewels."

I tense.

"What is it? What's wrong?"

"Nothing," I whisper. She looks at me intently. "It's nothing."

"Tell me," she says.

"Webb . . ." I take a rough breath. "Webb said we could have children. *I* could have a baby."

Emily frowns. "That's preposterous. He sensed your weakness and struck. Even if it were possible, this is not a life for children." Gently, she turns me around and zips me into my dress. Her voice softens. "Our lives are not fairy tales, sister. We must face reality." When she is done she spins me to face her and stares at me inscrutably. "Now you're even more impossible to resist."

Self-consciously I pull the dress down with my good hand, hoping to make it a little longer, but it's no use. I feel naked. "My boots," I say. "I want my boots." They are as worn and soft as lambskin. Emily helps me lace them and ties a tight double-knotted bow, easing my vulnerability with every pull of her strong, sure hands.

"It might be time for another pair," she offers, eying the ancient oiled leather. "I believe you've had these since Thorpe Green."

"Branwell gave them to me for Christmas. They're my only connection to him."

"The connection is in our hearts, not our boots. Are you cold?"

"I feel better. Em, I thought that was it. If Santos hadn't been there . . ."

Her brow darkens. "Do you think Webb wanted to kill you or keep you?"

"I don't know. He said he wanted to keep me, but I told him I'd rather die, and then he drank so long and hard, I thought he would never stop."

"He will stop. We will stop him."

"No, Em." I grab her by the arm. "You mustn't go anywhere near him. You must stay away. If he sees you, he will want you. He wants a companion to share the light with."

Her mouth sets in that stubborn way of hers that means her mind is made up.

I want to shake her. "He is too strong for you. He's a *Day* Walker. It's made him incredibly powerful."

"Shhh, Anne. Come rest by the fire. You're still cold as ice."

"You don't understand. He's unlike any I've ever seen before. Even in war. He's different."

"I know. He's a Day Walker. Come." Emily leads me toward the fire. When I enter the room, all eyes fall on me—William's feel like a torch against my skin.

"I'll be damned," Santos says. "I didn't think she was going to make it. You guys just don't fucking die, do you?"

"Stop talking like a heathen," snaps Emily. "Can't you see she's fragile? Your coarseness wears at her spirit."

"If she even has a spirit."

"She has one far nobler than yours, I promise."

He spins on her. "Anne killed Dana in cold blood. Stabbed her through the *heart*! You call that noble?"

"How many people have you killed?" Emily flares.

"Stop!" Vander says. "This bickering only distracts us from our goal."

"And what is that?" I ask, collapsing in a chair by the fire. Woody lies at my feet, an ear cocked to catch the argument.

William slams his hand on a table shaking the crystal. "To find this monster, hunt Webb down, and kill him."

Chapter 50

"No, William!" I exclaim. "You're not a hunter."

"You don't know what he is," Santos says, pacing like a caged tiger. "You don't know anything about us."

"And you don't know anything about Webb. You have no idea what you're dealing with."

"He has no idea what *he's* dealing with," says Santos.

Emily shakes her head in disgust. "You're not going against some malnourished goatherd in a Stone Age country. Drop the macho act."

"It's not an *act*."

"That's even worse." She stares Santos down across the room, and he shoots her a look that suggests any moment he might cross the silken Oriental rug and grab her by the throat. Emily smiles like she wants him to. Like she's *daring* him to.

I shiver and William brings me the softest fur throw, draping it over my shoulders, then begins to rewrap my broken wrist, discarding the wet, dirty bandage and replacing it with a long silk scarf that has somehow magically appeared. I don't want him to go. I don't want him to fight. No one in this room is strong enough or savage enough to take on a Day Walker. Not even Santos.

"You can't beat him," I say.

"Good thing you're not military." Santos spins on me. "We would have lost every fuc—" he stops himself "—every war we ever fought."

"You're doing a good job of that all on your own," Emily says.

Santos' eyes go ice-cold, silencing her. Yes, I think. See how romantic your Heathcliff is now.

"Stay on point," William demands. He ties off my bandage and turns to Santos. "Don't forget who you're talking to, Atticus. No matter how strong they may be, these are women, not twenty-year-old Rangers. Adapt to your audience or we will get absolutely nowhere."

Santos stops pacing the room and collapses into a chair, running his hands over his face. "This is crazy," he moans. "I don't know what's real. What the hell is a Day Walker? How many of them are there? Is the entire town crawling with . . . with . . . *vampires?*"

I sigh and close my eyes while William fills Santos in, bringing him up-to-date on what information we've pieced together. As I sit by the fire, Woody curls up and falls asleep in my lap. Vander brings me another goblet of blood that tastes of cinnamon. Already I am healing, but I sip to regain more strength. Emily refuses to drink or sit. Instead, she stands near the far side of the mantel, edged toward the exit, glancing continually toward the tall carved doors as if any moment they will slam shut, locking us all inside. Santos throws back a shot of ancient scotch from a nearby decanter followed by another in rapid succession. William takes nothing while calmly explaining to Santos what we know of Day Walkers and menarche while Santos looks on, bewildered. Thankfully, my first kill is not part of the story.

"Menarche?" Santos asks.

"A girl's first blood," William explains. "Apparently it's full of power. Strength."

"How did you ever figure this out?" Emily asks me quietly.

I whisper so softly only she can hear. "When you tell me about your lover, I will tell you about my first kill." Her eyes glide away.

"Did you kill Webb?" William asks.

Santos scowls. "I don't think so. I shot him twice and clipped him a third time as he ran off. He's fast. *Insane* fast."

I turn to Santos. "How'd you find me?"

"Your text. When I got there, Dana was dead and Webb was carrying you off. I didn't know what went down. Who was what and who killed Dana? With a *saber?* None of it made sense. I tried to follow, but Webb was too fast. Eventually I tracked him to Whisper Mountain and found him . . . *feeding* on you." He grimaces. "I thought he was going to kill you."

"I thought so too."

"How badly do you think he's injured?" William asks.

"Not as bad as Jadallah and he lasted three days."

"Jadallah wasn't a Day Walker," I remind them. "Dana told me that she was soon going to have her virgin and become a Day Walker too. They would live together in the sun."

"Christ. She really was a selfish bitch," Santos says.

Vander sits in an embroidered high-backed chair and drums his fingers against the carved armrest. "If Webb is injured, he'll want to feed again. Especially if he thinks people are coming for him. We heal fast, but it takes more than a few hours to heal from a gunshot wound."

Abruptly, Santos jumps up from his chair. "We've got to go now. While he's weak, before he feeds. We're wasting time."

I search for the moon through Vander's skylight. "There are only a few hours of night left. Webb's sun-strength is fading. He'll weaken with daylight."

"We'll make sure he's dead before daylight," William says.

"The only Night Walker you ever fought was Jadallah and he was severely injured. Webb is different. Don't rush into this. You need a plan."

Santos walks to the wall of weapons and surveys his choices. "The plan is to strike while he's off balance. We'll find him and gun him down. I'm a sniper. I'll hit him from downwind with a round not even he can survive. Vander's got an arsenal here. We don't *exit* until the parasite is dead. Resources: overwhelming firepower, three vampires and two combat-experienced vets."

"Oh, I'm not coming," Vander says.

Confounded, Santos stares at him.

"Anne is far too weak to fight," says Emily.

"You're not going without me," I protest.

"It's completely out of the question," William says, examining a shotgun before placing it in a black canvas duffel. "You're half starved and injured."

I set Woody down and stand. "Let me make something perfectly clear." I look at William and Emily. "I will not stay behind while you fight without me. If we do this, we do it together."

"You're not a fighter, Anne," William says gently. "You said so yourself just last night."

"But she *is* a paramedic," says Santos, turning his back on Vander. "We may need her. She can stay clear, out of the line of fire."

I nod, surprised Santos and I agree on something.

William gives me a worried look and I arch an eyebrow at him as if to say, *don't you dare refuse me.* With a darkened brow, he resumes stuffing the duffel full of weapons: rifles, pistols, knives. *Grenades.* He slides a German dagger beneath his belt and then reaches for a saber. Why not take along a nuclear bomb too? Maybe then they'd actually have a chance against this Alpha.

Santos reaches for ammunition, draping it over his chest like a glittering sash. "I don't see what she can do." He indicates Emily. "It's not like she's going to get into hand-to-hand combat with him. She can stay with Anne."

"I've handled a weapon or two in my time," Emily says, eying a rifle. "Though I prefer my bare hands. Guns are too easy. So little finesse is required."

"You obviously have no idea what you're talking about," says Santos.

"I've killed a hundred times more than you ever will," Emily counters.

"Not something to brag about."

"That's all your kind do." Emily sneers at Santos. "Brag. Wave your flags and nail your animal heads to the wall so everyone can see how many innocent beasts you've killed."

"I've never killed the innocent!" says Santos.

"That's what all killers say." Emily's anger toward him surprises me. He saved me from Webb. You'd think she'd show a little gratitude.

"Take her along," Vander advises Santos. "You will need her. Two mortal men are not enough for a Day Walker."

"It will have to be," William says. "I won't risk Anne's only surviving family. Santos and I have hunted and captured the most ruthless killers in foreign territory. This is *our* home. With the right weapons and strategy, we can take on Webb. He's a doctor, not a soldier. When Santos shot him, he fled. He preys on little girls with no worldly experience. He's never been hunted by the likes of us, and he shall learn it is an entirely different experience. One he will not survive."

I grit my teeth and remain silent. I'm not going to argue with William in front of others, but if he thinks Emily and I will stay in the safe zone while he fights, he's in for a surprise. It's always been my way to exert my will quietly, with little drama, and that's what I plan to do now. Smooth as a fox, I move to the kill wall and gather the few weapons I'm comfortable with—slender, sharp, elegant things. No one pays me any mind except Emily, who observes with approval.

"Should you call SWAT in on this?" asks Vander, staring darkly at the ground. His brow is creased in consternation, his hands clenched in his lap, as if he envisions perfectly well the carnage about to unfold.

"No." Santos shakes his head. "We deal with Webb ourselves." Santos throws the duffel over his shoulder. "Every minute we waste, he grows stronger. We must go *now*, before he regroups."

William nods grimly in agreement. "We'll start with his house."

The grandfather clock sounds, jolting my very bones with its four long chimes.

With a long sigh, Vander looks at us all, shaking his head as if he can't believe what's happening. "Your self-sacrificing nobility inspires and impels me to offer greater support." He rises like a grand aristocrat, striding to the fireplace and sweeping Woody up in a graceful arm. The little dog blinks at them. "Tonight, my intrepid friends, no one stays behind. I have one more thing to offer and where it goes, I must go as well."

"What more can you possibly provide us with?" William asks. "You've already given us so much."

"Every warrior must have the proper weapons *and* the proper steed."

"You have a horse in here?" Santos asks, looking around suspiciously.

Vander laughs. "Better than a horse. *Appropriate* transportation. Specifically designed for a rapid escape in case all hell ever broke loose."

I remember my car. "My Mini is at Lookout Point."

"No matter," Vander says with a tone that fashioned the Biltmore's very earth. His eyes glint wickedly. "The time has finally come to unleash the Beast."

Chapter 51

"The Beast?" Santos says. "Tell me there's not another monster locked up in this place."

Emily and I exchange curious looks.

Vander laughs. "What a vivid imagination you have, Sergeant. You and the professor run ahead in your squad car. The ladies and I will follow at a reasonable distance in my beastly RV."

"What's an RV?" asks Emily.

"A recreational vehicle," I say annoyed. "If you think I'm going to cruise along behind in an—"

"Anne, trust me," Vander says. "The Beast has important resources and you'll want to familiarize yourself with the medical equipment."

"Excellent idea," William exclaims as if it were settled.

I flash him my darkest look. His protectiveness is wearing at my nerves. I have the sudden urge to thrust him against a wall and show him how strong I really am. Or throw him into bed. Inwardly I blush. With everything going on, how can I even think of such a thing? Because now, despite his stifling chivalry, I want him more than ever.

If we survive this night I will claim him, not in blood, but in body.

As if sensing my thoughts, his gaze falls on me with fervent intensity. Obsession swims in his eyes and a trickle of unease crawls up my spine.

"Promise me, Vander," he says while staring at me. "Promise me you'll keep Anne safe."

Vander bows in acquiescence.

Emily has drifted toward the door, unwilling to follow behind Santos and William, but not wanting to leave me. Santos reaches for her and pulls her close. "Be careful. Webb doesn't know you exist. Let's keep it that way."

She doesn't reply, only looks at him with eyes the color of a lit universe, burning with stars and darkness. A tremble, invisible to him, begins in her but she catches it. She is at war with herself.

Why?

The whole world swims within her gaze. Santos seems to fall into it, mesmerized, then with a deep breath drags his eyes off her and steps out. Emily's eyes track Santos as he steps into the darkness.

William crosses the room, gathering me to him. His hands find my face and he looks at me, inside me, down into my very soul.

The world falls away.

"I've been searching for you my whole life, Anne, even in my dreams. To find you is the greatest gift. Perhaps there is a God." He drags his thumb across my mouth. "I love you," he whispers. "I will always love you."

Tears slide down my skin onto his fingers, all my sorrow falling into the palm of his hand.

He kisses me and before I can catch my breath, he is gone.

Chapter 52

I steel my courage for the battle ahead as Vander drives Emily and me for miles along a steep mountain road in the Beast—a black, gazillion-dollar RV tricked out against the sun—his getaway vehicle if one was ever needed, prepared for every contingency. It holds two dozen genetically modified rabbits, a weapons cache, top of the line medical equipment, plus a navigation and communication center linked to its very own space-launched satellite.

In a green down parka, Woody sits in the passenger seat.

The Biltmore's top secret security system is able to track every emergency response vehicle in the county and Vander has followed Santos' police vehicle to Whisper Mountain. He studies a blip on the screen before slowing and pulling over.

"Santos has parked somewhere close," he says. "He's hidden his car quite well."

Emily grazes her fingers over Woody's head as she steps out. I follow, but Vander stops me with a gentle hand on my arm. "I'll be waiting right here," he says. "If you can make it back by sunrise, I'll get us home."

I nod gravely. "Thank you, Vander, for everything."

He gives me a wistful smile. "Remember my dear, you two are no ordinary women. No ordinary Night Walkers. It is an honor to assist you."

I can't help but smile at our newfound kinship. I place my hand over his and squeeze, then turn and step out into the night.

With my sister by my side, I walk through the forest. It's like when we were girls roaming the moors, only this time we are better armed. Snow drifts down from above, obscuring the sky and a violet moon slants through the trees, cold and dim. The wind moans like a woman giving birth, while the scent of crushed pine breaks beneath our boots. I'm dressed inappropriately, wearing only a night-colored dress and ancient knee-high, lace-up boots and I shiver against the hard breeze. A sharp WWII dagger lies against my calf, snug in my boot, and I have a new saber on my hip.

Emily is tracking William and Santos through the softly fallen snow so that we can catch up with them after their head start. Like me, she never had any intention of waiting behind while they fought Webb without us. Her hunting skill is preternatural and she moves with a feline grace through the night. She's wearing her soft leather jacket, a thin taunt against the freeze. A knife is in her boot, a shotgun snug against her back, and an Uzi is grasped lightly in her hands. She looks ready for anything, while I, on the other hand, feel spectral as a wraith. A ghost walking. When I glance down at my hand poised above the snow, I barely detect a difference in shade.

Before us, high up Whisper Mountain, the great house looms, glowing like a demon camp. Its light leaks faintly through the night, straining toward us, swallowed by forest. Webb lives here, staring down on us, a malevolent king upon his throne. My hand goes to my throat where he bit me. It aches. My whole body aches at the horror of seeing him again.

I am cold and the night is black, but tonight I embrace the darkness and gather it about me like armor. A midnight owl watches from a gnarled tree limb then glances toward the house, blinking. A warning. The moon hovers above, brushing me, as if to say, *I am here, sister. I am here.*

What though the Sun had left my sky; To save me from despair
The blessed moon arose on high, and shone serenely there.

I have had friends all along. All this time, I have never been alone.

Emily suddenly stops, turning to me. "Anne, there's something I have to tell you. In case something happens."

"I assure you, Em, something is most definitely going to happen."

Her face is intent. Determined. "It's about Bran. Everything I told you is true. I've seen his art on walls and underpasses, broken-down warehouses, concrete roofs—"

"What's this have to do with anything?"

"It's all true, except—" she bites her lip, uncertain "—he's not what brought me here."

The wind has stalled and the forest is perfectly silent as if the earth is holding her breath. Even the owl barely breathes. "This can wait," I whisper.

"It was Santos."

"Santos?"

"I've seen him before in Afghanistan."

"So you told me." My impatience is growing. Our friends are about to be slaughtered and Emily has finally decided that now is the time to chat.

"He killed my . . . my . . ." She searches for the right word, then her shoulders sag. "Friend."

My breath catches. "Jadallah?"

Her eyes widen in surprise. "How did you know?"

"Jadallah was your *lover*?"

"Santos tortured him for three days then burned him alive," she hisses.

"He killed four of Santos' men."

"After they cornered and trapped him like an animal."

"He was an insurgent."

"Insurgent?" She gives me a bewildered look.

"What do you want with Santos?"

She looks at me sharply. "What do you think?"

I shake my head, astounded.

"To kill him. Once and for all. Tonight."

A blast shatters the night and I freeze. Emily pulls me behind a tree. "Don't get caught in the cross fire. Stay behind the trees."

Shrieking tears through the night, a crying and yelping sound, full of agony and fear. My memory is yanked back to the wilds of Scotland, hiding and scavenging, stumbling upon a great stray dog, all roiling eyes and long strings of red, frothing slobber, being systematically torn apart by wolves.

Only this time it is no dog that howls. It is a man.

"Wait here," Emily whispers. "I'll go."

"No!"

But she is gone, a shadow streaking through the night.

"Emily! Wait!"

The forest closes in on me, reeking with death. Screaming rends the air, trembling the trees, shaking snow from their limbs. In a panic, I run toward the cries, slipping wildly in the frost. Falling. Jagged stone rips my knees, scraping them raw. They sting with dirt and snow, but I am up, running toward gunfire and the scent of blood.

Wait for me.

They must all wait for me.

They must not leave this life without me.

Chapter 53

I find them beneath a cone of moonlight.

They are all grievously wounded.

William. Santos. Emily.

Savannah!

My dear God.

The Granger girl is there, apparently unharmed yet slack against a tree, scarlet hair flowing down her shoulders like blood. Guilt snatches my breath away. No. No. *NO!* Of all the girls, not Savannah! I led her to him. Handed her over to Webb like a sacrificial offering.

She trusted me. The Grangers *trust* me.

Shame, hot and thick, fills me with nausea. How could I be so blind? *How?*

Santos lies still as death on the ground, his body tossed like a discarded afterthought, weapons in pieces. William is standing, staked to a towering red oak with a saber shoved through his shoulder, deep into the ancient tree. Webb, riddled with bullets, snarls at him like a rabid dog, straining toward his throat with dripping teeth, held back by the double-barreled shotgun William presses into his shoulder.

He fires.

Flesh and blood splatter the snow, showering William, spraying my boots. The blast hurls Webb onto his back. William cracks open the shotgun to reload, sliding in a shell, but it snags and tumbles to the ground.

Impossibly, Webb begins to rise.

His eyes are demonic, hate-glazed and blazing, a hell-brother in his full glory. Bone-white muscle, livid and gleaming, writhes beneath his flayed shirt like a shark's. Wrath streaks his face in slashes of lurid pink. The good doctor is gone. Hyde is here.

Eyes locked on William, Webb climbs to his feet.

Beside Santos, Emily lies weaponless, femur fractured mid-thigh, fighting to sit up. Bone juts out of her flesh in wet, broken shards. She sees me and motions me away with a bloody hand. "Hide," she mouths. "Go."

I stop before her, gazing down. "Is he alive?" I indicate Santos.

She nods weakly, taking tiny, shallow breaths. With her good leg, she tries to push me away. "Please, Anne, *run.*"

Santos has a deep laceration across his skull. Fallen, he looks younger, vulnerable. *Human.* Even near death, his skin is earth colored. I remember how his blood smelled full of sunshine.

"Turn him," I order.

Understanding lights Emily's eyes. She bends to his throat like a dark Carmilla and piercing the flesh with her sharp teeth, she drinks long and deep. When I think she will kill him, she stops, bites her wrist hard and holds it to his lips.

Her heart-threaded blood smears Santos' mouth and she opens his lips wider with her fingers, letting it drip upon his tongue. Santos' lips twitch. He swallows. His hand moves to her wrist, grabbing and grasping it to him. In a flash, he is upon her, pressing her into the earth, sinking his teeth into her throat, tearing it open. She's too weak to stop him. He is drinking her, swallowing my sister, my greatest friend, before my very eyes.

Santos is killing Emily.

Why didn't I turn him? It should have been me.

Webb stalks his prey, smiling while William reloads. In a flash, he lunges for William's throat, hissing and spraying his face with blood. William slams the shotgun between them, holding Webb back, but unable to fire. A ring of crimson surrounds the two like a witches' circle as the sun begins its ascent. The heat and smell of blood crashes in my head, dropping me to my knees.

Webb's savage musk. William. Emily. Santos. Savannah's moon-time is here, lancing the air with a clean, pure scent. The forest is full of blood. They will die before me. All my loves and friends and guardians overcome by brutality.

The night is here and there is no grace.

If this is my fate, I will seize it.

On hands and knees I crawl to the Granger girl, eyes locked on her, snow stinging my raw knees. A glimmer of hope lights her eyes. She believes I have always been there when she needed me. Her blue angel. Safety.

Oh, the hell her father will wreak.

I reach for her hand and grasp it, shocked by its soft, blazing warmth, then notice she's tied, hand and foot. Her tiny fingernails sparkle blue in the moonbeams. I rip her free and she clings to me, surprisingly strong for such a little thing.

"Miss Anne," she whispers fiercely. "I knew you'd come. I knew."

Yes, my darling. Death always comes.

I thread my fingers through her hair.

"Have courage, my sweet. I'm here. No fear, only love."

I pull her to the ground.

Daughter of Carnage.

I turn her head aside.

Grief Bringer.

I sink my teeth into her throat.

Death Walker.

I suck.

The blood is hot between her legs. I squeeze my knee between her thighs until I feel it slick against my open wound. My lips press her honeyed neck. All her descendants lay against my tongue and with piercing love, I drink them down, one by one by one.

I swallow her life and am born again.

Chapter 54

In a rush, I'm on my feet, throwing Santos off Emily. He spins and moves for me in black fury.

I point to Webb. "Kill him."

His eyes follow my hand. Like an attack dog, he leaps, slamming Webb to the ground. He strikes hard and fast, pounding him in rapid fire before the Alpha can recover.

But Webb is a Day Walker, and Santos is no match.

Webb rises, shaking off the blows like a dog in a rainstorm. Each hit from Santos knocks him to his knees, but he is up again with a brutal smile.

I run to William. He's dropped the shotgun and torment is scrawled across his face. Carefully, I release him from the tree, stabilizing the blade in his shoulder. His breath comes ragged and blood drains down his shirt, drenching his chest. It smells so strong I can taste it. Fire and wisdom and moors riddled with grief.

"You shouldn't have come," he says through gritted teeth.

"I won't live without you," I whisper.

He shakes his head, refusing my words. "The shotgun," William rasps, nodding toward the fallen weapon. "It's chambered. Take it."

My eyes linger on his, not wanting to release him, but his gaze is hooded, his soul locked away. Beneath the trees, Savannah lies dead and nearby Emily struggles for life. William stumbles toward my sister and, sinking to his knees, presses the gaping wound in her neck with a handkerchief. They are both critically wounded.

Only Santos and I remain on our feet.

I reach for the shotgun. The metal is warm and light in my hands. Santos is slowing. He roars with every frustrated blow, yet Webb is like a bear shrugging off a rabid German shepherd. His strength is unnatural. Demonic. If Webb knew how to fight, Santos would be dead already.

With a violent kick, Santos slams him against a gnarled oak, then gulps at the air, struggling to breathe. He is faltering. I raise the gun for a shot, but Webb lunges up, charging his enemy. Santos stumbles out of the way and slips, his knee twisting. He crashes to the ground while Webb rushes at him like lightning.

I can't shoot Webb without hitting Santos.

In a blink, Santos scrambles up and pivots, sweeping Webb's feet out, hurling him back against the tree. Snow showers them like a baptism. Fog drifts across the moon casting the forest in shade. Santos gasps for air as if drowning.

I shove him aside.

The gun is unnatural to me and I toss it to my left hand and stand before the doctor, unafraid. He leans back against the tree as if resting a moment, unthreatened by my presence. He surveys me and a glimmer of pride flits across his face as if his little girl has finally grown up. A smile touches his lips.

It turns my stomach. The last thing I want is this monster's approval.

He looks at me almost seductively, blood dripping down his face as if he has a crown of thorns upon his head, and in that moment, Webb is beautiful. He wants me as I am and my heart leans toward him, desperate for acceptance. I feel a leap inside my chest like an addict who has unexpectedly stumbled upon her poison. With a wrenching of will, I gather my heart back to myself, enclosing it within my impenetrable dignity.

I need no acceptance from him.

I will be my own judge.

Not God.

Not family.

Only me.

Webb smiles. My entire body recoils upon itself, an instinct of spirit, for now he looks a lecherous Jesus. An abomination. A debasement of everything I hold selfless and pure. Medicine. Innocence. Savannah. Slowly, he moves toward me.

Grasping my saber, I drive it straight through Webb's chest.

"Payback," I hiss.

He growls, pinned like an insect, but bloody hell, I've missed his heart. The saber stakes the tree, sticking out the other side yet still Webb lunges for me. I slam my boot against him, pressing him back against the rough bark. His face is drawn, tight with fatigue, but I'm strong and new. Santos breathes hard beside me, hands on his knees, trying to catch his breath. Blood drips from his head onto the ground like tears. He glares at Webb.

"Tell me, *medic*," Webb snarls. "How did Savannah taste?"

Fury lights my veins like fire. "How dare you take her?" I growl. "She was *mine*."

"Why did you bring her to me when she was perfectly fine?" asks Webb. "Was it because you were *hungry*? Or because you're a weakling who preys on the sick and injured like a virus."

My throat closes in guilt. "I protect the weak."

"You're not strong enough to protect anyone. Not even a little girl."

Savannah.

She lives within me now: mountains and wildflowers, family and love.

I *ended* her.

Swallowed her like a drop of honey.

Ate her like a wolf.

But as the earth is my witness, not a child on my watch shall ever be slain again. I'm changed. Awake. Now I will guard my strength and fight for it, eternal hellfire be damned.

Webb's time is over. My time has come.

"I am the Day Walker now."

He grasps my boot and laughs. "You don't have the heart for it."

"I will adapt." Sliding my boot to the tree, I place the barrel of the shotgun hard against Webb's chest. The beat of his heart thrums through the metal, traveling up into my palm. I feel it in my bones. He reaches for the barrel and tries to pull it away, but I'm the stronger one now.

I look him in the eye. His breath smells like death. "This is *my* town and your behavior will not be tolerated."

He roars and I pull the trigger. Fangs bared, he takes the hit as blood and flesh explode, raining down upon me. His chest opens like a great red sun and the smell of a thousand virgins drains into the night.

Chapter 55

The sun is rising. I smell it like blood. I am safe, but not Santos, not Emily. Santos shakes violently, confusion breaking across his face, breath scrambling on the edge of panic. His turning came too fast, too rough. I grab him by both arms and force him to look at me.

"Hold it together. You are still yourself and we're not done here."

Emily lies broken in the moonlight, gazing toward the sky, waiting for death. Her breath is unspooling. Her jagged femur gleams through torn denim like wet ivory, but worse is the blood loss.

"Vander is waiting by the road. Take her to him. Quick."

Emily flinches from Santos as he moves toward her.

"My God, your throat," he groans. "I'm sorry. I'm so sorry." Gently he slides his arms beneath her and picks her up. "I didn't mean to. I couldn't stop."

She takes a ragged breath. "I know," she whispers, then rests her head against his chest and closes her eyes.

Hold on, sister! This time I can save you. Don't let go!

William's hand is cold in mine, but his breath is warm against my cheek. I kneel by his side. He looks at me grimly. "You always were the strong one."

"We are all strong." I place his good arm over my shoulder and raise him to his feet. "There are supplies ahead. I can fix this."

"I don't want to be turned," he says. "I'd rather die."

"I wouldn't." Hurt rings in my voice. "Never without your consent."

My mind turns to Santos. No one asked his consent. How will his ancestral spirits frame his rebirth? Who will they tell him he is? I don't know much about Santeria, but I know how it feels to believe your god has turned against you and thinks you evil. Fallen.

Oh brother, forgive me.

William and I begin the slow walk back. The forest is full of sounds I've long heard only in my dreams. Life is awakening. I hear the glide of a bat, a squirrel's breath, snow melting, the sun being born. Heat radiates from every tree I pass, each one with its own distinct signature: oak, pine, fir, maple and dogwood. Poplar. The earth smells radiant with fox and bear, snow and sun. The night softens on its way to dawn yet still the stars blaze like beacons.

Despite the horror, life is beautiful.

I look back.

Savannah lies on her back, staring into the forest. A small tender hand reaches out, open, and her hair spills like a flaming cloak upon the snow. In this world of grey and white, it sears the image upon my mind like a torch thrust at me out of the dark. She is whiter than the snow. Almost transparent.

Drained.

There is no happily ever after.

Yet if by some miracle heaven exists, I pray for my sisters Maria and Elizabeth to meet Savannah at the gates.

I will look at her and remember.
I will not turn away from what I've done.
I will face the darkness and own it.

✿

In Vander's Beast, I treat my patients as he drives us back to the Biltmore. Emily is too weak to feed. She lies on a narrow surgical table, drifting at the edge of consciousness while I give her a transfusion. Santos stands close, face tense. On an ebony dining table, William waits stoically. He too has lost a lot of blood. We are all alive yet he remains resolutely silent, caved over himself, an arm braced against the table, grimacing with every breath he takes. There is no joy in his face. No relief. He doesn't whisper sweet endearments or take me in his arms. His countenance is stone cold. Though he struggles to conceal it, I sense a repressed fury simmering beneath the facade.

I sentenced his best friend to eternal murder and killed a girl in front of him. Savannah was no marbled rabbit. She was a little girl and William witnessed it all.

My heart shatters in agony, but I refuse to ask for forgiveness. William is *alive*. Emily is *alive*. And I will bear all the hatred in the world for them to live one more day.

As blood streams into my sister, I leave her with Santos. Her leg must be reset but it can wait. William cannot. As I turn to him, I sense him recoil in anticipation of my touch. Pretending not to notice, I cut his shirt away, start an IV and suture his wound. His shirt is off, his skin streaked in blood, and I try to keep my hands from shaking. This is the first time I've seen him undressed, felt his naked skin beneath my fingers, traced the curve of his lean, bare muscles. I've ministered to a thousand unclothed men, but with him it feels different. Intimate. Personal. His burning warmth is gone, replaced with an icy coldness. I struggle to remain professional and not linger against his flesh.

He doesn't look at me.

With my newfound strength, I read his body with every touch. Deep within his rigid muscles, I feel restrained trembling. I sense the throbbing of his blood, the threads of his nerves touching, transmitting, the wash of chemicals flooding his brain and coursing through his body. Serotonin. Dopamine. Adrenaline. I can smell them all and I know he still wants me, physically at least, even if he is waging a great war against it.

Lust is small consolation in the wake of love lost, but it is something.

When I have bandaged him and given him blood, I return to Emily to reset her leg. The blood has revived her some and now she is watchful.

"This will hurt," I say, "but when it's done, you'll feel better." She nods bravely.

I take Santos' hands and place them on her hips. "Hold her firmly, so she doesn't slide when I pull traction."

Their eyes meet for a second, and I wonder if she will shove him away. A flash of vulnerability lights her face. She appears slender beneath his hands, strangely fragile, a look she quickly buries. Santos' face is hard, his hands firm. To my surprise, she surrenders beneath him.

"Hold on to the table," I say. "When the pain comes, don't let go." Her hands clench the sides and she stares up at the ceiling, expressionless. Santos takes a deep breath and looks at me as if to say, *I'm ready*. Firmly I grasp Emily's leg and apply traction. She doesn't flinch, but Santos does when I pull the bone straight and the jagged edges slip back into place.

Emily's knuckles are clenched white, but she doesn't make a sound, only takes small, shallow breaths.

"Goddamn," he mutters.

I brush a wild strand of hair off her face. "Breathe, Emily. Let the oxygen reach your bone and heal you." Her breath shifts, deeper and slower. I immobilize her leg with a splint. I tell Santos, "A human would need steel screws and antibiotics, but not a Night Walker. Once Emily feeds properly, she'll heal quickly."

"I can't hunt like this," she grumbles.

"For now, you will have to acquire a taste for rabbit," I say with a teasing smile.

She wrinkles her nose in distaste. Santos frowns. Clearly, the thought of hunting is no trifling matter to him.

I place a hand on his shoulder. "Have courage, Atticus," I say, using his given name for the first time. "You'll get through this." I give Emily a pointed look. "We will help you." She stares at him, her eyes like embattled stars, amazed and horrified. She is his maker. His creator. Now they are linked.

When I have finished splinting her leg, Emily insists on sitting up despite my protestations. She braces herself against the table and says in a pained voice, "Anne, there's something I need to tell you."

I give her a wary look, afraid she's going to re-declare her vendetta against Santos. He watches us with a strained expression. I wonder what Jadallah meant to her. Did she love him? Emily doesn't love easily and her forgiveness comes even harder.

"I didn't turn you," she says.

"What?" I draw back, surprised.

"I didn't turn you. You seem to be under the impression I did, but I would never. As much as I hated watching you die, I would never have stolen that peace from you."

"Then who did?"

"Our brother, of course. Branwell."

"Branwell?" I say, unease slipping into my belly. "Why would he do that? I was never his favorite." His words come back to me. *Anne is nothing. An absolute nothing.* But, that was when I was so shy as to be almost mute and long before we lived and worked at Thorpe Green together. Before he betrayed our reputation and made love to our master's wife.

"I'm not sure," Emily says. "We discussed it. He agreed you weren't suited for eternal darkness. You adored the light. Your poetry was bathed in it. When I visited you on your deathbed, I only wanted to give you comfort. The kind of comfort in my selfishness I denied you from giving me." Her eyes tighten and I know this is the closest she'll ever come to an apology for pushing me away. "But you didn't need it. You were already halfway to God. If anyone deserved heaven it was you, so I left you in peace. I never imagined Bran would turn you. I suppose he was afraid of being alone." Her drawn white skin colors with anger. "He always was a selfish bastard, enslaved by his attachments."

My mind is whirling. "But why did you leave?"

If she'd stayed, I might have grown to love the sweet dark. Instead, I rejected the galaxy's glow, worshipping the sun as if it were a false idol, believing God lived only in the light and not in the darkest places too.

Emily shifts and flinches with the pain. "Branwell said he wanted a moment with you alone. I'd said my goodbyes and I couldn't bear to watch you any longer, so I left. I didn't know he was going to turn you." She holds my gaze, something she was never very good at in life. "I *never* would have left you, Anne. I only found out later, after you ran. I found the drained girl and Branwell, beaten by his little sister! I couldn't believe it. Oh, how I wanted to kill him. I almost strangled him right there in that dungeon, but he was my only brother, so I left him to walk the earth alone and think on his sins. I tried to find you, but I must say, sister, you are strangely good at hiding."

My voice comes out a whisper. "All this time I thought you'd turned me and left."

"You're my sister, Anne. I will never abandon you. *Never.*" She pulls me to her and holds me tightly, something she did only when I was a very little girl. For a moment I feel the strong beat of her heart, then she releases me and pulls away.

I smile.

Emily is here. My sister is here and she is safe, as are William and Santos, Vander and even Woody.

For the first time in a life of darkness, I'm not alone.

I glance around the luxurious, hi-tech RV strewn with weapons and bloody bandages. Santos, with arms crossed, stands tensely a few feet from Emily, staring at her as if she's an alien from outer space, dangerous and mesmerizing. Her t-shirt is ripped from when he attacked her, revealing the hard white curve of her shoulder splattered with blood. She turns and looks at him and his eyes flash with blackness but he remains still, trapped in his new purgatory.

William has edged near a window with his back to us, staring out into the dying night. He looks so alone my heart breaks. The sole human amongst immortals. Possibly the only human to have ever fought a Day Walker and lived. His tangled hair is streaked with blood and his lean, bruised body is covered in lacerations. His hands are scarred and clenched. I long to go to him and kiss him until they open and reach for me. Until they claw and tear me open. With the newfound sun in my blood, his beauty stands in stark relief against the darkness of my memories, stunning me with hunger.

I move toward William, but he tenses, and I stop. Torment transfigures his face and his brilliant burning light is dimmed down low.

I have broken his heart. William's vision of a pure, gentle Anne is dead. His true love no longer exists. His Anne is soiled. Stained. But that is a price I willingly pay if it means my loves live.

Such a harsh price love reaps.

I want to heal him with my body, and it takes all my strength not to kiss him until he thaws and reaches for me. Until he submits. But though I'm a Day Walker, I refuse to be a demon. And what have I learned in all these years if not Night Walker patience?

With an iron will, I keep my distance and force down my desire.

Up front, behind the wheel, Vander picks up Woody from the passenger seat and sets him in his lap, scratching the little fox terrier's ear. Together they squint through the tinted front window as the sun slowly ascends over the mountains. I slide into the newly vacated seat, still warm from Woody's body, and watch the forest flash by in streaks of color only I can see. Umber, violet, emerald, red. Snow, a bright blazing white.

There's work to be done, graves to be dug, but for now I will savor our victory.

My eyes fall upon Woody. Once upon a time in England, he was a hunter of foxes. Now he sits enrobed in his swirling twists of grey and white, poised with an alertness that surges for bright moments in those whose allotted days are dwindling. My heart squeezes. The little fellow is winding down and soon will be embarking upon the greatest journey of all. A changing of worlds. But tonight he sits up straight and with milky blue eyes, gazes out the front window as if he can envision the curving mountain road leading us all toward home.

Chapter 56

The night sky is brighter than I've ever seen it. Stars illuminate the heavens like a trillion brilliant flames. The universe brims with life. It pulses down at me, filling the void with its howling song. The wild unsayable. The moon is ripe and the air is tinged with heat. Winter is passing and spring is being born.

I stand with Emily and Atticus by O. Henry's modest grave in historic Riverside Cemetery. This boneyard seems the only place in town Emily is truly comfortable. She likes it here. Her leg is healing and she is clad in new black jeans and a thin t-shirt. Santos stands beside her, eyes shining like a wolf. They search the night incessantly, looking for threats or a way out. Since the night of the turning, he has fallen unusually quiet.

He has secured a leave of absence from the sheriff's department, claiming he needs a mental health break. No one was really surprised. The murders, he told them, on top of a decade of war, had taken their toll.

Officially cleared of suspicion, Lucien has assumed Dana's place as my partner at work. I'm glad for his company and this way

I can more easily protect him. Though investigators have assigned blame for the murders of the two girls, and the disappearances of Dana and Savannah, to the vanished Dr. Webb, not everyone is convinced.

Mr. Granger, especially. He's unable to accept that a respected white doctor took his daughter and not the young black man who openly desired one of the victims. Others are unsure as well and Lucien walked a hard road until detectives discovered mementos of Webb's other victims in his home on Whisper Mountain. Delicate locks of hair in wisps of gold and amber, jet and flame, were tied with silken thread, kept under glass like specimens of butterfly. *Las Mariposas,* Santos calls them. Webb even had a lock of Savannah's, which he might have snipped the night I brought her to the hospital. I can easily imagine him sliding a scalpel out of his white coat and slashing free a tendril of her hair when she and her father weren't looking.

They trusted us.

Mr. Granger is on the hunt, armed with a rifle and moonshine. His kin dust these mountains like blue smoke and have come forth to search for Savannah. Law enforcement is looking as well, but no one will find her. With my sun-strength, I buried her three fathoms deep on a high bluff looking down upon the Grangers' valley. I wanted to get her closer to home, but with the bloodhound noses of her kin, it wasn't wise.

No one must ever find her. No one will ever find Webb. I incinerated him where he fell, and I will confess that I took alarming satisfaction in it. All it took was one little match and his sun-ravaged corpse erupted in ash.

In the cemetery, Santos now shifts uneasily on his feet. While it soothes Emily, the setting seems to unsettle him. He does not know how familiar Emily and I are with graveyards. We grew up with one right outside our parsonage window. For us, they are a comforting reminder that the dead are never far.

His skin is a shade paler, but the darkness still remains. It glows more blackly in his eyes, shining. How will he adjust to constant killing without losing his soul?

Emily and I won't let him.

"You're his maker," I say to my sister. "Don't run from this." *Don't slip into fantasy and hide.* "Teach him. Contain him. Show him how to survive. If anyone is strong enough, Emily, it is you."

She looks at me with a wide, deep gaze. There is an anguished look to her I haven't seen since Branwell died. Her eyes are a sea-grey storm, crashing with frightening currents. I have never known a male and female Night Walker to live as equals, but Emily will be subjugated by no one.

Beside her, Santos looks savage and on edge. Fear in him swirls, shifts to anger, filling me with dread. Depending on his heart, he can become a dark guardian or a blazing demon, and I'm unsure which path he'll take. He stays close to Emily as if her presence offers security, and this gives me solace.

I long to reach out to him, to comfort him, but his taut wrath holds me back. I pray Emily will grant him a little warmth. A soothing touch. An impassioned embrace? I smile inwardly at the thought. Perhaps that is asking too much, but Santos is a physical creature and if there's any chance of saving him, she mustn't live too fiercely in her mind, withholding reassurance, refusing to forgive.

He saved me. He saved *her.* Surely sentencing him to a life without daylight absolves him of Jadallah's death. So why this dread in my heart? Because my sister doesn't forgive and she *never* forgets, even when it defies all reason.

Yet if I can be so thoroughly transformed, then surely the possibility exists for her as well. To soften. Open. Atticus is angry and scared, but mostly he is confused. He doesn't understand why Emily bristles in his presence and remains so resolutely cold. I long to explain, but that is for her to do when the time is right. She'll tell him someday, but not yet. He has enough to contend with now.

"Have courage, Atticus." His eyes alight on me and I feel their force against my skin. So much intensity burns within. How will he ever contain it? "You are worthy of the night. You have the strength and discipline for it. Learn to love it. Don't shun it as I did, rejecting its mysteries and wisdom. The darkness is beautiful and Emily is one of the brightest souls I've ever known. She will light the way."

With a jaded stare, he studies her to see if this is true. Only I can hear her heart quicken. She glows beneath the moonlight, untouchable, but I smell the fear in her. Santos has no idea who she is. He knows not her brilliance or her strength and cannot conceive the depths of her brutality. Her poise turns his gaze hot with anger. I don't know if he's forgiven us, but when he looks back to me I glimpse a slender thread of hope. Perhaps I am proof this life does not condemn one to a fiend, and even amidst the carnage we can do some small measure of good.

I relinquished his mortality, but I will not relinquish his soul. "You are at a crossroads, Atticus. Although we walk in darkness, we are guardians of the light. But you must *choose* it. We are condemned to be free and *you* must decide which path to walk. Excuses are irrelevant. Only choice matters."

His eyes rest on me a moment before turning away, looking across the graveyard. Roaming, scanning, sweeping for danger, but *he* is the danger now.

"What will you do?" Emily asks me.

"I'll stay here. It's my home now. William is here and my work." He hasn't forgiven me yet, but I feel his desire and I'm unwilling to relinquish that either.

Emily shifts uneasily and stares down at my new boots. They are gleaming black leather, supple and sleek. Not a drop of blood stains them, which is how I'd like them to stay if I can help it.

She kicks at the ground and says, "I never told you I was sorry. For abandoning you." I'm not sure if she is referring to our first life or second, but it doesn't matter. I forgive her everything, for even with her blood-drenched heart she is the most beautiful of souls. Primal and true. She needs no rules to guide her way. No laws or religion. Emily is her own compass, her own flame carving a path through the darkness.

A beacon unto herself.

Oh, how I love her.

And suddenly I know that love is *immortal*. Death cannot end it. Time—space—mortality cannot contain it. Love *transcends*. Long after our bones have melted to dust, our memories decayed, despite madness, betrayals, loss—it still abides. Shattered hearts *bleed* with love. We can't help it. It's how we're made.

In the image of divinity.

Emily looks at me, eyes fierce. "I should have found you sooner. I should have looked harder." Her voice breaks. She rubs her brow in frustration while Santos watches, mesmerized by her sudden vulnerability. "I will never run again, I swear it. If you need me, call and I will come."

"I'm glad to hear it." I reach into my jacket pocket. "Here." She stares uncomprehending as I hand her a flip-phone. "Charge it occasionally. I'll take care of the rest."

Her shoulders drop as if I have yoked her with a great burden. "I guess I'll have to figure out how to use this."

"Atticus will show you." I laugh. "It won't hurt you to step into the 21st century."

"They can track us with it," Santos says.

"Who's 'they'?"

"The police," Emily says. "The government."

"It's not the government I worry about, it's other Night Walkers," I tell them. "Regardless, I'll no longer be careless with my safety. From here on out, all technology our group uses, including this phone, comes from Vander. He's tightened his security and doubled his satellites. Our messages are encrypted and locations blocked. William is tracking other Night Walkers in our area and we're strengthening our medical and blood supplies in case of an emergency. You'll have to trust us," I tell Atticus.

"I trust you," he says.

My heart leaps. Emily shifts, aware he has not granted her this gift and I want to pull her into my arms and kiss her, but she would detest it. Instead, I squeeze her hand.

"Emily, I forgave you a long time ago. Branwell, too. Even Charlotte." I smile. What is a slandered manuscript next to eternity? "We had a love that was epic. *Is* epic. It will never die."

Grief illuminates her gaze, but she does not let the tears fall. I'm glad of it. She will need great strength if she is to save Santos from the darkness of his own heart.

Embarrassed, she turns to leave, but I stop her. I must be strong too.

"Emily Brontë and Atticus Santos." My voice turns formal, capturing their attention. "You are more savage than me, but know this, Asheville is my town now. I am its Alpha. Its blood is off-limits to you. If you hunt here or harm a living soul, I will kill you."

Atticus glares at me, hurt flooding his face.

Emily reaches a hand out, softly grazing my cheek. "My little fawn has learned to fight. As you wish, my love."

And they are gone.

I walk the streets toward home. Voices drift through windows, laughter, the sleepy murmur of a child. A father tucks his daughter into bed. A mother whispers the words of a fairy tale to her little boy. *Once upon a time there was a sweet little girl.* A dog looks up, but doesn't bark.

I turn down a block until I stand outside William's door. Through the window, I see him bent over his desk, scribbling away in feverish concentration on a new manuscript. He no longer shares his work with me and in a brilliant fury threw his first novel in the fire. Bless the gods I was there to snatch it from the flames despite his best efforts to stop me. Against William's will, I've stowed it safely away.

Tonight his eyes are bruised from insomnia, his thick locks a long, tangled disaster. Beside him is a stack of crisp, clean paper and a laptop, cold and closed. At his feet, Woody dreams restlessly.

Longing shatters my soul. My professor hasn't thawed for me even though I sense his desire thrumming through him. Vander says to be patient, in time William will come around. He's been exposed to violence before and always recovers. *But not this kind of violence*, I think. Not from a woman. Even so, I suspect it's not violence that shakes him, but something far worse. Shame. Shame at his failure to protect me. Shame at his fragile sense of mortality. Shame at his humanity.

But he didn't fail me. He saved me. He gave me the strength and courage to fight. He gave me a reason to face the darkness and own it. I've tried to tell him, but he won't listen. He refuses to see past his injured pride, and his sense of honor is not as flexible as Vander thinks.

I have read his masterpiece. I know his soul. Honor and duty cut in unexpected ways and it is the noblest among us who bear the deepest wounds.

Yet what do I have if not patience?

I am no longer blind to my powers and someday William will know them too.

He believes I am a fallen angel; Emily thinks I'm a risen one. I have tasted the forbidden fruit and swallowed the blood of self-knowledge and such nourishment has triggered the dream's dissolution.

I know who I am.

William glances up and stares out into the night, his mind a multiverse away, lost in dreams, the gods of his religion. And in this moment, *he* is the creator, infinitely more powerful than any destroyer. He shakes his hand as if to ease a cramp, then bends back to his work, writing with quick, fluid strokes. His skin is pale, his eyes tortured, but they burn with an incandescence I know fully well.

I want to go to him, to ease his doubts and slay him with love, but in my family it is a sin to break a writer's deep thoughts, so I let him be.

For now.

I turn toward home. Soon the sun will rise and I will meet it in tearful awe, but for the first time in a life of darkness, I do not want the night to end.

At home, Ivanhoe greets me with a look that says, "You are the same, but different, and I approve." Sweeping him up, I give him a kiss, go inside and build a roaring fire.

Then I sit before my ancient desk, pick up a pen and begin to write.

The End

ACKNOWLEDGEMENTS

It has taken me years to write this book, and many generous and patient souls have helped me along my journey. I am extremely grateful to the following people: Dana Isaacson, Ayesha Pande, Shelby Ozer, and Randy Brooks for their invaluable insight and guidance on this manuscript; Madison Smartt Bell and Judy Sternlight for their wisdom and support; Ericka Adams Cole and Julie MacKenzie for their sharp eyes and edits; and Patrick Knowles for his deadly cover design.

Heartfelt thanks to Marinda Williams for her insight on the Biltmore Estate; John Hinton, Joe Havel, Ruben Munoz, Jack Murphy, and Loren Schofield for answering my questions on hunting or the military; and Rick Rizzo for his input on law enforcement. Any mistakes I've made in the details of this story are solely mine. Thanks also to George Izquierdo whose insane imagination emboldened me to share Night Walker's story with him. As a result, Vander will never be the same.

Thank you to Asheville, NC, for being a vibrant source of inspiration. Note that I took liberties with Buncome County EMS and the Sheriff's Office, changing their names and expanding their territories for reasons of artistic license. As a firefighter/paramedic myself, I know with what fanatical specificity EMS and law enforcement know their territorial boundaries and it was in the spirit of story that I expanded them to encompass my narrative.

Thanks also to the fabulous female firefighters of Triple F for encouraging my writing and inspiriting the women of my story.

Enormous love and gratitude to Bob and Shirley Haff for their unfaltering support. I know a safe and loving space is always to be found with them.

All poetic passages in italics belong to Percy Bysshe Shelley, Emily Brontë, or Anne Brontë. Authorship is indicated by the text. I've attempted to remain true to the known Brontë biographies, allowing my imagination to fly freely only when describing the time following their deaths.

"*The wild unsayable*" is from Mark Doty's book of poetry, *Deep Lane*.

"*Once upon a time there was a sweet little girl*" is from Jacob and Wilhelm Grimm's "Little Red Cap."

"*Lost in dreams, the gods of [his] religion*" comes from a letter written by Charlotte Brontë.

Of course this novel would not exist without the immortal presence of the Brontës. Every single one of them is utterly unique and essential to the genius of the others. I am forever indebted to Branwell, Charlotte, Emily, and Anne, for being endless sources of inspiration, and to Reverend Patrick Brontë for so radically allowing his children to follow their own paths.

Deepest love to Woody. I will miss you forever.

And to my Mother who taught me that art *matters* and a life without dreams is meaningless—so fight for your dreams.

And to my husband, Rob, who makes all my dreams possible. For you, I would do anything.

ABOUT THE AUTHOR

Gea Haff is a firefighter, paramedic, rescue diver, and special ops flight medic with Miami Dade Fire Rescue. She holds an M.A. in Women's Studies in Religion from Claremont Graduate University, a B.A. in Humanities from University of Southern California, and an A.S. in Emergency Medical Services from Miami Dade College. She's written for Fire Rescue Magazine and JEMS, and she blogs for Triple F—Fabulous Female Firefighters! She lives in the Florida Keys with her husband and creative partner, Rob Haff.